Heads You Lose

Rob Johnson

XERIKA PUBLISHING

HEADS YOU LOSE

Published by Xerika Publishing

Cover design by Brian Ground from an original painting by Penny Philcox.

First published 2015 by Xerika Publishing
10 The Croft, Bamford, Hope Valley,
Derbyshire S33 0AP

ISBN 978 0 9926384 4 3

http://www.rob-johnson.org.uk

For my namesake,
Rob Johnson.
"I not call you nephew..."

.

ACKNOWLEDGEMENTS

I am indebted to the following people for helping to make this book better than it would have been without their advice, technical knowhow and support:

Nuala Forde, Jim Jones, Penny Philcox, Petros Stathakos, Dan Varndell, Chris Wallbridge, Elizabeth Wallbridge, Nick Whitton, Patrick Woodgate.

Many thanks also to retired West Yorkshire Police Inspector Kevin Robinson for technical advice on British police procedures.
https://crimewritingsolutions.wordpress.com/

And finally, my eternal gratitude to Penny Phillips for her unfailing support, encouragement and belief and for losing her head sufficiently to marry me in July 2014.

COVER DESIGN

Special thanks to Penny Philcox for the original artwork and to Brian Ground for the overall design of the cover.

GREEK LANGUAGE NOTE

There are a few Greek words and phrases used in the text, and these have been transliterated into the Latin alphabet. Where a word has more than one syllable, an accent shows which is the stressed syllable. For instance, the Greek word *póso* (meaning 'how much') is pronounced with the stress on the first 'o'.

The letter 'i' has no dot above it and is written 'ι'.

When you address someone directly by name in Greek and their name ends in an 's', the 's' is omitted. For instance, a man called Dimitris would be addressed as Dimitri. For the sake of simplicity, however, this rule has not been observed in the text.

1

Careful now, Trevor. Careful. You know what'll happen if he sees you. — Pain. That's what'll happen, Trev. And I'm not talking about the brain-freeze kind of pain you get from eating ice cream too quickly. No, Trev, I'm talking about the kind of pain that you probably never even *imagined* that one human being could possibly inflict on another. The kind of pain Dustin Hoffman felt when Larry Olivier drilled through his front teeth in *Marathon Man.* — Maybe even worse. It'll be like passing kidney stones and giving birth at the same time. Have you ever known anybody do that, Trev? Have you? — Well, okay, maybe not at the same time, but that's the kind of pain you can expect if he sees you, Trev. You mark my words.

The voice in Trevor's head was starting to get seriously annoying and was only adding to his already off-the-scale anxiety level. One good clean shot was all he needed, and then he was out of there. But first he had to get his hands back under control. And not just his hands either. His whole body had developed a sudden and severe attack of the shakes, and the night was nowhere near cold enough to blame it on impending hypothermia. It was fear that was giving him the jitters. And who in their right mind wouldn't have been afraid? The guy was enormous. The guy in the knee-length black leather coat with the upturned collar on the opposite side of the street who'd just come out of the Pontiac Club. The guy that Sandra had persisted in calling "the target".

Ethan "Mountainman" Machin was a recently retired heavyweight boxer with a reputation for swinging his fists almost as often outside the ring as in it. This had resulted in a couple of periods when he'd been detained at Her Majesty's pleasure, and according to most of the pundits, it was these interruptions to his career that had prevented him from making it to the very top of his profession. Still, he'd done pretty well for himself in terms of prize money, and judging by the way he was chatting and laughing with the young woman he currently had his arm draped around, he didn't appear to harbour any regrets.

She must have been a good fifteen years younger than Machin and was well over a foot shorter. She was wearing one of those creamy-grey fur jackets that ended above the waist, and the blue silky dress underneath was cut low at the front. The hair and the eyes said she was probably Japanese or Chinese, but Trevor couldn't remember the rhyme about how you tell the difference. Not that it really mattered. Sandra would no doubt have given him a bollocking for being politically incorrect anyway.

Machin stuck out a dinner plate hand to hail a passing cab, but it failed to stop. If he got lucky with the next one, Trevor would have missed his opportunity. Another wasted night — the third on the trot — trailing round after a retired boxer when he'd much rather have been at home watching the telly. He'd come close the evening before, but at the very moment he'd had Machin and his girlfriend crystal clear in his sights, some bloody autograph hunter had stepped into the firing line and stayed put until they'd disappeared inside yet another of Mountainman's favourite watering holes.

Trevor took several deep breaths to try and steady his nerves and braced his elbows against the frame of the open car window. Now or never, Trev. Now or never.

He rested the tip of his finger on the button and focused, but a sudden tremor made him apply a little more pressure than he'd intended, and there was a loud "click" and a burst of white light, which momentarily illuminated the entire area.

'Oh, bloody Nora,' he said aloud, realising that he'd forgotten to turn off the flash before taking the photograph.

He fleetingly considered firing off another couple of shots but decided against it. Mountainman Machin had obviously clocked the camera flash, and it didn't take him long to figure out that he and his girlfriend were the photographer's unwilling subjects. He'd already set off across the street, and given the length of his stride, he'd be on top of Trevor in seconds.

Trevor dumped the Pentax onto the passenger seat and turned the key in the ignition. There was a dull, whirring noise from the engine but nothing that even faintly resembled a throaty roar. He tried again, but the engine merely churned in chorus with his own stomach. He stole a glance to his right. Machin was more than half way across the road by now, and if it had been a sunny day, his huge frame would easily have created its own eclipse.

'Come *on*, you bastard,' said Trevor, and at the third time of asking, the engine fired into life.

He slammed the Peugeot into gear, but before he could let out the clutch, a tree branch of an arm had thrust itself through the open side window and what felt like a steel claw had grabbed him by the front of his padded anorak. Trevor's foot slipped off the clutch pedal, and the car lurched forward, coming to an abrupt halt six feet later when it smashed into the back of a parked BMW. Machin staggered and fell but was back on his feet again inside a count of two and had yanked open the Peugeot's door before Trevor had time to even think of backing up and making his escape. The Mountainman had to bend almost double to bring his face in front of Trevor's and was about to speak when he suddenly snapped himself upright again at the sound of a voice from behind him.

'Ex*cuse* me.' The voice was public school, loud and indignant, but Trevor couldn't see who it belonged to through Machin's vast bulk.

'You just tap me on da shoulder?' For a man of his size, Machin's voice was curiously high pitched. A couple of octaves higher and only dogs would have been able to hear him. And either he had a very bad cold or his nose had been broken so many times he'd lost the ability to pronounce his dental fricatives.

'That's my BMW you just smacked into,' said its invisible owner.

'Beamer, eh? Well, ain't you da lucky boy den,' said Machin and was beginning to resume his bent double position when there was another tap on his shoulder.

'I'm going to need the driver's insurance details.'

'No, man. I dink you gonna need da casualty department before dat.'

Trevor heard a loud crack and then briefly caught his first sight of the BMW owner as he catapulted backwards and bounced off the bonnet of the Peugeot and onto the ground.

'You!' There was no escaping who it was that Mountainman was addressing now since he'd stooped down again and was staring into Trevor's face. 'Outta da car unless you want some o' da same.'

Trevor definitely didn't want "some o' da same" or something that even vaguely resembled it, so he did as he was told. It was a fairly safe bet that he was going to get "some o' da same" whether he got out of the car or not, but for now, compliance was probably the better option. Machin had left him little room to carry out the manoeuvre, however, and he stood with his back pressed against the doorframe of the car and his nose almost touching the Mountainman's barrel of a chest. A strong smell of whisky drifted down from above.

'You takin' pictures of me?'

Trevor craned his neck upwards, but the overhang of Machin's Desperate Dan chin made any eye contact impossible. 'Pictures?'

'You pepperoni creeps really piss me off, you know dat?'

Trevor assumed he meant "paparazzi" but decided against correcting him. 'No, no, I'm not... one of what you just said. I'm a er...'

Come on, Trevor, *think*. You're a what? You're working for a private detective agency and you've been paid to get divorce snaps of the guy hanging out with his latest floozy? Yeah, that ought to do it.

'I'm er — I'm putting together a book. Photographs. Coffee table sort of thing, you know? Hundred best nightclubs from all around Britain. That sort of thing. And you just happened to be—'

'So show me.'

'Show you?'

'All dese pictures of all dese nightclubs you got on da camera.'

Trevor swallowed. 'Well, obviously I haven't got all the—'

The larynx-crushing grip around his throat prevented him from completing the sentence, and his feet lost contact with the ground. For the first time, he was able to look into Machin's blue-black, red-rimmed eyes, and as far as their being the windows to the soul was concerned, things weren't looking too promising.

'Show. Me. Da. Camera,' said Mountainman, emphasising each word by ramming Trevor's back against the side of the car.

Trevor felt himself being slowly lowered back down to the ground, and fighting to get some air back into his lungs, he reached in and grabbed the Pentax from the passenger seat. It was a big, expensive piece of kit with a telephoto lens, but in Machin's hand, it looked like a compact.

'Nice,' he said, holding it up to his face and pointing it towards the club entrance across the street. 'Gimme a smile, honey.'

Trevor shifted his head to one side and peered round him. The Oriental-looking woman struck a pose that was more like Rodin's *The Thinker* than anything you were ever likely to see at a Kate Moss photo shoot. Then there was a "click" and a flash, followed by half a dozen more, and for every shot, Miss Japan (or China) came up with a pose that was equally as absurd as the first. But all the time Machin seemed to be enjoying himself, he wasn't bothering to check through the pictures Trevor had taken and discover he'd been lying. The great lummox probably didn't have a clue how to do it anyway, and Trevor certainly wasn't about to offer him a tutorial.

'Hey, Kazumi, I got an idea,' the lummox shouted. 'Get your cute little butt over here, yeah?'

'What for?' came the heavily accented reply.

Machin's tone hardened. 'Just do it, yeah?'

Kazumi gathered up the skirt of her silky blue dress and stepped off the pavement, only narrowly avoiding being crushed by a passing black cab.

'And watch da damn road,' Machin yelled over the blare of the taxi horn.

She looked left and right and then hobbled her way across the road, her forward movement impeded by the pencil skirt of her dress and the height of her stilettos. The whiff of an expensive scent heralded her arrival, and Trevor could see that she was even better looking than she'd appeared through the viewfinder of his camera. In fact, she was a stunner and could very easily have made it as a model if it wasn't for her rubbish posing ability. Her features reminded him of the woman in that *Green Lady* print which used to be all the rage back in the seventies, except her complexion wasn't in the least bit green or even blue.

'Quit your gawping and take holda dis,' said Machin, thrusting the Pentax at Trevor's chest. 'You gonna dake some nice pics of me and my girl.'

Trevor took the camera and waited while Mountainman threw his arm round his girlfriend's tiny waist and pulled her close. How very odd, he thought. He's actually *ordering* me to do exactly the same thing that a minute ago he was about to batter me to a pulp for.

He raised the camera and framed the happily smiling couple in the viewfinder. Focusing was tricky, though, as his hands were trembling even worse than before.

'Hold da ding steady for Christ's sake,' said Machin. 'I don't want dese comin' out all blurry.'

Trevor took another deep breath and tried to reassure himself that there was nothing to be anxious about. Surely what this meant was that Machin had changed his mind about inflicting any actual — or quite possibly grievous — bodily harm on him? He clicked away while Machin and the woman alternated between gazing lovingly into each other's eyes and beaming into the camera lens. There was even a couple of shots of the pair of them kissing. Sandra's going to be well impressed with this, he thought. Not to mention Mrs Mountainman — although for rather different reasons of course.

'Okay, dat's enough,' said Machin, his joyful smile suddenly transformed into a glower which he no doubt usually reserved for the boxing ring.

Trevor lowered the camera. 'If you give me your address, I can send you prints if you like.'

The glower intensified.

Bit too cocky with that one, wouldn't you say, Trev?

Machin held out his hand. 'Gimme da camera.'

Trevor handed it over.

'Get in da car and take da handbrake off.'

'Wh—?' Trevor didn't even finish the syllable. Machin's raised eyebrow and slight inclination of his head towards the open driver's door was enough to freeze it on his tongue.

He got into the car and released the handbrake while the Mountainman crouched down and then uncoiled himself just far enough to make eye contact with Trevor, the Pentax no longer in his hand.

'Now reverse,' he said. 'But slowly.'

Trevor braced his ears for the inevitable sound of splintering metal and plastic as he rolled the car backwards. Less expected was the sharp hiss of air from a newly punctured front tyre.

'Oh dear,' said Machin, his tone dripping with insincerity. 'Now nobody'll get to see any o' dem lovely pictures. Still, da main ding is nobody got hurt, right?'

'Er, right.'

'So no hard feelings den, yeah?'

Machin held out his gorilla paw of a hand, his grin not even close to the beaming smile he'd worn for the camera a couple of minutes earlier. Trevor hesitated but realised he had no choice but to reciprocate.

The pain was immediate and excruciating as Machin mangled and crushed his fingers with no more apparent effort than most normal people would use to squeeze a tube of toothpaste. A reflex howl of agony only made it halfway up his throat before the Mountainman wrenched him from the car, and when Trevor glanced down at what was left of his hand, he caught the briefest glimpse of Machin's right fist thundering up towards his face. An explosion inside his head. Then blackness.

2

Contrary to the old proverb that a watched pot never boils, Jackie Summerfield had been staring at the electric kettle from the moment she'd turned it on, and it had long since come to the boil and switched itself off. But she was far too busy rehearsing her lines to notice. Today was the day. She couldn't put off telling him any longer. He'd make one hell of a fuss of course, but that was nothing out of the ordinary these days. Only yesterday, he'd kicked up a right old stink just because she'd suggested he ought to wear a hat if he was going to sit in the sun for much longer. Then there was the time when—

'You making tea?'

Her husband's voice snapped her out of her contemplation, and she let go of the marble worktop and turned towards him. He wasn't even looking in her direction but was rummaging through the contents of the cupboard beneath the sink. The patch of skin amongst the greying brown hair on the crown of his head was definitely getting bigger. At least twice the golf ball size it had been the last time she'd noticed, although she couldn't remember when that might have been.

'You seen the insect spray?'

Questions, questions.

Jackie added one of her own. 'What's it for?'

'Bloody great hornet in my study. Can't get rid of the bugger.'

'You've tried shooing it out of the window?'

'Of course I— Ah, here it is.'

Simon pulled himself upright, clutching a large aerosol can and shaking it next to his ear. As he did so, his sunglasses dislodged themselves from their perch on top of his head, and he grabbed them as they fell. 'You told him yet?'

'I'm just taking him his breakfast,' said Jackie and flicked the switch on the kettle to reboil it.

'We can't leave it any longer, Jack. I mean there's all the—'

'Did you know we were out of honey?'

'What? — Oh yeah, there was only a bit left. I had it with my yoghourt.'

Jackie sighed and put two slices of white bread in the toaster, then crossed to the other side of the kitchen and took a jar of raspberry jam from the fridge. She was aware that Simon was watching her every move and wondered why he was still there.

'I thought you had a monster hornet to deal with,' she said, returning to the fridge to fetch butter and a carton of milk.

Simon looked at the aerosol can in his hand as if he was surprised to find it there.

'Yes indeed,' he said. 'Let battle commence.'

He held the can aloft as if it were the aerosol equivalent of Excalibur and set off across the open-plan living room, his flip-flops flip-flopping against the pale grey marble tiles.

Chirpy really didn't suit him, thought Jackie, but she knew exactly why it was. There was a shitty job to be done, but this time there could be no argument about which one of them would have to do it. It was entirely her responsibility, so Simon was completely in the clear for once and loving every minute of it.

* * *

Not for the first time, Jackie recoiled at the smell of pee and stale cigarette smoke when she opened the door to her father's bedroom. In the gloom, she could just make out his tanned and heavily lined face above the top of the bedclothes, and as far as she could tell, his eyes were closed. His breathing was deep and laboured, almost as if he were snoring, but more than likely he was only faking it. It was something he often did, probably because it gave him something else to shout at her about when he pretended she'd woken him "at some godforsaken bloody hour" for no good reason.

She set his breakfast tray down on a low wooden chest at the foot of his double bed and opened the blinds of both windows. Her father groaned and hauled the bedclothes up over his head when the bright sunlight blazed into the room, and Jackie would have smiled to herself at the repetition of the daily ritual if it hadn't been for her anxiety over what she was about to tell him.

'Morning, Dad,' she said, returning to the tray and collecting a tumbler of water and a small plastic cup which was almost full with a dozen or so tablets of various colours, shapes and sizes.

'Bugger off,' came the muffled reply from beneath the bedclothes.

Jackie moved to the head of the bed, taking care not to trip over the metal stand of the catheter bag and its nightsworth of cloudy urine.

'Pills first, then breakfast,' she said, looking down at the gnarled and nicotine-stained fingers which kept a tight grip on the bedclothes, the only parts of him that were now visible.

There was no response, so she used up a few seconds mentally rehearsing the bombshell she was about to drop.

'Dad?' she said when she felt she'd got the words clear in her mind.

'What?'

'You need to take your tablets.' Yes, better to get them down him first and then tell him.

'I thought I told you to bugger off.'

Jackie put the glass of water down on the bedside table and took hold of the bedclothes with her free hand. After a brief tug-of-war, which her father won easily, she deposited the tablet cup next to the glass of water and resumed the battle with both hands. For a man in his early seventies, Marcus Ingleby was much stronger than he liked people to think, but he was still no match for his daughter's two-handed assault on the bedclothes.

She avoided the venomous glare she knew he was giving her by turning away and picking up the tablets from the bedside table.

'You want to sit up now?' she said, taking him gently by the upper arm.

Ingleby brushed her aside. 'I can manage. I'm not a bloody vegetable.'

He hoisted himself up into an awkward approximation of a sitting position and snatched the plastic cup of tablets from Jackie's hand, almost spilling the contents in the process. He tipped a few onto his palm. 'Water?'

She passed him the tumbler and strolled over to one of the windows. It was tempting to throw it open to let some fresh air into the room, but she knew he'd throw a fit, and this was no time to upset him any more than she had to. Instead, she folded her arms and stared down at the reflection of a single small cloud on the mirror smooth surface of the swimming pool.

She cleared her throat. 'Simon and I have been thinking.'

There was a loud grunting sound from the bed behind her.

'The thing is,' she went on, 'we've got a few things we really need to do back in England, and we can't put them off any longer.'

She waited for the expected tirade, but none came. Either he was thinking over what she'd said or he had a mouthful of pills. She glanced over her shoulder as he glugged back the last of the water and screwed up his face in distaste.

'Breakfast?' he said, unusually articulating the word more as a request than a command.

'Do you need your teeth?'

'What is it? Rump steak?'

'Toast.'

'Then, no, I don't need me sodding teeth, do I?'

Jackie transferred the breakfast tray from the chest at the foot of the bed to his lap.

'It might even be for a few weeks,' she said, 'but obviously we'd get someone in to look after you while we're away, and we'd—'

'Where's the honey?' Ingleby was holding a triangular piece of toast between forefinger and thumb and eyeing it's generous covering of raspberry jam with deep suspicion.

'We've run out. Sorry.'

'Jesus,' said Ingleby and took a large bite out of the toast with his few remaining teeth. 'This is Greece, for Christ's sake. Whole bloody country's awash with the stuff and you run out?'

Jackie ignored the remark in the interests of resolving the real matter at hand. 'So what do you think?'

'I think it's bloody incredible. That's what I think.'

'I mean about Simon and I going to—'

'D'you know,' said Ingleby through a mouthful of toast, 'that when bees find a good place to get pollen — or whatever else it is they make honey from — they do this little dance inside the 'ive which tells all their mates where to find it? Amazing thing, Nature.'

He grinned up at her, chewing the toast with his

mouth wide open.

'The thing is, Dad,' said Jackie, undeterred from her course of action, 'we need to get someone in that you're going to be happy with. Somebody who can do all the cooking and stuff and make sure you take all your medicine on time and—'

'Oh dear.' Her father's grin morphed into an expression of palpably insincere embarrassment.

'What is it?'

'I think maybe...' Ingleby began and then lifted the breakfast tray from his lap. ''Ere, take this, will yer?'

She took the tray from him, and he raised the bedclothes to peer underneath.

'Oh yeah. Seems like me catheter tube got disconnected somehow,' he said, then shifted his gaze upwards to meet Jackie's, his grin back in place and spread even wider than before. 'Oops. Bit of a damp patch, I'm afraid.'

3

Someone had hammered a blunt chisel into the centre of Trevor's forehead and then poured molten lead into the hole so that it channelled its way to every part of his brain. That's how it felt anyway.

Okay, so he'd be the first to admit he had an exceptionally low pain threshold. He couldn't even bear to watch hospital dramas on the TV in case his synapses started to over-empathise with whatever body part happened to be under the knife at the time. His ex-wife, Imelda, used to tell him he was a wimp or an attention-seeking wuss or something equally unsympathetic whenever he complained of being unwell or in pain. But what did she know? Two-faced, deceitful cow had had the bedside manner of Vlad the Impaler's more evil sister.

But surely even she would have been forced to concede that what he was going through now was about as excruciating as agony could possibly get and way beyond the point where even the likes of Rocky Balboa would have thrown in the towel and begged for mercy.

He stared up at the ceiling and contemplated reaching behind him to adjust one of the three pillows which had slithered down to a less than ergonomic position just below his right shoulder but decided that such a movement would almost inevitably slosh the molten lead to some other part of his head that it hadn't yet explored. Sighing was also out of the question since this seemed to cause the ball bearings in his neural pathways to run amok with their own particular version of pinball croquet.

And where the hell was Sandra? She'd promised she'd call in on her way home from work, and it must be at least... He swivelled his eyeballs sideways as far as they would go, but there was no way he could see the clock on his bedside table without turning his head.

'Bollocks,' he said and instantly regretted the involuntary sigh which followed.

It was mostly her fault he was in this state in the first place. If she hadn't have got him to—

The front door opened, and Sandra's voice drifted up the stairs: 'You still in bed up there?'

'Yes.' — *Course I'm still in bed. I'm in a serious amount of pain in case you hadn't noticed before.*

'Trevor?'

'Yes.' The effort of increasing his volume made his brain rattle.

'I'll be up in a tick. You want a cuppa?'

He wasn't sure.

'Trevor?'

— *Oh God, I don't know. Stop asking me these questions, will you?*

He closed his eyes but opened them again when he heard footsteps on the stairs.

Sandra appeared in the bedroom doorway with a kind of mocking grin that Trevor considered highly inappropriate. More annoying still was that the grin accentuated her already prominent cheekbones and added a sparkle to the intense electric blue of her eyes. In his present mood, the last thing he wanted was for Sandra to be looking quite that attractive. They saw each other on an almost daily basis, working together, socialising together and even occasionally bickering as if they were a long-married couple, but nothing could have been further from the truth. In the eighteen months they'd known each other, they'd become nothing more than very close friends. And now here she stood, smirking and looking... well, perhaps not quite making it into the "drop-dead-gorgeous" category but definitely worthy of something slightly less life-threatening. There was something else about her too. — Yes, that was it. She'd had her hair done. A bit of a trim to keep it an inch or so from being shoulder length and a shade more honey-coloured than her usual blonde. So that was why she was late.

'It's a tossup, I know,' said Sandra, 'but I have to say Ralph Fiennes did it for me rather more in *The English Patient* – even *with* all the bandages.'

'Oh yeah? Well, I've got more plasters and bandages on me than he ever did. — In fact, I've got more plasters and bandages than Tutankhamun's mummy.'

'Not sure they actually had plasters in the days of the pharaohs, but never mind. How you feeling?'

Her tone was still much too chirpy, but there seemed to be real concern behind the question.

'Bad,' said Trevor. 'Worse if anything.'

'Oh.' Sandra approached the bed and held out a brown paper bag. 'Here. I got you some grapes.'

Trevor felt himself go almost cross-eyed as he forced his eyes downwards to peer into the bag without tilting his head. 'Seedless?'

'Of course.'

'Not sure I can.'

'What?'

'Eat anything. Everything hurts. When I move.'

Sandra scanned the room. 'Where's Milly?'

'Bathroom.'

'Washing her hair, is she?'

'Wouldn't stop jumping on me and licking my face—'
He tensed rigid at the sudden blaze of fire somewhere near his frontal lobe. 'So I shut her in.'

25

'Pity. They say dogs' saliva is a very effective antiseptic.'

Trevor didn't respond.

'She's being incredibly quiet,' said Sandra, taking off her cream cotton jacket and dropping it onto the bed. 'Normally she'd be—'

'I gave her one of my sedatives.'

'You did what?'

'She'll be fine. She's had them before.' He made a half-hearted attempt to reach one of the wayward pillows behind his shoulder but gave up with a scowl.

'You want a hand with that?' Without waiting for an answer and ignoring his yelps and groans, Sandra managed to ease his upper body far enough forward so she could drag the pillow up behind his head.

She stood looking down at him for several seconds, and Trevor saw that the chirpiness had vanished from her expression. She perched herself next to him and took hold of his hand. 'You don't... blame me, do you?'

He summoned the courage to raise an eyebrow.

'For what happened?' she added.

Trevor thought about it. — *Well, yes, I do blame you actually, but only in a round about sort of way, I suppose. You didn't exactly* force *me to become a partner in your private investigator business, and it was the luck of the draw that I'd got the job of tailing an ex heavyweight boxer to try and get evidence that he was, as Mrs Mountainman Machin put it, "throwing a few jabs outside the ring". And, to be fair, it was probably my own fault that Machin had spotted me with the camera and used my face for pummelling practice.*

'So you obviously do blame me, or you wouldn't need so much time to think about it,' said Sandra after he'd failed to answer straight away.

'No, of course I don't. It's just that I don't know if I'm cut out for this kind of work, that's all.'

'You'd rather go back to Dreamhome Megastores, would you?'

The very thought of working at that shrine to mind-numbing tedium gave Trevor the sweats, but at least nobody beat the crap out of you there. Not physically anyway.

'They made me redundant if you remember.'

Sandra helped herself to a handful of grapes from the bag. 'Thing is, Trev, unless the trade in jealous spouses picks up, you might have to. Look for another job, I mean. If not Dreamhome, then somewhere else. Me too.'

'Eh?' He knew that they'd been subsidising the detective agency with what was left of the cash from the Harry Vincent business, but he'd assumed there was still plenty left in the kitty. 'What about the Vincent money?'

She shrugged. 'Down to the last couple of grand.'

Trevor gave a low whistle, but he cut it short when his teeth started to throb. 'Maybe we need to... What's the word? Diversify.'

'Into what exactly?'

It was Trevor's turn to shrug. 'Perhaps we could...' he began but tailed off when all that came to mind were phrases like "thinking outside the box" and "horizon scanning" which he'd picked up when he'd been forced to endure those godawful training sessions at Dreamhome Megastores. In any case, thinking even *inside* the box made his brain hurt, and talking sent spasms of shrieking pain to every part of his body from the knees upwards. From now on, if he needed to communicate, he'd use mime for the simple stuff and paper and pen for anything more complicated.

'Well, oh wise one?' said Sandra. 'I'm all agog to hear this earth-shattering idea of yours.'

Trevor drew an imaginary zip across his lips and then pointed to his face before holding his palms close to the sides of his head and moving them back and forth several times. He'd always been rubbish at charades, but Sandra seemed to get the message.

'Oh great,' she said. 'So now I've got Harpo Marx for a partner. — I may as well go and put the kettle on.'

She got to her feet and was almost at the door when the opening bars of *Mamma Mia* blared out from her mobile. Trevor's instinct was to cover his ears to blot out the din, but he knew the agonising price he'd have to pay for such a rapid movement, so he waited patiently while Sandra came back to the bed and fished the phone out of her jacket pocket. She checked the display and then waved the mobile in his direction.

'Aha,' she said — which was kind of appropriate, given her choice of ringtone. 'What you were saying just now about diversifying? This might be precisely the sort of thing you were on about.'

4

Eric took off his heavy-rimmed spectacles and huffed and puffed on the circular lenses before polishing them with an immaculately pressed powder blue handkerchief from the top pocket of his jacket.

'It's like when you see funerals in films,' he said, returning the spectacles to the bridge of his nose and staring fixedly at the massive wooden gates of the prison through the persistent grey drizzle. 'Always pissing it down. — Or snowing. Sometimes it's snowing. Never in bright sunshine though, are they? Like prisons. They just don't look right if they're bathed in sunlight, do they?'

He waited a few seconds for his granddaughter to answer, and when she didn't, he turned towards her. She was still reading the magazine that she'd propped open against the steering wheel when they'd first arrived nearly an hour ago. Since then, she'd hardly spoken more than a couple of words. It wasn't that she was sulking exactly, although this was one of the rare occasions when she'd made it abundantly clear she wasn't happy about giving him a lift somewhere. No, not sulking. Not like her mother. Her mother could sulk for England and never did anything for anybody unless she could see some benefit in it for herself. Physically though, Kate had inherited almost every aspect of her mum's good looks. The long, sleek black hair. The pale, flawless complexion. The ever so slightly upturned nose and those grey-green eyes that could wither or delight you, depending on how she felt at the time.

He wiped a patch of condensation from the windscreen with the back of his hand and turned his attention back to the prison gates. They were still only just visible through the film of rain that had settled on the outside of the glass.

'Give the wipers a dab, will you, sweetheart?' he said. 'Don't want to miss him, do we?'

Without even looking up from her magazine, Kate switched on the ignition and let the windscreen wipers run for a few seconds before turning it off again. She flicked over a page. 'How much longer, d'you think?'

'Should be any minute now. They're usually fairly prompt.'

Eric had scarcely finished the sentence when a door in the prison gates opened and out stepped a grey-haired man with a ruddy face and a belly the size of which his long, shabby overcoat couldn't disguise. The door slammed shut, and he dropped his canvas holdall to the ground and pulled his coat tighter around him.

'There he is,' said Eric and threw open the car door.

He hurried towards the man in the overcoat, who spotted him immediately and came to meet him, limping heavily and walking with the aid of a stick.

'Frank, you old bugger,' said Eric, throwing his arms out wide as the gap narrowed between them.

The two men hugged, and then Frank took a step backwards.

'Eh up,' he said. 'You've not turned queer, have yer? I had enough o' that malarkey in there.'

Eric laughed. 'What, *you*?' he said, giving Frank the once-over. He was in his early seventies — a couple of years younger than Eric — but his time inside clearly hadn't been kind to him, and he could easily have been taken for nearer eighty.

'Aye well, 'appen I've let meself go a bit lately, but I weren't a bad looker when I went in.'

'Didn't need a walking stick either, as I recall.'

Frank raised his stick and eyed it with contempt. 'Fookin' arthritis. Knee 'urts like buggery some days.'

Eric pulled a sympathetic face, and Frank tilted his head to look past him. 'You got a motor 'ere or what? I'm getting bloody soaked out 'ere.'

'Your carriage awaits,' said Eric with a flamboyant gesture in the general direction of Kate's car.

Then he picked up Frank's holdall and led the way across the rain-soaked parking area, listening to the tap-tapping of the walking stick behind him and wondering whether Frank was actually going to be of any help at all with the task at hand.

5

For a dead man, Harry Vincent didn't look too bad at all. In fact, apart from the roll of belly spilling over the waistband of his brightly striped swimming shorts, he appeared to be in remarkably good condition. His skin was tanned to a pale teak colour, and his thick sandy hair, combed backwards from his forehead, was only just starting to show signs of thinning.

He was playing to the camera, strutting around the swimming pool like a dressage pony and performing a variety of bodybuilder-type poses which failed to display any great prominence of muscle. Then he froze, his ear-to-ear grin abruptly replaced by an expression of wide-eyed terror as he appeared to notice something — or someone — beyond and to one side of the camera.

He threw up his hands in mock surrender. 'No, no. Don't shoot. Please. I can explain every— Aaargh!'

The first imaginary bullet struck him in the centre of the chest, and his hands clutched at the apparent point of entry. A second imaginary bullet caught him just below the left shoulder, and he reeled backwards, his body then contorting and twisting under a hail of imaginary machine gun fire. This was followed by a prolonged and outrageously hammy dying scene which culminated in his toppling sideways into the pool.

The resulting splash spattered the lens of the camera with droplets of water, and there was the sound of a woman laughing. 'Oi, watch the camera, Harry.'

But Harry couldn't hear her, his head still under the

surface of the water as he swam back towards the edge of the pool.

'Al Pacino, eat yer heart out,' he said when he clambered out and grabbed a towel from a nearby sun lounger. He began to dry himself, and staring directly at the video camera, came swaggering towards it. Then he tossed the towel aside and hooked his thumbs into the waistband of his swimming shorts, easing them downwards a fraction of an inch at a time whilst humming the tune to *The Stripper*.

'Hang on a sec,' said the woman. 'I'd better switch to full zoom if you're gonna do that or it won't show up.'

But at the very moment Harry was about to reveal all, the camera switched to a shaky close-up of the marble tiled floor.

The woman giggled. 'Harr-eee.'

The image on the enormous flat-screen TV dissolved into the visual equivalent of white noise, and Donna reached for the remote on the settee beside her without taking her eyes off the screen. When it didn't come immediately to hand, she searched for it among the small pile of used tissues and then rewound the tape. Freeze-framing it at the moment where Harry is approaching the camera towards the end, she took a fresh tissue from a half full box and wiped the mascara stained tears from her cheeks.

'You all right, Mrs V?'

The man's voice came from behind her, but she kept her gaze fixed on the TV screen and stifled a sob. 'Yeah, I'm okay thanks, Eddie.'

The ever dependable Eddie, who Harry had unofficially adopted twenty-odd years ago when the lad was no more than fourteen and living rough among the lowlifes and down-and-outs in some of the shittiest parts of London. He was already a heavy crack user by then and was financing his habit by turning the occasional trick as a rent boy whenever he got the chance — which wasn't that often, given the filthy state he was in most of the time. Harry always used to get embarrassed when people told him he'd saved the kid from a short and miserable life, and he'd insisted that all he'd done was got him cleaned up and given him a job.

Eddie had turned out to be quite an asset to the firm as it happened and became the automatic first choice whenever a getaway driver was needed. Then, later on, when Harry'd decided to go into a kind of semi-retirement and he and Donna had bought the villa in Greece, Eddie had come with them. Minder, chauffeur, secretary and all round "walking bloody miracle" as Harry called him.

He sauntered round in front of the settee, his short-sleeved Hawaiian shirt hanging open and amply revealing the results of his daily workout routine. 'Mrs Snobbydrawers is here to see you.'

'Eddie, you really shouldn't call her that.'

'It's what Harry used to call her,' said Eddie, flicking a thumb towards Harry's image on the TV screen. 'Anyway, she's out by the pool. You want me to get rid of her?'

'No, it's fine.' Donna dabbed at her eyes with the tissue. 'How do I look?'

'You might want to…' Eddie made a circling gesture with his finger around his own eyes.

'Oh shit,' said Donna, uncurling her legs from beneath her. 'Tell her I'll be out in a few minutes. Get her a drink or something, yeah?'

As Eddie left the room, she took the box of tissues and went over to the empty fireplace next to the TV screen. She inspected her reflection in the mirror above it and set to work repairing the damage to the smudged mascara. When she'd finished, she took a step back and combed her fingers through her thick auburn hair. Colour needs a bit of a touch-up, she thought. Still, not bad for a fifty-two year old, wouldn't you say, Harry?

She picked up a framed photograph from the mantelpiece and stared at the picture of her and Harry on their silver wedding anniversary. A candlelit dinner for two at a fancy restaurant in Paris, holding hands across the table. She was laughing, and Harry was leaning forward, a big grin on his face and saying something. — Something? Even now, she could remember exactly what he'd said, word for word. "You know what, darlin'? Twenty-five years wed, an' I still bloody loves yer just as much as the day I first clapped eyes on yer."

Donna smiled and lightly kissed the photograph before replacing it on the mantelpiece.

'Right then,' she said. 'Better not keep Mrs Snobbydrawers waiting, had we?'

6

The pain was still there, particularly in his ribs and his lower back, but the only visible signs of his mauling at the hands — or rather, fists, knees, forehead and feet — of Mountainman Machin were a plaster above one eye and another across the bridge of his nose. At least the pain was almost bearable now, although he hadn't felt ready to leave his sickbed quite so soon until Sandra had told him to quit his malingering and damn near dragged him out of it. Whatever happened to the idea that women were supposed to be the caring sex?

Trevor trudged behind the supermarket trolley, hunched over with his forearms resting on the handle and with more than an air of the bored teenager about him. This would have given entirely the wrong impression, however, because he was far too deep in thought to have been bored. In fact, so deep in thought was he that he was only vaguely conscious of the direction Sandra was heading in as he traipsed behind her from one aisle to another. Nor had he even noticed that she was dropping things into the trolley that weren't actually on the shopping list — a practice he would normally have condemned vehemently as bordering on anarchy.

'This the one?' said Sandra.

Trevor brought the trolley to a squeaking halt, inches short of bashing into her, and looked up. She was holding out a jumbo-sized tin of dog food for his inspection.

'But where's it all gone?' he said.

'Well, my guess would be Milly ate it all. Unless of course you were feeling a bit peckish one night and—'

'No, the money.' Trevor stole a furtive glance back over his shoulder and whispered, 'Harry Vincent's money.'

'Why you whispering?'

Trevor glanced back over his other shoulder and continued whispering. 'We can't have spent twenty-five grand in... what? Eighteen months?'

Sandra counted the expenses off on her fingers. 'Holiday in the Maldives? New car? Not much business coming in?'

She deposited six tins of dog food into the trolley and carried on along the aisle. Trevor followed, slouching a little less than before but his mind still occupied — at least at that particular moment — with matters he considered to be far more important than brands of dog food.

Even after all this time, the very thought of Harry Vincent never failed to induce what amounted to a mild panic attack — sweating, trembling and the sensation that a group of Japanese taiko drummers had started to pound out an up-tempo rhythm inside his chest. Vincent had been a semi-retired gangster that Trevor and Sandra had crossed, entirely by accident, and who had come terrifyingly close to doing them serious physical harm — or worse. The last they'd seen of him had been in a flat in Bristol when Vincent had been lying on the floor with a bullet hole in each foot and two MI5 agents standing over him. What had happened to him after that was anybody's guess, and although Sandra had always insisted the guy must be dead, Trevor had never been entirely convinced. Eighteen months later and he still had the occasional nightmare about Harry Vincent suddenly turning up and demanding his twenty-five grand back — with menaces. The twenty-five grand that Trevor and Sandra — or more precisely, Sandra — had waltzed off with, and of which, apparently, very little now remained.

Two aisles further on, Sandra stopped and took a large packet of Weetabix from the shelf. Then she changed her mind and swapped it for a small packet.

'I don't see we have much choice,' she said.

'Big packet's cheaper, weight for weight,' said Trevor distractedly as if the remark was instinctive rather than resulting from any conscious deliberation.

'I'm talking about the Greek job. It's about the only offer we've got at the moment, and the money's not bad. At least it'll tide us over for a while till business picks up again.'

She strode off ahead, and Trevor hurried to keep up with her.

'So how bad is he exactly?' he said.

'Who?'

'This old bloke we're supposed to look after.'

'Not sure, to be honest. Probably just old age stuff. Arthritis, rheumatism, whatever.' She paused by the refrigerated section and added two cartons of milk to the growing pile of groceries in the trolley.

'We won't have to... you know... do bedpans and stuff like that, will we?' said Trevor.

'No idea,' said Sandra.

Trevor screwed up his face at the prospect of the bedpan aspect of the operation, which created another doubt in his mind.

'Why us though?' he said. 'We're a detective agency, not a nursing agency, so how come they want *us*?'

'She didn't say.'

'She?'

'Donna. The woman who wants to book us.'

'Donna who?'

Sandra took a pack of butter from the cold cabinet. 'She didn't give a second name.'

'All sounds a bit mysterious if you—' Trevor began but suddenly noticed what she'd done. 'Hang on, hang on,' he said and grabbed a twinpack of margarine tubs, taped together and labelled with a "2-for-1" sticker. 'Look.'

'But you hate margarine,' said Sandra. 'In fact, *I* hate margarine and come to think of it, even Milly hates margarine.'

'Should last even longer then.' He was about to drop the marge into the trolley when he caught a direct hit from one of Sandra's famous withering looks and tossed the twinpack back into the refrigerator.

They carried on in silence as far as the deli counter, where the sight of a dozen or so plastic trays piled high with various cuts of bloody red meat flashed another thought into his mind. 'And while we're on the subject, what about Milly?'

'We take her with us of course.'

'On a plane?'

Sandra had just opened her mouth to speak to the woman behind the deli counter but instantly switched her attention back to Trevor. 'A *plane*? — Listen, Trevor, if you think for one moment that I'm going to set foot on a plane with you ever again in my life, then you are seriously mistaken. That Maldives trip was a bloody nightmare.'

'I told you I hated flying.'

'Yes, but you didn't tell me you were going to howl like a banshee all the way.'

'I was in pain,' said Trevor, forcing back the pout that he knew was about to surface. 'Pressure on my eardrums. I thought my head was going to explode.'

'Flight crew thought it was some weird kind of air rage.'

'Can I help you, madam?'

It was the woman behind the counter, but Sandra kept her eyes on Trevor when she said, 'Somehow I doubt it.'

Then she ordered a quarter pound of sliced ham and headed for the drinks section with Trevor wheeling the trolley beside her.

'So if we're not flying, how *do* we get there?' he said.

'The camper van?'

Trevor felt a warm glow and the rush of something that almost amounted to excitement. It was always the same whenever a trip in the van was on the cards, and he'd never taken it out of the country before, so the Greek job was beginning to sound far more appealing until another potential snag occurred to him.

'But don't dogs have to have all sorts of documents and jabs and stuff if you take them abroad?'

'No time for all that,' said Sandra. 'We'll just have to smuggle her through.'

'Milly? Are you serious?'

Sandra said it was highly unlikely that anybody would bother to check anyway, seeing as they were only travelling through EU countries, but Trevor wasn't so sure. And while they continued to discuss the issue of how best to get Milly to Greece without the usual mayhem associated with even taking her from one end of the street to the other, they were only dimly aware of the announcement which came over the supermarket's tannoy:

'This is a customer announcement. Would the owner of a blue Peugeot, registration number LG 12 TBR, please return to their vehicle immediately as their, um... dog appears to be destroying the upholstery. Thank you.'

Sandra's awareness became instantly less dim at the mention of the registration number, and she grabbed Trevor's arm to silence him. At the end of the announcement, their eyes met for the briefest of moments before Sandra said 'Oh Jesus', and they raced towards the checkouts, abandoning the shopping trolley in their wake.

7

There weren't many moments in Jackie Summerfield's life that she would have described as blissful, but this one was certainly close. Sitting on the edge of a swimming pool under the hot sun and dangling her legs in the cool, shimmering water was hardly a new experience, but this was different. This was Donna's pool, which meant she was away from her own house and out of earshot of her father's abusive demands for attention. If he wet himself now, someone else would have to deal with it — specifically Simon — although she knew from experience that he'd probably leave her to do the cleaning up when she got back. Still, as long as Donna came up with the goods, she'd be able to escape for a whole three weeks or more, even though it meant spending most of that time with her dope of a husband.

She took a sip from her gin and tonic and felt a tiny spasm of pleasure at the piney taste and the comforting clink of the ice cubes inside the glass. It was the perfect drink to accompany her near-bliss-experience, which was enhanced still further by the view in front of her. Not that it was much different to the view from her own villa. The rolling expanse of olive groves which drifted gently down to the crescent of the bay, flanked on either side by two small mountain ranges, was almost identical except for one crucial addition. — This was the young Greek god whose day job appeared to be as Donna's pool boy, scooping leaves and dead insects from the water with a long-handled net, his shoulder-length black hair too often falling forward and tantalisingly obscuring much of his face. Jackie slid her sunglasses down the bridge of her nose by a fraction of an inch to get a more realistic image of the darkness of his skin, most of which was exposed apart from a pair of low-slung, blue and white checked swimming shorts that ended just above his knees.

She took another drink, but the spasm of pleasure this time had less to do with the taste of the gin and far more to do with the way the lad's muscles ebbed and flowed beneath the surface of the taut young skin. She was especially taken with the tattoo on his left upper arm. Some kind of helmeted warrior holding a sword that quivered with every twitch of his biceps.

'Hot, isn't it?'

The words had barely left her mouth before she flushed with embarrassment. Of all the banal things to say, she'd blurted out the most inane comment about the state of the weather. Six years living in Greece, and it seemed she still hadn't shaken off that particular British obsession. But at least she hadn't been thinking out loud and said "Hot, isn't he?" instead. Not that she needed to worry. The lad obviously hadn't heard her as he didn't so much as glance in her direction but studiously continued with his pool cleaning duties. Then she spotted the earpiece through the tumbling black hair and the thin white cables which traced their way down the front of his torso and disappeared into a pocket in his swimming shorts.

'I see you've met our Manolis then.'

Jackie turned to see Donna standing behind her, and even the enormous sunglasses she was wearing couldn't conceal the smirk on her face. She was dressed in a short white bathrobe, the silky material of which was so sheer that her black swimsuit was clearly visible beneath.

The heat had only just subsided from Jackie's cheeks,

but it returned now with a vengeance.

Donna laughed. 'It's okay, Jackie. I've had the same thoughts myself. — Drink all right?'

Jackie looked down at the glass in her hand, grateful for the opportunity to turn away from Donna's gaze. 'Fine thanks. You not having one?'

'Trying to cut down,' said Donna, patting her stomach, which was already flat enough to be the envy of a woman half her age. It was certainly the envy of Jackie, who could never understand how much younger her friend looked even though they'd been born within a few months of each other.

Donna perched herself on the end of a nearby sun lounger. 'So how's the old bugger doing then?'

'Dad or Simon?'

'I suppose I meant your dad really.'

Jackie took a slug of gin and tonic. 'Difficult as ever. Worse since I told him we were going away. First thing he did was wet the bed, and I know he did it deliberately. — You sure these people of yours are going to be able to cope?'

'All I can say is they come highly recommended. A friend of mine's used them a few times now, and she's not the easiest to please. Not by a long chalk.'

'But they're still not a definite?' said Jackie.

'I told them I needed to know by the end of today.'

'Here's hoping, eh?' said Jackie and drained her glass, taking the remains of one of the ice cubes into her mouth at the same time.

'Same again?'

'Go on then,' Jackie said, her voice slightly distorted through the ice. 'I *am* nearly on holiday after all.'

Donna shifted her position on the sun lounger and called out towards the house, 'Eddie?'

During most of their conversation, Jackie had kept her eyes fixed on Manolis, albeit from a sideways angle in the hope that Donna wouldn't notice.

'Yes, he's quite a treasure, our Manolis,' said Donna, who obviously *had* noticed.

'How often do you have him?' said Jackie and immediately regretted her choice of words when both of Donna's eyebrows appeared over the top of her sunglasses. 'I didn't mean that,' she added hastily. 'I meant— Or maybe I did mean that.'

'Jackie, he's nineteen. You're old enough to be his—'

'I know. I know. But you can't help—'

'In fact, the way some kids carry on these days, you'd be old enough to be his grandmother.'

Jackie knew it was only a joke, but the remark still stung. 'Oh thanks.'

'I'm only pulling your leg. God, you're the same age as I am.'

'Yes, but you always look—'

'Mrs V?' Eddie had appeared as if from nowhere. It was a knack he seemed to have, which Jackie always found disconcerting.

'Get Mrs Sno— Summerfield another G and T, will you?'

Eddie stooped to pick up Jackie's empty glass. He also seemed to be keeping a close eye on Manolis, but for an entirely different reason.

'You not finished that yet?' he called out to the young Adonis at the far side of the pool, but when he got no response, he snatched up a pebble from the top of an ornamental plant pot and tossed it into the water a foot from the scooping net.

Manolis looked up and removed one of his earpieces.

'*Pisína*,' said Eddie, pointing at the surface of the pool. 'Why you not… *térma*?'

Manolis grinned cheerily back at him, said 'Okay', replaced his earpiece and carried on with his work.

'Christ's sake,' Eddie muttered.

'Eddie doesn't think Manolis is quite the treasure I do,' Donna said to Jackie in a stage whisper.

'He's an idle little—' Eddie began, but Donna cut him off.

'Any phone calls?'

'Just the one. Somebody called Sandra Gray. I said you'd ring back.'

'Ah,' said Donna, getting to her feet.

Jackie took off her sunglasses. 'Is that...?'

'Fingers crossed, eh?'

Donna followed Eddie across the terrace and up the marble steps to the veranda. When they'd disappeared through the sliding patio door into the living room, Jackie kicked her legs back and forth in the cool water of the pool and stared down at her crimson-painted toenails. At least her *feet* didn't look old, she thought. Perfect if Manolis happened to have a foot fetish.

She looked up to see that he'd worked his way round to her side of the pool and was now no more than three or four yards from her.

'Hard work in this heat,' she said, but as she'd expected, he hadn't heard her over whatever music he was listening to, so she waved her arm to get his attention.

Once again, Manolis removed one of the earpieces, and he smiled at her with his head cocked slightly to one side.

'I was wondering how much you charged for pool cleaning,' said Jackie. 'I've got a pool just like this one and I—'

She broke off when Manolis's smile gave way to a frown, and she realised he couldn't understand a word she was saying.

'*Póso kostéezei*?' she said, resorting to her faltering Greek. '*Ya...*' But her basic vocabulary let her down, so she pointed at the pool and then attempted a mime which was supposed to represent scooping up leaves and dead insects with a net. '*Pósa evró*? You. *Mia óra.*'

Manolis pointed a finger at his chest. '*Egó?*'

'*Nai.*'

There was a pause while he appeared to seek inspiration from the handle of his scooping net, and then the smile returned, revealing even more of his dazzling white teeth than before. He gabbled something in Greek, but the only words Jackie could make out were *pénde* and *evró*. Five euros an hour for pool cleaning was probably a bit on the steep side, but what the hell.

'What — day — could — you — come?' she said, falling back on the time-honoured British habit of speaking English to foreigners as if they were not only deaf but half-witted as well.

This was met with another frown and a blank expression of complete incomprehension, so she tried again. '*Ti méra boreís na*... er, come to *spíti mou ya*... Oh never mind. I'll wait till Donna gets back.'

Manolis's frown deepened, and his shoulders came up towards his ears.

'Do you speak any English at all?' said Jackie. '*Miláte angliká?*'

'*Óchi*,' said Manolis with a backwards tilt of his head.

'So you wouldn't know what I was saying if I were to tell you I'd pay you a sight more than five euros an hour just to be able to—'

'Jackie? Start packing.'

Jackie swivelled round to see Donna hurrying towards her across the terrace, a glass in one hand and giving her a thumbs up signal with the other.

8

Frank's mouth dropped open the moment he stepped over the threshold of what used to be The Dog and Duck but had now been renamed Monty's. And not just renamed either. The saloon and public bars had been knocked into one long room with a bar running almost the entire length of the far wall. Neat rows of tables and chairs filled most of the floor area, interspersed here and there with settees and matching armchairs. Bright lights reflected off every gleaming surface, giving a hospital laboratory atmosphere to the place. The pool table had gone, as had the dart board, the fruit machine and Frank's favourite old settle where he used to spend many a happy hour drinking with his mates.

Scanning the unfamiliar surroundings as he went, he followed Eric and Kate to a table near the far corner of the room, his feet slapping against the highly polished wooden floor where an age-worn, and often sticky, carpet used to be. He flopped down onto a chair with a heavy sigh. 'What the fook 'appened 'ere then?'

'I told you it had changed,' said Eric. 'Paddy was losing money hand over fist, so he sold up.'

'Who to? Little Lord Fauntleroy?'

Eric laughed. 'It's the fashion these days, I'm afraid. Nobody wants the old pubs any more.'

'Still sell beer though, do they?' Frank said with a nod towards the bar. 'I'd go, but I'm a bit skint as it 'appens.'

'It's waiter service,' said Kate without looking up from the menu she'd been studying since they'd sat down.

As if on cue, a young man in a white shirt and apron arrived at their table, notebook and pen in hand. 'Welcome to Monty's. And what can I get you today?'

'What you got on draught?' said Frank, eyeing the waiter with suspicion.

'Pardon me?' said the waiter.

'You know. *Draught*.' Frank pulled an imaginary pint with an imaginary handpump and then added, 'Bitter?'

Understanding flooded the young man's face. 'Oh, I'm sorry sir, we don't sell bitter. But we do have a rather good *weissbier* which you might enjoy.'

'Vice *what*?'

'Wheat beer,' Kate muttered.

'Wheat?' said Frank. 'Fook me, did they run out of hops since I were inside?'

Before the waiter could even begin to think how to answer, Eric stepped in and ordered two wheat beers, and Kate opted for a Chardonnay with ice.

'Christ almighty,' said Frank. 'Ever since I got me release date, all I could think about was sitting down in me old local and how good that first taste were gonna be. And what do I find? Some poncey gaylords' knocking shop where you can't even get a decent pint o' beer.'

He snatched up a menu from the table and squinted at it, alternately holding it at arm's length and then close to his face before settling on a position midway between the two.

'I take it you're not too keen on the place then,' said Kate.

Frank ignored the remark. 'And what 'appened to the steak and kidney pies Paddy's missus used to do?' With considerable difficulty, he read aloud from the menu. 'Goo-acka-mole and core-eetso brushcutter. Salmon rilette. Angel hair pasta with prossycuto and shaved ricotta. Chicken queasy-dilla. — What's a bloody queasy-dilla when it's at 'ome?'

Kate leaned forward and pointed to the relevant sentence on Frank's menu. 'Quesadilla. Chargrilled tortilla filled with a red pepper and chili salsa and Monterey Jack cheese, served with tzatziki.'

'Bollocks to that,' said Frank and twisted round in his chair. His gaze fell on the plate a middle-aged woman was eating from at the next table. ''Scuse me, love, but what you got there?'

'I'm sorry?'

Frank nodded towards her plate. 'What you eatin'?'

The woman glanced at her male companion as if seeking guidance on how to respond and then down at the food in front of her. 'Um, it's calamari with saffron aioli.'

'Nice, is it?'

'Um, yes. Very.'

'Looks bloody disgusting to me.'

'Frank,' said Eric in a heavily chiding tone.

Frank spun round to face him. 'What?'

'Look,' said Eric, 'I know you've been away for a while, but you'll have to—'

'A while? Fifteen fooking years and you call that "a while"?'

'All I'm saying is—'

'What did you do? Nine, wasn't it?' said Frank, taking a battered tobacco tin from his overcoat pocket.

'Oh, come off it, Frank. You know as well as I do you'd have been out at the same time as me if you'd behaved yourself. But no. You had to go and—'

Kate ostentatiously cleared her throat and tipped her head at the minutely thin cigarette Frank had placed between his lips.

'You can't smoke that in here, Frank,' said Eric.

'I know, I know,' said Frank. 'I been in prison, not livin' under a fookin' rock on the far side o' the moon.

— I just forgot, is all.'

He took the cigarette from his mouth and put it back in the tobacco tin, slamming the lid shut with the palm of his hand. His eyes ranged around the room once again, and he shook his head, his expression conveying both bewilderment and contempt. 'Jesus. What's 'appened to this country since I been away?'

'We discovered the wheel?' said Kate.

'Fun-nee,' said Frank with a menacing curl of his lip. 'All I can say is I 'ope the bars in Greece are a bloody sight better than this craphole.'

Eric lowered his voice. 'Frank, if we get what we're after, you'll be able to buy a whole chain of bars and turn them into whatever you like.'

'Yeah, well, first we 'ave to—'

'Are you ready to order?' The waiter had returned with a tray of drinks, and he set two wheat beers and a Chardonnay down on the table.

'Yes,' said Frank. 'I'll have the steak and kidney pie with mash and peas.'

A cloud of confusion passed across the waiter's face as if he'd never heard of such a dish, but before he could respond, Eric intervened once again. 'It's okay. He's pulling your leg.'

'Oh, I see,' said the waiter with the briefest and most unconvincing of laughs and took his notepad and pen from his back pocket.

Frank was holding his glass up to the light and closely examining its contents. ''Ere, this ain't right. It's all cloudy.'

'It's supposed to be like that,' said Kate. 'It's a wheat beer.'

Frank took a tentative sip and his features instantly bunched into a grimace of disgust. 'Not only does it look like piss, it bloody tastes like it an' all.'

The waiter shifted his weight from one foot to the

other. 'Shall I give you a couple more minutes to decide?'

'No need, son. I've decided already,' said Frank, taking the cigarette back out of his tobacco tin and rummaging in his overcoat pockets for a box of matches.

The waiter poised his pen over his notepad in readiness to write down the order.

'And you won't be needing that either,' said Frank. 'Not unless you're gonna draw me a map of where I can find the nearest chippie.'

With that, he got to his feet, lit the cigarette and blew a lungful of smoke into the waiter's face. Then he grabbed his walking stick from the back of his chair and hobbled off towards the exit.

9

The atmosphere inside the van was stifling, not only from the heat but also from the tension that had been brewing steadily between Trevor and Sandra for the past hour or so. According to the dealer who'd sold it to him, the converted VW Transporter was "what we in the trade call an *entry level* camper van". This meant that it was lacking in some of the finer luxuries, such as a toilet, a shower and anything approaching an efficient system for cooling the inside of the van in a hot climate. Even with all the windows open, Trevor's T-shirt was wringing wet, and the sweat from his brow periodically dripped into his eyes, stinging them with its salt. Sandra, on the other hand, seemed to be deriving some relief from the battery powered mini-fan which she held constantly beneath her chin. Trevor had asked her to "Give us a go on that, will you?" soon after they'd driven out of the ferry port, but she'd refused, saying, "I told you when we were on the boat that we should get one each from the shop, but you said they were a waste of money".

Trevor grabbed an already damp towel from the dashboard and wiped another cascade of sweat from his eyes. But the moment his vision was restored, he spotted a dog lying asleep near the edge of the road, and he swung the steering wheel sharply to the right to avoid it.

'Shit, that was close,' he said.

'Would have been a lot less close if you'd been driving on the right side of the road,' said Sandra, returning her gaze to the map which was spread out on her lap.

'Oh, bloody Nora. Not again,' said Trevor, rapidly veering the van into the right-hand lane after a brief glance in his wing mirror. 'I'm never going to get the hang of this.'

'Well, I rather hope you do for all our sakes. I don't think turning up in the back of a hearse would give our new employers the right impression somehow.'

The sideways lurch of the van had apparently woken Trevor's lean-looking black and tan mongrel, Milly, who until now had been curled up nose-to-tail and snoring softly on the floor behind them. She lunged forward into the gap between the driver and passenger seats and in so doing, managed to knock the gear stick into neutral.

Trevor slammed it back into gear again before the van could come to a complete stop. 'Thanks, Milly. That's a great help.'

Milly responded by wagging her tail like it was an out-of-control metronome and licking the perspiration from Trevor's forearm with feverish enthusiasm.

'Oh good,' said Trevor. 'Sweat *and* saliva.'

Sandra lifted her head from the map and twisted round in her seat to look out of the back window. 'What was the name of that village we just went through?'

'No idea,' said Trevor. 'All the signs are in Greek. — *Neo* something, I think.'

Sandra frowned and went back to studying the map. 'It's got to be round here somewhere.'

'You said that an hour ago.'

'Ten minutes, to be precise.'

'Why don't you just phone her?'

'And say what exactly? "Hello? Mrs Summerfield? We're the people you've entrusted to look after your elderly father for the next few weeks and we're totally unable to follow even the simplest of directions".'

'And turning up in the middle of the night is going to

look good, is it?'

Sandra turned the map through ninety degrees and traced a thin wiggly line on the map with her fingertip. 'Gotcha,' she said and turned to Trevor with a triumphant smile. 'I told you we had to be close.'

'How close?'

'Five or six clicks.'

'God, I hate that expression,' said Trevor. 'This is Greece, not the Vietnamese jungle.'

Milly, who had presumably absorbed all of the salt she required from Trevor's arm, now turned her attention to the road ahead, planting her front paws squarely on the dashboard and letting out a persistent series of whining sounds.

'She'll need a pee first,' said Trevor, giving the dog a reassuring couple of pats on the head.

'Her and me both,' said Sandra, roughly folding the map and dropping it onto the dashboard next to Milly's left paw.

Trevor steered the van onto what seemed to pass as a hard shoulder and switched off the engine. He stretched expansively and wiped his face with the damp towel as Sandra opened the passenger door and jumped out. Through the open side window, he watched her hurry towards the nearest clump of bushes.

'Watch out for snakes,' he called out after her. 'And that goes for you too,' he said, tapping Milly lightly on the tip of her nose and clipping a lead to her collar.

* * *

The enormous living room of Marcus Ingleby's villa was similar, if not quite identical, to Donna's, which was hardly surprising since both houses were designed by the same architect and built about the same time. The interiors lavishly demonstrated the architect's apparent obsession with pale grey marble and burnished chrome, and in the Ingleby living room, the furniture blended in rather than contrasted with its surroundings. A long L-shaped settee and three armchairs were all chrome-framed and upholstered in pale grey and occupied almost half of the floor space. The remainder was taken up by a large, oval dining table and chairs and a kitchen area, which was separated from the rest of the room by a marble-topped breakfast bar.

Ingleby was slouched in the armchair that was furthest from the kitchen and was using a remote to channel-hop the seventy-inch plasma TV on the wall in front of him. He took a drag on his cigarette and, without looking, casually flicked ash in the general direction of the onyx ashtray on the occasional table beside him. The ash missed its target and fell instead onto the arm of the chair, joining another half dozen deposits of cigarette ash.

Despairing of ever finding anything interesting to watch on the TV, he clicked it off and dropped the remote onto his lap, then bent down to adjust the Velcro straps on his half-full catheter bag, which was almost entirely visible below the left leg of his khaki knee-length shorts.

'What time you say they were coming?' he shouted.

'Any minute now,' said Jackie, who was busy unloading the dishwasher in the kitchen.

Ingleby grunted and stubbed his cigarette out in the ashtray as if he was trying to grind it into submission.

'You sure you don't want to get dressed before they get here?' said Jackie.

He glanced down at the deeply tanned skin of his bare chest and stroked the sparse sprouting of white hairs. 'I *am* dressed.'

Jackie came towards him, drying her hands on a tea towel and wearing a full length butcher's apron and a simpering expression. 'It's just that... you know.'

Her eyes drifted down to the catheter bag, and Ingleby followed her gaze.

'What?' he said. 'They never seen a piss bag before? I thought you told me they were medically trained.'

'Yes, I know, but you don't want to make a bad impression on the—'

Ingleby pulled himself into a more upright position in the armchair. 'I'm not asking them on a sodding date. I'm paying them shedloads of cash so you and Simple Simon can piss off to Blighty, so as far as I'm concerned they're just the hired help.'

'Yes, but—'

Jackie got no further with her next point in an argument she was never going to win because Simon called out from the top of the marble staircase. 'Darling, have you seen my Ray-Bans?'

'Prick,' said Ingleby, not caring less whether his son-in-law could hear him or not. 'Why doesn't he call them sunglasses like everyone else?'

'In the kitchen, next to the wine cooler,' Jackie shouted.

An impish grin swept across her father's face. 'Speaking of which,' he said. 'Be a good girl and fetch us a drink, will yer?'

'It's a bit early, Dad.'

Ingleby's grin vanished as quickly as it had arrived. 'Sod you then. I'll get me own.'

He got up from the armchair with rather more agility than he usually displayed and padded across the marble floor to a semi-circular glass and chrome bar in the corner of the room. Selecting a thirty year old malt whisky from the shelf behind the bar, he poured himself a moderate measure and was about to replace the cap on the bottle when Jackie said, 'Just don't go mad then, eh? We don't want you to...'

Her voice tailed off as Ingleby doubled the quantity of whisky in his glass and took a generous slug. 'Cheers, darlin'. Happy holidays.'

He crossed the floor back to his armchair and had just sat down when there was the blast of a vehicle horn from outside.

'Sounds like my nannies have finally made it then,' he said, taking a cigarette from the pack on the table next to the chair.

Jackie was already halfway to the terrace door by the time he'd finished the sentence.

'What?' he said. 'You gonna greet 'em in your pinny? Tut tut. Don't want them thinking you're the maid, do we?'

His daughter stopped in her tracks, paused for a moment and then removed her apron, dropping it onto the arm of the settee along with the tea towel. She turned back towards the door, but hesitated again and stuffed the apron and tea towel behind the nearest cushion.

'First impressions and all that,' Ingleby called out after her as she stepped out onto the terrace.

* * *

Trevor parked the van on the gravel driveway in front of the villa and tooted the horn.

'What did you do that for?' said Sandra.

'Er, let them know we'd arrived?' said Trevor with heavy sarcasm while fending Milly off with both hands when she attempted to climb over his head and out through the open side window.

'So they don't have doorbells in Greece?'

Trevor shrugged. 'How should I—?'

He was interrupted by a loud yawn from the back seat of the van and the words 'What's happening?'

They both turned towards the sound and watched as

Sandra's nephew threw off the thin sheet under which he'd been fast asleep for the past couple of hours. His short dark hair was heavily gelled and the thinness of his moustache stood in stark contrast to his unusually prominent eyebrows. Knotted around his throat was a red neckerchief, and below this, he wore a blue and white hooped T-shirt.

'Hey, Herbert. Glad you could join us,' said Sandra.

Herbert grabbed a black beret from the top of the fitted unit next to the back seat and placed it on his head, adjusting the angle to something that resembled rakish.

'*Zut alors, mais je suis très faim,*' he said in an accent far closer to Margate than Marseille.

Trevor caught Sandra's eye and scowled.

10

A faint breeze managed to find its way into the olive grove, but it brought little relief to Frank, who on numerous occasions that afternoon had complained that he was "sweating like a bastard". Eric had no idea why people of doubtful parentage would perspire any more than those who had been conceived within wedlock, but he decided not to contest the issue as he knew he would inevitably regret having wasted his breath. Besides, there were far more important matters to attend to, which, at that particular moment, involved keeping a close eye on the front of Marcus Ingleby's imposing — but to Eric's mind, somewhat tastelessly designed — villa. The large, flat-roofed block of white-painted concrete with its uPVC window shutters could scarcely be described as aesthetically pleasing, and the deep purple bougainvilleas climbing up each corner were its only mitigating feature.

'Don't these bloody crickets ever shut up?' said Frank, who was standing at the base of the olive tree which Eric had climbed into an hour or so earlier.

'It would appear not,' said Eric without taking his eyes from the binoculars. Until then, he had mostly been able to block out the incessantly loud chattering noise from his consciousness, but now that Frank had mentioned it, the din returned like a bout of particularly irritating tinnitus. 'It's called stridulation, the technical term.'

'Oh yeah? Well, I calls it fooking annoying, that's

what I calls it.'

Eric shifted his position from one branch to another to try to ease the cramp in his legs. It was way past time that Frank should have taken a turn on lookout duty, but Eric had little faith in his ability to concentrate on the job in hand. It would also mean having to put up with an even more intense barrage of moaning, which would no doubt be primarily focused on how being perched up in a tree played havoc with his rheumatoid arthritis.

Frank hadn't always been a whinger. On the contrary, when Eric had first met him more than twenty years ago, Frank had been the proverbial life and soul of the party whose glass was always more than half full — both metaphorically and literally. Well, maybe not when he'd *first* met him. That had been in Glenfield Prison when the two of them had shared a cell. Eric had never been to prison before and shouldn't have been there at all if there'd been any justice in the world — or at least in the Crown Court where he'd been convicted. It was his car all right, but it hadn't been him who was driving it when the lad had got knocked down. It had been stolen on the night of the hit-and-run, and the first Eric had known about it was when the police had come knocking on his door early the next morning. By then, the lad had died of his injuries, and what made matters a whole lot worse was that he was the nineteen year old son of a local bigwig who also happened to be one of the Chief Superintendent's regular golfing partners. Not surprisingly, the police had been keener than ever to make an early arrest, and since there was apparently no indication that his car had been broken into and he'd had no alibi to speak of, Eric had been the most likely candidate.

When he'd been released after serving two years of his sentence, he'd already been sacked from his job as head of English at a secondary school and had little prospect of finding similar employment now that he had a criminal record. Six months later, Frank was out, and the two of them had met up for a drink. Frank already had a job lined up to rob a post office in some sleepy market town up north and wanted Eric on the team because it needed somebody with "a posh accent and a bit of brain". But Eric had turned him down flat. Although he still harboured a deep bitterness towards the British system of justice that had treated him so shabbily, there was no way he was about to embark on a life of crime as a misguided and futile gesture of vengeance.

A year down the line, however, he was still unemployed, his wife had left him, and his house had been repossessed, so he'd given Frank a call. After all, he'd reasoned, if I'm to be treated like a criminal for the rest of my life, I may as well act the part and reap some of the benefits.

His first job with Frank was a supermarket robbery, and everything went exactly to plan. No-one got hurt — which was a strict condition of Eric's for any job he was to be involved in — and his share of the proceeds was enough to pay off the debts he'd accumulated and with a fair few quid to spare. There was also the adrenaline rush — something he'd never once experienced during all his years of teaching the Romantic Poets or the Victorian Novel to the likes of Form 4B — and he became more and more addicted to it with each new job.

But their luck finally ran out the day they robbed a jewellery shop, and Eric and Frank were both sent down for fifteen years. Eric had got out after nine, but Frank had served the full term, and the experience had clearly damaged him irreparably. The happy-go-lucky Yorkshireman with the perpetual cheery smile had been transformed into the bad-tempered whinger who was now standing beneath an olive tree in Greece and moaning his head off.

'I still don't see why we can't just go straight up and knock on the bastard's door,' Frank was saying.

Eric lowered the binoculars and wiped the sweat from his eyes with a handkerchief. 'Casing the joint is what I believe we used to call it in the good old days.'

Frank continued to complain about the heat, the crickets, his arthritic knee and a range of his other current annoyances for the next ten minutes until Eric spotted an elderly VW camper van pulling up on the driveway in front of the house. He adjusted the focus on the binoculars to get a sharper image and watched as the passenger door opened and a blonde woman in her early forties jumped down onto the gravel.

'There's a van just turned up,' he said.

'Oh yeah?' said Frank, his tone brimming with indifference.

'Woman and two men. And a dog. Looks a bit French, one of them.'

'A poodle?'

'What? — No, not the dog. One of the men.'

The dog — a black and tan mongrel — was hurtling around the driveway and in and out of the flower borders on either side of it as if it was being chased by a swarm of hornets. The non-French-looking man was shouting at it in what was clearly a vain attempt to bring it under control, and at exactly the same time as the dog squatted down in the middle of a clump of geraniums, another woman appeared from around the side of the house. Her bright, welcoming smile faded instantly when she caught sight of the dog, and although Eric couldn't hear the words, it was obvious from her expression and her pointing finger that she wasn't at all happy about the desecration of her flowerbed.

'I think that's Ingleby's daughter just come out of the house,' said Eric when she turned her face a little more in his direction. It was donkey's years since he'd last

63

seen her, but even from a distance, her posture and slightly raised chin gave her an air of haughtiness which was all too familiar. 'What was her name again?'

'I dunno,' said Frank. 'Maureen? Monica? Summat like that.'

'Jacqueline. That was it. Jackie. Doesn't seem to have aged that badly.'

'Well, bully for her,' said Frank. 'I need a slash.'

Eric heard the faint sound of a fly being unzipped and looked down to see Frank spreading his feet at the base of the tree.

'Not there,' he shouted. 'Go and find another tree. There's plenty enough to choose from.'

Frank stared up at him, his face an even brighter shade of red than normal in the heat. 'Jesus, Eric.'

'It's bad enough having to sit up in this damn tree for hours on end without having to put up with the stench of your piss as well.'

Frank muttered something inaudible and shuffled off to another olive tree about three metres away, and Eric resumed his surveillance with the binoculars. But there was nothing much happening other than a fair bit of chat and people shaking hands. Eric felt the cramp in both of his legs returning yet again and began to wonder whether there was much point in staying where he was. They'd probably seen all they were going to see, and it was doubtful now that Ingleby himself was going to make an appearance as they'd hoped.

When Jackie and the others disappeared from view around the side of the house, he lowered the binoculars and let them hang from the leather strap round his neck. Twisting himself round on the branch and gripping the one next to it with both hands, he was about to call out to Frank to come and give him a hand down when there was a shriek of terror, followed by a brief flurry of footsteps and the appearance of the top of Frank's head a few inches below Eric's dangling feet. Taking hold of the lowest substantial branch, Frank launched himself upwards and, defying his bulk and distinct lack of athleticism, managed to swing his backside onto it and stay put.

'Now what are you doing?' said Eric, tightening his grip on his own branch for fear of being dislodged by Frank's sudden ascent.

'Fooking snake.'

'What?'

'Fooking snake,' Frank repeated.

'Where?' said Eric and scanned the ground in their immediate vicinity.

'Over near that tree where I were 'avin' a piss. Gimme a lift up for Christ's sake.'

Eric reached down and grasped Frank's outstretched forearm, the veins standing out in his neck as he helped him clamber up onto the branch beside him. Frank's breathing was heavy and laboured, and despite its thickness and solidity, the entire branch vibrated from the effect of his shaking.

Once again, Eric surveyed the ground beneath them, paying particular attention to the area around the tree he presumed Frank had been referring to. 'Can't see it.'

'I'm telling you.'

'Any idea what kind?'

'How the fook should I know?' said Frank, swivelling his head towards him and almost losing his balance.

'Well there's a lot of different kinds of snake in Greece, and most of them aren't dangerous. Did it have diamonds on its back, for instance? They're the ones you need to look out for.'

'Diamonds on its back? Listen, David Attenborough, I don't give a monkey's whether it were wearin' a ginger wig and 'ad the crown bloody jewels up its arse. Snake's a snake, far as I'm concerned.'

'And if it's got a bit of a—'

'*Eh! Ti kánete páno sto théndro mou?*'

Eric and Frank looked down through the lower branches of the tree to see who it was that was shouting at them. It was a man of similar age to themselves — although possibly much older — with a face as gnarled as the olive trees around him and wearing a flat cap, checked woollen shirt and dark baggy trousers held tight at the waist by a thick leather belt. All of his clothing, including the cap, seemed in need of several hours' boil washing and some serious attention with a darning needle. But far more disturbingly, he had an ancient-looking double barrelled shotgun slung over his shoulder.

Eric and Frank exchanged glances.

'What he say?' said Frank.

'No idea,' said Eric, 'but I'm guessing these are his trees and he doesn't want us up in them.'

The old man moved closer to the foot of the tree and shouted something else in Greek.

'Tell him about the snake,' said Frank.

'Oh yes, because he obviously speaks perfect English, doesn't he?'

Undeterred, Frank pointed to the spot where he'd seen the snake and made a wriggling motion with his other arm. 'Snake. Over there. Big bastard. Snake-o. There.'

The man took off his cap and scratched his head. '*Ti?*'

'Jesus,' muttered Frank and then repeated his arm wriggling gesture, adding a strange hissing sound for good measure.

'*Fíthy?*' said the man, replacing the cap on his head, his expression appearing to register some understanding of what Frank was trying to communicate.

Frank shrugged. 'Probably.'

'*Okyá?*'

'Er… *si*.'

66

The old man spat on the ground, unslung the shotgun from his shoulder and marched towards the spot Frank had pointed to. Almost immediately, there were two very loud bangs and a small but impressive mushroom cloud of blood and snake shrapnel.

Eric and Frank held each other's wide-eyed gaze.

'Blimey,' said Eric.

'Fook me,' said Frank.

11

Marcus Ingleby could not have made it more obvious that he was taking no notice of his daughter whatsoever as she went through the motions of introducing him to his new temporary carers. Instead, he remained slumped in his armchair, taking frequent sips of his whisky and focusing his attention exclusively on Milly, who was standing on her hind legs on the other side of the sliding patio door, scratching manically at the glass with her claws.

Jackie touched Herbert lightly on the elbow. 'And this is, um...'

'Herbert, *monsieur*,' he said and took a step forward, his hand outstretched. '*Bonjour.*'

Ingleby ignored him.

'And this is Sandra.'

Ingleby shifted his position in the armchair and winced.

'Please,' said Sandra. 'Don't get up.'

'I've no intention of getting up,' he said, setting his whisky down on the table beside him. 'Just sorting out this bloody catheter thing.'

Both his hands worked away at the groin area of his khaki shorts, and his wince turned to a full-scale grimace. 'Bloody nightmare these things. Ever had to use one?'

'Well, I—' Sandra began.

'Not you,' he snapped. 'The blokes.'

'Er, no,' said Trevor, and Herbert shook his head.

'Ah, that's better,' said Ingleby, sitting back in his chair with a sigh of relief. 'Still, saves me having to trot to the khazi every few minutes.'

He sat forward again and patted the catheter bag on his leg as if it was the head of a favourite grandchild. 'Oops,' he said. 'Gettin' a bit full by the looks o' things. — Jacks, be a good girl and fetch us the bucket, will yer?'

His daughter's face flushed crimson. 'Dad! You know perfectly well you never use a bucket in public.' She turned to the others with the hollowest of laughs. 'He's just trying to embarrass me, that's all.'

Trevor and Sandra chorused a faint smile in response, while Herbert was apparently so mesmerised by the catheter bag that he'd failed to hear anything of the previous exchange.

'So you mean the other end actually goes into your...' he said, tailing off with a barely perceptible nod in the direction of Ingleby's groin.

'Perhaps this would be a good time to take us through your father's drug regime, Mrs Summerfield,' Sandra said quickly before Ingleby had a chance to reply.

'Well, I—'

'That's a lie,' said Ingleby, interrupting his daughter and rounding on Sandra with an expression of intense anger.

'Sorry?' said Sandra.

'I've done some bad things in my time, but no-one — and I mean *no-one* — can ever accuse me of having had a drug regime.'

He held Sandra's gaze for several seconds, then smirked at her with a theatrically exaggerated wink.

'Such a joker,' said Jackie, once again resorting to the hollow laugh of embarrassment.

Ingleby lit a cigarette and inhaled deeply. 'That your dog outside?' he said, smoke billowing from his mouth as he spoke.

The others all turned towards Milly, who had taken a short break from scratching at the patio door and was now sitting and steaming up the glass with her panting breath. But as soon as she realised that all eyes were upon her, she resumed her scratching with renewed vigour.

'Er, yes,' said Trevor. 'But it's okay. Mrs Summerfield has already explained that—'

'I've already explained that we can't allow pets inside the—' said Jackie, in the apparent belief that he'd be unable to finish the sentence unaided, but was then interrupted herself.

'Oh, let the bugger in for God's sake,' said Ingleby. 'I could do with some intelligent company for a change.'

Trevor frowned. 'I'm not sure that'd be such a—'

'Housetrained, is it?'

'Well, yes, but—'

'In he comes then,' said Ingleby, bringing his hand down sharply on the arm of his chair.

'"She", actually.'

'Can't blame the dog for that.'

Milly dropped down onto all fours when she saw Trevor approaching, and the moment he slid open the door, she hurtled into the living room, her paws scrabbling for traction on the marble tiles. With her nose close to the floor, she scurried in every direction, seemingly intent on carrying out a preliminary examination of her new surroundings in the shortest possible time. Trevor could hardly dare to watch as he waited for the inevitable calamity, which almost came about when Milly skidded into a tall podium, on top of which was a large — and very probably priceless — porcelain vase. The ornament rocked from side to side until it reached the point of no return and began its rapid descent to the ground, where it would no doubt have ended up as mosaic fodder if it hadn't been for Sandra's sideways lunge and perfectly timed two-handed catch.

Oblivious to how close she'd come to destroying an irreplaceable *objet d'art*, Milly then extended her area of olfactory interest to the kitchen area at the far end of the living room and disappeared behind the breakfast bar for a good minute and a half. All the while, the assembled human company waited in silence until she finally reappeared and paused momentarily to sniff the air as if trying to decide which of the previously encountered scents were worthy of further investigation.

Ingleby leaned forward in his armchair. 'Come on, girl,' he said with a click of his fingers. 'Come and say hello.'

The decision made for her, Milly loped casually over to him and instantly thrust her nose at his almost full catheter bag, snuffling at it with unabashed enthusiasm.

'Bit whiffy, eh?' said Ingleby, gently stroking the top of her head. 'I keep telling 'em it needs emptyin'.'

Trevor was wondering whether this would be an appropriate moment to intervene and try to establish some kind of control over the situation when Milly spotted the dangling end of one of the catheter bag's straps and grabbed it between her teeth. The ensuing tug-of-war between a laughing Ingleby and a grunting Milly came to an abrupt end, however, when Trevor sensed the need for immediate intervention and took a firm hold of Milly's collar, the dog finally obeying the "Leave!" command at the fifth time of asking.

'Well, that could have been seriously unpleasant,' said Ingleby, his continued laughter giving the lie to any genuine concern he may have had about the matter.

Sandra looked across at Jackie, who seemed to be frozen to the spot, her mouth equally motionless in the half open position.

'You were going to tell us about your father's

medication,' said Sandra.

It took a second or two for Jackie to register that she was being spoken to. 'Sorry, what? — Oh yes, of course. I'll fetch his chart.'

She set off towards the kitchen area, but she'd gone no more than half a dozen paces when the telephone rang.

'It's okay,' she called back over her shoulder. 'I'll take it out here.'

* * *

Donna stood by the fireplace, a cordless phone held to her ear, and in the other hand the framed photograph of her and Harry on their silver wedding anniversary.

The ringing tone clicked off, and Jackie's voice came on the line. '*Hello?*'

'Are they there yet?' said Donna.

'*Oh, hi, Donna. Yes. A few minutes ago.*'

'How do they seem?'

'*Er, okay I guess.*'

'You don't sound very sure.'

'*It's just that they've got a dog and there's three of them.*'

'Two people and a dog?'

'*No, three people and a dog.*'

'Who's the third then? I thought there was only supposed to be two.'

'*Sandra's nephew. He's only just left school apparently, so I can't see he's going to be a lot of use.*'

Donna could hear clattering sounds on the other end of the line and then a man's voice in the background: '*I thought you said they were by the wine cooler.*'

It was Simon.

'*Well, that's where they were the last time I saw them.*' Jackie's voice. Irritated.

'Hello?' said Donna.

'*Sorry, Donna. What were you saying?*'

'How's your dad taking to them?'

'*Hard to tell just yet, but I don't think he's planning on giving them an easy time of it.*'

'No surprise there then.'

The background noises had become increasingly louder with what sounded like the opening and closing of cupboard doors and drawers being slammed shut.

'*Bloody hell, Jackie. What have you done with them?*' Simon again.

'*I haven't done anything with them. And in case you hadn't noticed, I'm actually on the phone. — Sorry, Donna. You still there?*'

'Uh-huh.'

Donna heard Simon say something about "damned tidying sprees" and then Jackie's voice again.

'*I'm going to have to go, Donna. Major crisis here at the moment as you can probably tell, and I still haven't finished packing.*'

'Not to worry. I wanted to make sure everything was okay, that's all.'

'*Thanks. I'll see you when we get back.*'

'And have a great time, you hear?'

'*Bye then.*'

Donna clicked off the phone and set it down on the mantelpiece, satisfied that she'd put just the right amount of sincerity into "I wanted to make sure everything was okay". She couldn't give a toss whether everything was okay or not, other than to make sure that her plan was still on course and that her quarry had entered the trap. As far as she was aware, neither of them had the slightest experience of looking after incontinent old codgers like Marcus Ingleby, but so what? Ingleby's welfare hadn't exactly been a priority when she'd recommended them.

They hadn't been easy to track down, but when Harry had disappeared, she'd sent Eddie to England to do some digging, and he'd managed to get some information from a hired hand of Harry's called Jimmy MacFarland. He'd been reticent about saying anything at first, but Eddie had bunged him a few quid, and MacFarland had told him everything he knew. Well, maybe not everything. Eddie had been fairly sure that he'd held back on some of the details, but one thing MacFarland had been clear about was that a pair of interfering busybodies by the names of Trevor Hawkins and Sandra Gray had stitched Harry up, and it was at least partly down to them that he'd ended up in the hands of the Secret Service. And since that was the last anyone had heard of Harry, it wasn't much of a stretch to assume that MI5 had wasted him and then got rid of the body. There wasn't much Donna could do about the MI5 agents themselves of course, but Sandra Gray and Trevor Hawkins were a different matter altogether.

A faint smile crept across her face and, holding the photograph of her and Harry in both hands, she brought it to her lips and kissed his image through the glass.

'So far, so good, Harry darling.'

Putting the photograph down next to the phone, she wandered over to the patio window and stood for several seconds watching Manolis half-heartedly sweeping the terrace and creating more dust than he was removing.

'Eddie?' she called out eventually, her eyes still fixed on the young Greek.

Almost as if he'd been waiting for the summons, Eddie appeared instantly in the living room doorway, and although he'd arrived without the slightest sound, Donna knew he was there without even looking round.

'It's time,' she said.

Eddie joined her at the window and followed her gaze. 'You want me to fetch him?'

There was a brief silence before Donna replied. 'Pity really, but needs must, I suppose.'

12

The taverna was buzzing. The small interior was empty, devoid not only of customers but also any tables and chairs, all of which had been taken outside onto the L-shaped terrace, which thronged with men, women and children of all shapes and sizes. They were an eclectic mix of locals and tourists — mostly British and German but with other Europeans and a smattering of Americans — and almost all seemed intent on the common purpose of having "a great night out". To this end, the proprietor had cleared one area of the terrace to make way for dancing, and a dozen or fifteen revellers were currently taking full advantage of it.

The traditional Greek music was loud and mainly up-tempo and provided by an amplified three-piece band consisting of a young man with a bushy black beard on guitar, a slightly older woman with close cropped hair on bouzouki and — between the two of them — a singer in a floral-patterned cotton dress who looked like she'd far rather be at home with her feet up or even doing the ironing. Her lack of enthusiasm was more than made up for by the spirited performance of the other two musicians, however, and none of the dancers appeared to notice nor care about the po-faced apathy of the vocalist in the middle. On the contrary, most were far too busy concentrating on their dance steps, particularly the handful of foreigners who were being patiently tutored by some of the local Greeks. By far the least adept of these students was Frank Phelan, who was circling the dance floor in a group of ten, each dancer linked to the person on either side of them with an arm across their shoulders. On his right was the old farmer with the shotgun who they'd met in the olive grove earlier that day and who was now shouting unintelligible instructions into Frank's ear at almost every second step.

'Well, Frank looks like he's enjoying himself,' said Eric.

He and Kate were sitting at one of the tables furthest from the musicians, but he still had to shout to make himself heard.

'Must be the ouzo,' said Kate, who, along with the singer, looked as if she'd rather be elsewhere.

'That and his new Greek farmer pal egging him on. Thought the old devil was going to shoot us at one point.'

'Pity I missed it.'

'Us being shot?'

'Frank talking your way out of it. Especially as he doesn't speak a word of Greek and the old farmer guy doesn't speak any English.'

'It was certainly quite a performance, I must say. The "my father fought with the Greek guerillas during the war" part was a joy to behold. — Myo father fight...' Eric paused briefly to mime someone boxing. '...with you-o Greekoes in war-o.' This was followed by a mime of rifle shooting and dramatic explosions complete with vocally produced sound effects.

Kate laughed. 'At least he didn't try and do "guerilla".'

Eric responded with a wry smile.

'Oh my God,' said Kate. 'Don't tell me—'

Before Kate could finish her sentence, Eric pointed at her and then performed the traditional impersonation of a monkey, grunting and scratching his armpits with his arms pivoting at the elbows.

76

'That's when I really thought the guy was going to shoot us,' he said.

'I'm not surprised. — But I didn't think Frank even knew who his father was.'

'He doesn't,' said Eric, mildly distracted by a man of about Kate's age who had been looking in their direction — or more specifically, Kate's — for the past couple of minutes.

Catching Eric's eye, the man smiled and nodded, and Eric reciprocated, albeit in the understated and warily polite manner of the reserved Englishman. But this was apparently more than enough for the man to interpret the gesture as an invitation, and he rapidly approached their table.

'*Kalıspéra,*' he said, bending forward from the waist and raising his voice above the music.

'*Kalıspéra,*' said Kate, a strong note of suspicion in her tone.

The man's face lit up in surprise. '*Ah. Mıláte Ellınıká.*'

'*Léego, naı.*'

'*Brávo.*'

After another brief exchange in Greek, Kate smiled faintly and translated for Eric's benefit. 'He asked me if you were my husband, and when I told him you were my grandfather, he said you didn't look old enough.'

'I like him already,' said Eric. 'Does he speak any English?'

'Ah, I am sorry, *kírıe,*' said the man. 'You don't have the Greek like your wife— granddaughter?'

'I'm afraid not.'

'Then I try my English. It is good for me to practise.'

There then followed a short but awkward silence, during which the man shifted his weight from one foot to the other, obviously waiting to be asked to join them, and Eric carried out a quick appraisal. It was abundantly clear that the man was far more interested in Kate than the opportunity to improve his English, and although she was a grown woman and perfectly capable of making her own decisions in these matters, he couldn't help feeling protective towards her. Still, he seemed well-mannered and smartly turned out in a pale blue polo shirt and pressed jeans with thick black hair brushed back and neatly groomed. You could probably even describe him as "ruggedly good looking", Eric thought, as long as you were the type who went for the swarthy Mediterranean Heathcliff look.

'May I?' said the man, indicating one of the two vacant chairs at their table and presumably having grown impatient with the length of the awkward silence.

'Please do,' said Eric, mirroring the man's chair-indicating gesture and pretending not to have noticed Kate's look of disapproval.

'Thank you,' said the man, sitting down and extending his hand to Eric. 'My name is Pericles.'

'Like in the play, eh?' Eric shook his hand, which felt surprisingly dry considering the heat of the evening. 'I'm Eric.'

'William Shakespeare, yes,' said Pericles, beaming as if he was delighted that Eric had made the connection.

'And this is my granddaughter, Kate.'

Pericles took Kate's hand between both of his. 'Kiss me Kate,' he said, his smile even broader than before.

Kate snatched her hand back. 'What?'

Pericles's smile evaporated quicker than an ice cube in a Turkish bath. 'Like in the musical. Also Shakespeare, I think.'

'Ah yes,' said Eric. '*The Taming of the Shrew.*'

Pericles's smile returned. '*Étsı, brávo,*' he said and sat back in his chair, patently relieved that a potentially embarrassing misunderstanding had been averted. 'Now what will you drink with me? Ouzo? Tsiporo? Whisky?'

Kate covered the empty wine glass in front of her with her palm. 'Thank you, but—'

'Well, that's very kind of you,' Eric cut in. 'Just a beer for me, please.'

'And for Kate?'

'Er, red wine then, please.'

'Oraía,' said Pericles and twisted round in his chair in search of some service.

The moment his back was turned, Kate gave Eric a light kick under the table and stretched her face unnaturally wide to mouth the word "Why?".

Eric couldn't decide between a sheepish grin, a wink or a shrug as an appropriate response, but realising that any one of these would probably antagonise his granddaughter even more, he opted instead for bending down and stroking the skinny ginger cat which had been pestering them for food most of the evening.

'Sotiris!'

Eric sat upright again to see Pericles half standing and half sitting, staring into the middle distance with his right arm stretching vertically upwards like a small child asking permission for a desperately needed visit to the toilet.

'Sotiris!' Pericles shouted again, and this time, a middle-aged man with a double chin and quadruple bags under his eyes sidled over to their table.

Pericles gave him their order, and Sotiris headed back inside the taverna without so much as a nod of acknowledgement.

'So,' said Pericles, 'you are on holidays here in Greece?'

'Kind of,' said Eric. 'Bit of pleasure and a bit of business really.'

'Ah, but I thought you English say they should never be mixed — like malt whisky and Coca Cola.'

Pericles laughed a little too heartily at his own joke,

Eric smiled politely and Kate stared down into her empty wine glass.

'And where do you stay? An hotel in the town perhaps?'

'No, we've got an apart—'

Eric was interrupted by the unceremonious arrival of Frank, who slumped down in the only remaining vacant chair and wiped sweat from his face and neck with a once white handkerchief.

'Fook me, I'm roastin'.'

'And this is our friend, Frank,' said Eric. 'Frank, meet Pericles.'

Frank dutifully shook hands with Pericles but without making eye contact.

'Eh, but that Thanassis has got some go in 'im for an old'un,' he said.

'Thanassis?' said Eric.

'The old Greek farmer we met this afternoon.'

'Ah yes,' said Kate. 'The one who nearly shot you.'

'Bloody pillock keeps shoutin' at me 'ow to dance, but I can't understand a bloody word he's on about.' Frank stuffed the grubby handkerchief into his trouser pocket and rubbed at his leg. 'Fookin' knee's giving me some gip though. Reckon I could do with some more o' that rocket juice. What's it called? Ouzy?'

Kate sniffed. 'I think you'll find an Uzi is a submachine gun. You might have a bit more success if you ordered an *ouzo*.'

'Whatever,' said Frank and waved his hand in the air to dismiss the remark just as Sotiris got to the table with a tray of drinks for the others.

Fortunately, Sotiris was lighter on his feet than he looked, and with a reflex sidestep, managed to avoid Frank's hand sending the tray and its contents flying.

'Oh, there y'are,' said Frank, totally unfazed by the narrowly averted catastrophe. 'Ouzy please, mate. Make it a large 'un and plenty of ice.'

Sotiris's forehead creased into several folds of skin. '*Ouzy*?'

When Pericles came to his aid with a translation of Frank's order, he gave a slight shrug and once again set off back inside the taverna.

Frank nodded his appreciation at Pericles. 'What was the name again, mate? I weren't really listening before.'

'Pericles.'

'Like as in Perry Mason, yeah?'

Eric assumed this was meant to be a joke but then realised there wasn't the faintest flicker of a smile on Frank's face. Pericles clearly had no idea what Frank was talking about, but Kate shook her head at him to indicate that the remark really didn't merit any further consideration.

Apparently reassured, Pericles added some ice cubes to his whisky and raised his glass. 'So then, everyone. *Yámass.*'

All except Frank clinked their glasses together, and even Eric joined Kate in a '*yámass*' since it was one of the half dozen Greek words he actually knew. No sooner had they toasted their healths than Thanassis the farmer appeared, a drink in one hand and dragging an empty chair behind him with the other. He'd clearly made a considerable effort with his appearance since the episode in the olive grove, although his "Sunday best" was effectively a freshly laundered version of the checked shirt and dark baggy trousers he'd worn earlier in the day, but minus the cap and the shotgun.

'*Ethó eísai, kírie* Frank,' he said, clapping him on the shoulder and scanning the faces of the other three people at the table. The last of these was Pericles, and when Thanassis's eyes met his, the old farmer's demeanour of jovial *bonhomie* instantly gave way to a scowl of deep and bitter loathing.

'What's he say, Perry?' said Frank, tapping Pericles on the arm to get his attention.

But Pericles ignored him, his unblinking and expressionless gaze focused entirely on Thanassis. The two men locked stares in an ocular variation of a Mexican standoff, which continued for several seconds until Thanassis capitulated and stomped away, muttering under his breath.

'Something wrong?' said Eric.

Pericles spun round to face him, his features taut with a simmering anger. 'You know this *malákka*?'

'Not really. We bumped into him this after—'

'If you take my advice, you will— What is the expression? Drive clear of him. He is not a good man.'

'In what way?'

Pericles was about to answer when Sotiris came with Frank's ouzo and a small bowl of ice. He waited until Sotiris had moved out of earshot and then took a generous slug of his whisky. 'Let us just say I have had... dealings with him in my work.'

'Which is?' said Kate, more out of politeness than any genuine interest.

'Oh, did I not tell you?' said Pericles, his anger beginning to subside. 'I'm a police officer.'

* * *

Besides Kate and the singer in the band, the only other person who was clearly not enjoying himself that evening was sitting alone at a table close to the outer corner of the terrace's L-shape and almost continuously rolling a coin back and forth across the knuckles of his right hand. From here, he had a good view of Eric and Frank's table but without being too close for them to take any notice of him. They would also have had to make a special effort to peer through the sea of gyrating bodies on the dance floor, and even then, he doubted they'd recognise him. It had all been a very long time ago.

But Detective Chief Inspector Bruce Reynolds (retired) wasn't someone who left anything to chance, so he'd obscured most of his face with a baseball cap pulled low over his eyes and a two-week-old grey beard deliberately cultivated for the occasion. Not that he was as inconspicuous as he would have wished. The very fact that he was the only person sitting alone made him an object of curiosity, but there was little he could do about that. He wasn't by any means the gregarious type, so although he realised that wheedling his way onto someone else's table would be the ideal way of blending in, the very thought made the hairs prickle on the back of his neck. Then there was the single beer he'd been nursing for the past hour and a half, which, given the quantities of booze everyone else had been knocking back, also had the potential of drawing attention to himself. But he was even less a drinker than he was gregarious, and although he'd contemplated buying more beers and chucking most of them away in the flowerbed next to him, his abhorrence of waste prevented him. Soft drinks were another option of course, but he had an idea that a man on his own drinking lemonade or fruit juice would set him apart even more.

The beer bottle in front of him was still almost a third full, and he poured it into his empty glass and took a hesitant sip. He winced at its warm flatness, but he'd had much the same reaction when it had been fresh from the fridge. Dabbing at his moustache with a paper napkin and shifting slightly on his chair to ease the numbness in his arse, he wondered whether there was much point hanging on any longer. Nothing much seemed to be happening other than Frank Phelan making a twat of himself on the dance floor and Eric Emerson sitting there like the pompous full-of-himself git he always had been. The pretty young woman with the long black hair was a bit of a mystery. She'd been with them when they'd left their apartment earlier, but surely she couldn't be with either of those two old farts. Not in that way. Although Emerson did seem to be a bit touchy-feely with her every now and again. Relative maybe? Certainly not Phelan's though. He was way too bloody ugly to be sharing any genes with this little cutie.

The swarthy looking bloke who'd joined them later on was even more of a mystery. He was much too young to be the third man from all those years ago, so who was he? A fence perhaps? Could be worth keeping tabs on, although it'd probably turn out he was just some local Lothario desperate to get inside the young woman's pants.

Reynolds's musings were abruptly interrupted when one of the dancers clattered backwards into his table, almost upsetting both beer bottle and glass. The man — a blonde Scandinavian type — mouthed a grinning-faced apology and shifted his absurd twirling movements back into the midst of the other pissed-up Dervishes.

'Sod this for a game of soldiers,' Reynolds said to himself and got to his feet, taking care to keep the bulk of the dancers between him and the table he'd been watching. Slipping his lucky coin into his trouser pocket, he pulled out his wallet and looked around for somebody to pay.

13

The silver-coloured Mercedes crunched its way along the gravel driveway with Jackie shouting back out of the window. 'If there's any problems, you've got Donna's number. She's only a few minutes away. — Oh yes, and don't forget to...'

The end of the sentence was drowned out by the increasing distance and the noise of the taxi's engine as Trevor and Sandra stood watching its departure.

'You get that last bit?' said Trevor when the cab turned left at the end of the drive and disappeared into the night.

Sandra shook her head. 'Something about not forgetting something.'

She set off around the side of the house, and Trevor followed.

'What d'you reckon then?' he said.

Sandra looked back at him over her shoulder with a blank expression.

'The old bloke,' he explained. 'Think we can handle him?'

'I was expecting a lot worse, to be honest. If it wasn't for the catheter, you wouldn't know there was much wrong with him.'

'Maybe there isn't. Maybe he's faking it.'

Another blank look from Sandra.

'For the attention,' Trevor went on. 'Get everyone waiting on him hand, foot and finger.'

'You think?'

Trevor shrugged. He didn't really have any evidence to support his theory, and it was more of a gut feeling than anything else. But what did it matter anyway? They were being paid to look after the guy, and if there wasn't much wrong with him, their job would be all the easier.

By now, they'd reached the back of the house, and they sat down side by side on a sun lounger next to the swimming pool, the underwater lights giving the terrace area an eerie greenish glow. From here, they could see into the living room where Ingleby was bending forward in his armchair and rubbing Milly's upturned belly as she writhed on her back with evident delight. Herbert was perched on the arm of the nearby settee, his mouth opening and closing occasionally but his words unheard through the patio glass.

'He seems to be getting on okay with Milly anyway,' said Trevor.

'Herbert too by the looks of things,' said Sandra.

As they continued to watch, Trevor pondered on the conundrum that was Herbert. He'd been against bringing him along from the start, but Sandra had been insistent, pointing out that it might well be to their advantage to have a third member of "the team".

'His mum says he's really into cooking, so that'd be a bonus,' she'd said. 'And what if we want a day off some time? Herbert could look after the old man while we went off and... I don't know. Spend the day on the beach or whatever.'

Trevor had known there was little point in arguing, so he'd given in without bothering to put up any kind of a fight. He'd also been aware that Herbert's usefulness wasn't the real reason for Sandra's insistence, and that, in reality, she herself had been almost as reluctant as Trevor about taking him with them. No, the truth was that Sandra's older sister was one of those people who could persuade you to do pretty much anything they wanted you to, and using a highly effective combination of pleading, conniving and gentle bullying, she'd made Machiavelli look like an incompetent amateur. In this particular case, she'd also held a trump card in the form of a number of not insignificant favours she'd done Sandra in recent months.

When they'd first been offered the Greek job, Herbert had finished his A-levels and was hoping to go on to study French at university. The only problem — at least as far as his mother was concerned — was that he'd be "under her feet" for the whole of the summer, and he was already driving her crazy. Not that Carol — Sandra's sister — actually *disliked* him or anything. Far from it. She doted on the lad, and when it came to maternal pride, she glowed incandescent with it whenever she talked about him. It was simply that Herbert was absolutely fine in small doses, but after only a few hours in his company, he could get — not to put too fine a point on it — pretty bloody irritating as Trevor had soon discovered on their trip over from England. The whole pretending to be French thing was totally weird for starters, and when he'd asked Sandra about it, she'd told him that it had all begun when Herbert was about fifteen and he'd watched some Truffaut film on the telly. Ever since then, he'd been smitten by all things French.

'D'you think the old boy should be drinking quite that much?' said Trevor, who'd been watching as Herbert had gone over to the bar and refilled Ingleby's whisky glass.

'I was thinking the same thing,' said Sandra, getting to her feet.

She hurried towards the patio door, and Trevor went with her. By the time they stepped inside the living room, Ingleby was already taking his first swig of freshly poured whisky.

'Mr Ingleby, I really don't think that's a good idea, do you?' said Sandra, hands on hips like a school matron who'd just caught Fortescue Minor having a quick one off the wrist in the shower.

Ingleby slowly raised his head and eyeballed her. 'And you are?'

'It's just that your daughter told me to—'

The old man silenced her with a click of his fingers in Herbert's general direction.

'Marcel,' he said. 'Call the police and tell them we have intruders on the premises.'

Then he leaned forward and opened the small plastic tap at the bottom of his catheter bag, releasing a rapidly spreading puddle of urine onto the marble tiles. Sitting back in his chair, he gave Sandra a wicked grin and raised his glass as if in a toast. 'Oops.'

14

The apartment that Eric, Frank and Kate were renting was high up in the old part of the town with a picture postcard view of the entire sweep of the bay. It was late in the morning and already blistering hot even in the shade of the awning. Eric picked up the local map he'd been studying and fanned himself as he listened in on what Kate was saying on her mobile at the far end of the balcony.

'Another time perhaps... Okay, yes... Hard to say really... Okay then, bye... *Yássou.*'

She ended the call and leaned her forearms on the metal railing, staring out across the bay.

'You turned him down?' said Eric. 'Always assuming of course that it really was our friendly neighbourhood Sergeant Pericles asking you on a date.'

'Lunch,' said Kate, still gazing at the view.

'Pardon?'

'He wanted me to have lunch with him.'

There was a note of irritability in her voice, which Eric interpreted as a clear indication that she didn't want to discuss the issue, but he pressed on regardless. 'You know, far be it from me to interfere, Katie, but I think you might have made the wrong decision there.'

Frank, who was leaning back in his chair with a cold flannel covering his face, spoke for the first time in nearly an hour — a sure sign that he was seriously hung over. 'What's the matter? Do yer not fancy 'im?'

'Shut up, Frank,' said Kate.

'Yes, shut up, Frank,' said Eric and switched his attention back to his granddaughter. 'The thing is, sweetheart, it mightn't be a bad idea to cosy up a little with an insider from the local constabulary... given the circumstances.'

Kate shot him a glare. 'Cosy up?'

'Sorry. Bad choice. — Make friends with.'

'You don't necessarily 'ave to shag the bastard,' Frank added.

'Frank,' said Eric, turning towards him. 'How would you like some nice fried eggs and bacon with a large dollop of black pudding, all swimming in oil and washed down with half a pint of ouzo?'

There was a brief pause before Frank slid the flannel from his face, his normally florid complexion tinged with a greyish green, his eyes bloodshot and vacant. He stared into the middle distance for a couple of seconds as if trying to come to a decision, and then his hand flew up to cover his mouth. Jumping to his feet with uncharacteristic alacrity and knocking over his chair in the process, he scuttled off inside the apartment.

'Seriously though, Kate,' said Eric as soon as he'd gone, 'you know I wouldn't ask you to do anything you didn't want to do, but if you could bear to, it'd be very useful to know what the police are up to. Keep a couple of steps ahead of them in case things go wrong.'

Kate returned her gaze to the view of the bay. 'I'll think about it.'

'That's all I ask, sweetheart. That's all I ask.'

A silence followed, during which Eric unfolded the map he'd been using as a fan and spread it out on the plastic table in front of him. Although they'd been within spying distance of Ingleby's villa the day before, he wanted to get a better idea of what else was around and make sure he knew the route to the house itself.

'Better out than in,' said Frank as he stepped back out

onto the balcony, wiping his mouth and chin with toilet paper.

'Did the trick, did it?' said Eric without looking up from the map.

'Must've been summat I ate last night. — I told yer this foreign food didn't agree with me.'

'Well, I'm glad to hear you're feeling so much better, Frank, because I reckon it's about time we reintroduced ourselves to our old pal Marcus Ingleby.'

Eric prodded at a point on the map, then folded it neatly and sat back in his chair. Removing his spectacles, he misted one of the lenses with a sharp exhalation of breath and began to clean it with his handkerchief.

15

The flies and various other winged insects were winning hands down, and if anyone had been bothering to keep score, by now it would have been something like Insects 352, Milly 0. Seemingly impervious to the heat, she'd been cavorting around the pool for the past half hour, leaping into the air every now and then and snapping her jaws shut a nano-second too late to catch a single one of them. For roughly the same amount of time, Herbert had been swimming up and down the length of the pool, and Trevor and Sandra had been making full use of the intended purpose of a pair of sun loungers.

Sandra reached for the tumbler of freshly squeezed orange juice on the low table between them and took a long pull on the straw. 'Told you this'd be a cushy number.'

'Apart from cleaning up half a gallon of piss,' said Trevor.

'And who did that?'

Trevor scratched idly at the crotch of his fluorescent green and yellow swimming shorts. 'Yeah, okay, but I bet it won't be the last time.'

'At least you're not likely to be beaten to a pulp by a deranged heavyweight boxer round here.'

'"Beaten to a pulp" is putting it a bit strong.'

Sandra was about to remind him of the extent of the injuries inflicted on him by Mountainman Machin and the fuss he'd made during the long-drawn-out recovery period when Herbert clambered out of the pool directly in front of them.

'*Ça va bien?*' she said.

'Do you have to encourage him?' muttered Trevor.

'*Mais oui. L'eau est magnifique,*' said Herbert, grabbing a garish beach towel from a third sun lounger and vigorously rubbing his hair with it.

'You want to check on Mr Ingleby when you're done?' said Sandra.

'He still not up yet?' said Herbert, shifting the towel rubbing to his chest and back.

'His daughter said he doesn't usually stir much before lunchtime.'

'He had his pills yet?' said Trevor.

'Of course,' said Sandra as if this were a personal affront to her efficiency.

Still drying himself with the towel, Herbert padded away across the marble tiles and disappeared inside the house.

'Well, you can't say he doesn't have his uses,' said Sandra.

'So does a dishcloth,' said Trevor. 'But a dishcloth doesn't yatter on in French all the time.'

'Unless it's a French dishcloth.'

Trevor ignored the remark. 'And does he always have to be quite so chirpy? I mean, he's expecting his exam results any day now, isn't he?'

'End of the week.'

'Yeah, so if that was me, I'd be stressed to hell, not going round like a loved-up teenager who'd swallowed half a bottle of happy pills.'

'Then we should all be grateful it *isn't* you.'

Trevor was thinking about challenging the implicit personal criticism in Sandra's statement, but he was interrupted by a woman's cheery voice saying, 'Nice work if you can get it.'

A woman in supersized dark glasses and a floppy-brimmed straw hat strode towards them. She was clutching a bulky carrier bag in both hands, and she transferred it to one hand while she stretched out the other in front of her. 'I'm Donna. Jackie's friend. Sorry for barging in unannounced.'

Trevor and Sandra stood up, and they all shook hands.

'Donna. Of course,' said Sandra. 'And thanks for getting us the job by the way.'

Donna accepted the gratitude with a dismissive wave of her hand. '*Cigár t'avgár,*' she said and, in response to Trevor and Sandra's quizzical looks, added, '"Think nothing of it" in Greek. Literally something about slow eggs. No idea what the connection is, but that's Greek for you.'

She re-established her double-handed grip on the carrier bag, which had now attracted the attention of a small swarm of flies that had presumably tired of teasing Milly and were finding the bag of much greater appeal than winding up a deranged mongrel.

'Can I help you with that?' said Trevor. 'It looks rather—'

He held out his hand to take the bag from her, but Donna quickly snatched it out of his reach.

'No, it's fine. Thank you,' she said, cradling the bag in her arms. '*Karpóozi.* Er, watermelon. It's for Marcus. Mr Ingleby. He loves them. Is he up yet?'

'Herbert's just gone to check on him,' said Sandra and nodded at the bag. 'Must be a ripe one.'

'Hmm?'

'The watermelon. Seems to be attracting a lot of flies.'

Donna flapped at them in a vain attempt to shoo them away. 'Ripe. Yes. Very. — Anyway, I just thought I'd pop by and see how you were getting on — and deliver this of course.'

'All okay so far, thanks,' said Sandra, 'although we

did have a bit of a—'

'I'll go up then, shall I? Take Marcus his…'

Instead of finishing the sentence, she raised the carrier bag by a couple of inches as a visual clue to what she was talking about and then hurried off towards the house. She was within two paces of the patio door when Herbert appeared from inside, blocking the doorway. They exchanged brief, polite smiles, and Herbert took a step backwards to let her pass.

'*Qui est-elle?*' he said, glancing back over his shoulder as he came to join Trevor and Sandra by the pool.

'Friend of the family,' said Sandra. 'She's the one who got us the job.'

'Ah,' said Herbert. 'So what's *dans le sac?*'

'Watermelon,' said Trevor, mentally kicking himself for humouring the French nonsense.

'Old boy loves them apparently,' said Sandra. 'Is he up then?'

'Nope. *Il dit qu'il veut* lunch in bed.'

'Fair enough.' She checked her watch. 'And speaking of which, we probably ought to—'

There was a sudden loud splash, and all three of them turned to see Milly floundering in the pool with each one of her legs thrashing at the water in a different direction to the others.

'Jesus, Milly,' said Trevor. 'What the hell are you doing?'

He crouched down at the edge of the pool, and Milly managed to coordinate her limbs sufficiently to propel herself towards him. When she arrived, Trevor reached down and grabbed hold of her collar, then hoisted her up out of the water and onto dry land. But there was no time to react before Milly immediately shook herself and showered them all with water.

'*Merde*,' said Herbert. 'I'd only just got myself dry.'

'Shame,' said Trevor, taking Herbert's towel and giving Milly a thorough rubdown.

16

It was five months, two weeks and three days since DCI Reynolds had quit smoking, but the craving for nicotine had shown little sign of abating even after such a long period of abstinence. Patches, pills, chewing gum — he'd tried the lot, but none of them gave him any relief. He'd even resorted to one of those electronic cigarette things which looked like you should be playing a tune on it rather than smoking it, and this had helped for a while until he read about a guy in the States who'd had half his face blown off because of a dodgy battery. — Straight in the bin. Rolling his lucky coin back and forth across his knuckles gave him something to do with his hands but was totally useless when his need for a nicotine fix got particularly desperate, and one of those occasions was right at that very moment.

He was sitting at a table outside a grubby looking café which would have been closed down in a flash by the health and safety Gestapo if this had been England. But it wasn't. This was Greece, and despite the ban on smoking in public places, nearly every other bugger in the country apart from him seemed to be puffing away like it was against the law *not* to smoke. One of the very few exceptions was one of the two old geezers at the next table, who had a string of brightly coloured plastic beads like a rosary that he constantly flicked around his hand, first one way and then the next. Reynolds guessed it fulfilled a similar purpose to his coin rolling — to take the bloke's mind off the craving for a fag — but at least his own method didn't involve the incessant click-clacking noise that was beginning to get seriously annoying. Equally irritating was the racket blaring out of the ancient TV set mounted high up on a plinth at the edge of the pavement. It was some news programme or other, and the screen was divided into six sections with an angry-faced politician type in each of the boxes, all shouting at once. Reynolds didn't speak a single word of Greek, but he very much doubted that even a native would have the slightest idea what any of them were banging on about.

He looked down at the tiny white coffee cup that had been brought to him five minutes earlier, but which he had so far left untouched. He'd been putting it off because he was all too aware of the inevitable reaction that the first taste would trigger — his system's instant, screaming demand for nicotine. But the midday heat was making him drowsy, and he needed a jolt of caffeine to sharpen him up. At the first sip, his taste buds went into spasm. The thick, syrupy liquid tasted like it had been made with twelve teaspoons of coffee and three of water. He remembered watching a documentary once about the most expensive coffee in the world, which was produced from coffee beans that had been eaten and then shat out by monkeys. This stuff tasted like it had been ingested and then shat out after it had been brewed. He took a couple of gulps from the glass of water that had been brought with the coffee to try and dilute the effect, but that tasted like it had been scooped up from the nearest swimming pool.

Christ almighty, he thought. Isn't it possible to get *any* kind of drink in this country that's actually fit for human consumption? Apart from the need to keep himself awake, the only reason he'd ordered coffee was because the tea he'd had here yesterday was like gnat's piss with added vinegar. And the only reason he'd come back to this godforsaken shithole of a café was that it was the only place where he could sit in reasonable anonymity and watch the comings and goings at the apartment block along the street where Eric Emerson and Frank Phelan were staying.

Nothing of interest had happened so far today, and the previous day had been a complete cockup. He'd taken up position outside the café as soon as it had opened and had eventually spotted the pair of them coming out of the flats and heading off in a silver Toyota. His own hire car was parked just around the corner, and he'd set off after them, keeping a discreet distance and a car or two between them as they turned this way and that through the town's logically bankrupt one way system. All went well until the driver of the clapped-out old pickup in front of him decided to block the road by stopping to have a lengthy chat with the fishmonger who was hosing down the pavement outside his shop. Reynolds had tooted his horn a couple of times, but apart from a cursory glance in his direction, the pickup driver and the fishmonger had studiously ignored him. By the time they'd finished their yakking and he could finally get going again, Emerson and Phelan had vanished.

Returning to his lookout post at the café, he'd waited with mounting impatience for more than two hours until they'd eventually come back to the flats and disappeared inside. It had then taken him only moments to saunter casually up the street and fix the magnetic tracking device to the underside of their car, but another couple of hours had passed before he could put it to the test. It was almost dusk when Emerson and Phelan had reappeared from the apartment block and driven off up the street — this time in the company of the attractive young woman with long black hair. The tracking device had proved itself to be functioning perfectly, and its only fault was that it had led him to the taverna in some village or other where he'd spent a fruitless evening sipping warm beer and watching Frank Phelan make a dick of himself on the dance floor.

Today wasn't exactly turning out to be a whole lot of fun either, and more out of reflex than anything else, he picked up the coffee cup and had raised it almost to his lips before he realised what he was doing. He smacked the cup back down onto the table, spilling some of the thick black liquid onto the plastic cloth, and at the same moment, his lucky coin fell from his fingers and bounced on the ground close to his feet. He bent down to retrieve it, and as he straightened back up again, his ever vigilant peripheral vision caught the heavy wooden door of the apartment block being swung open. He narrowed his eyes to focus better, and out stepped Emerson and Phelan, looking for all the world like a dressed-down geriatric version of Laurel and Hardy. The theme tune hummed in his head as he watched the pair of them cover the dozen or so yards to their car, Emerson walking like he had a poker up his arse and Phelan limping along beside him and clacking at the pavement with his stick.

'Action at last,' Reynolds said to himself, putting his lucky coin into one trouser pocket and reaching into the other for whatever euros he needed to pay for the shit that passed for coffee in this place.

17

'What about paella for lunch then?' said Herbert.

From his prone position on the sun lounger, Trevor had to shield his eyes from the sun when he looked up at him. 'Paella's Spanish, isn't it?'

'So?'

'So if it's Spanish, it isn't French. *N'est-ce pas*?'

'Now who's encouraging him,' Sandra muttered from the lounger next to him.

'I was being sarcastic,' said Trevor.

'Really?' said Sandra and flicked over a page of her magazine.

'Anyway,' said Herbert, 'my tastes are *très éclectiques* when it comes to *la haute cuisine, mon ami*.'

He ignored Trevor's grunt of disdain and added, 'There's loads of rice, and there's plenty of seafood stuff in the—'

'You've got my number if you need anything,' Donna interrupted as she came out of the house with a now empty carrier bag and hurried towards the side of the house without breaking stride.

'Yes,' said Sandra. 'Mrs Summerfield gave—'

'Ring me if there's any problems,' Donna called back over her shoulder. 'Sorry, must dash. Bye.'

And with a perfunctory wave, she was gone.

'Bit odd,' said Trevor. 'Seemed kind of... flustered about something.'

'Maybe she's highly strung,' said Sandra. 'You know the sort. Lives on her nerves. I had a friend once who—'

'Good morning.'

'God, am I ever gonna get to finish a sentence today?' said Sandra, more to herself than anyone else, and they all turned to discover the source of the latest interruption.

It was two men of a similar age to Ingleby. The taller of them was dressed in a pair of lightweight, beige chinos and a short-sleeved cream shirt, while the other wore calf-length tartan shorts with a black T-shirt and had a large bumbag strapped to his front, which seemed to be there to support the overhang of his belly.

'Sorry to disturb you,' said the taller man. 'I'm Eric and this is Frank. We've come to see Marcus — Mr Ingleby.'

'I'm afraid he's still in bed,' said Sandra.

'Oh, that's a pity. — Still, I'm sure he won't mind. We're very old friends of his, you see.'

'Well, I—' Sandra began before being interrupted yet again.

'Haven't seen the old devil in years,' said Eric. 'Be a shame to miss him after we've come all this way.'

'Perhaps I should nip up and see him first,' said Trevor, 'and ask him if—'

'Actually, we were rather hoping to surprise him,' said Eric, removing his heavy horn-rimmed glasses and polishing the lenses with a pristine white handkerchief. 'See the look on his ugly mug when we turn up out of the blue after all these years.' He put his spectacles back on and treated each of them in turn to a pristine white-toothed smile.

Probably false, Trevor thought. Almost certainly the teeth and very possibly the smile as well.

'Well, I don't suppose it'll do any harm,' said Sandra. 'But if he gets, you know, over-excited, we'll have to ask you to—'

'Of course, of course, we—'

Sandra held up her hand to silence him, clearly having

lost patience with the constant interruptions. 'As I was *going* to say, if he gets over-excited, we'll have to ask you to leave.'

'Yes indeed,' said Eric, obviously pissy about being interrupted himself. 'Don't want to give him a heart attack, do we?'

'No,' said Frank, although Trevor thought he detected a slight note of insincerity from even this one syllable.

'Trevor can show you the way,' said Sandra. 'He was going up to empty Mr Ingleby's catheter anyway.'

'I was?'

Sandra's raised eyebrow was indication enough that this was precisely what he was about to do.

'You want to follow me then?' he said. 'I just need to get a bucket from the kitchen.'

'Thank you,' said Eric. 'Very decent of you. And I promise you he'll be over the moon to see us, won't he, Frank?'

'Oh yeah. Over the moon. Definitely.'

They followed Trevor into the house, and while he headed off to the kitchen area, Eric wandered round the spacious living room, his hands clasped behind his back and occasionally tut-tutting at a particular painting or ornament.

'I see Marcus's taste hasn't improved over the years,' he said and then spun round when he heard a "click" from behind him.

Frank was holding a semi-automatic pistol in one hand and its magazine in the other.

'Jesus, Frank,' said Eric in a hoarse whisper. 'Where the hell did you get that?'

'Me new farmer pal, Thanassis. I thought it might come in 'andy.'

'For what exactly?'

'Precaution.'

'Against what?'

103

'Against Ingleby pullin' a gun on *us* is what.'

'Oh, for goodness' sake. Put the damn thing away and don't let me see it again. Not under any circumstances, okay?'

Frank grunted and fed the magazine back into place, then zipped the gun into his bumbag just as Trevor reappeared carrying a plastic bucket.

* * *

The small red dot on his tablet computer was blinking away to itself but had remained stationary for the last couple of minutes. Reynolds had followed Emerson and Phelan until they'd turned into a gravel driveway about three miles out of town, and he'd caught only a fleeting glimpse of the swish-looking villa at the end of it as he'd driven slowly past. He'd turned his car round and parked up, far enough from the entrance to the drive to be inconspicuous but close enough to keep it in sight. It wasn't the ideal spot for surveillance purposes, however, as a high wall and a dense planting of oleander rendered the house invisible. The only other possibility would have been to skirt the perimeter on foot to try and find a better vantage point, but it was too bloody hot to be rummaging about in the bushes. Then there was the snake issue of course. Bound to be dozens of the slimy little bastards in this sort of place. Not to worry though. He could always check the house out later after Phelan and Emerson had buggered off.

But was this really the Holy Grail he'd been after for all these years? Was he at long last going to find out the identity of the third man? Better still, was he about to discover the whereabouts of all the loot they'd squirrelled away?

'Christ knows,' he said aloud and notched up the aircon to full blast.

18

Kate leaned forward over the bathroom sink and stared wide-eyed into the mirror as she set to work on the final application of mascara. It was a standard procedure and not at all for his benefit. She couldn't have cared less if Pericles found her attractive or not. He was pleasant enough and certainly wasn't lacking in the looks department, but he was just a bit too clean cut for her tastes. The sort most mums would have drooled over if you'd brought him home for tea. Not hers of course. *Her* mum had tended to go for something a little rougher round the edges. Maybe that's where she got it from.

Besides — and far more importantly — it had only been a couple of months since a rather messy breakup with her boyfriend. She'd dumped him after she'd found out he'd been sleeping around, but the guy couldn't take "piss off out of my apartment and don't ever contact me again" for an answer. An incessant stream of pleading phone calls, texts and emails as well as hammering on her door at all times of the day and night had him marked down as a vindictive and unrelenting stalker in her book, which was one of the reasons the trip abroad had been so appealing. And not just abroad either. This was Greece. A country she'd been to many times before but had never grown tired of visiting, so she hadn't needed much persuading.

She still wasn't entirely sure why her granddad had asked her to come along, although the most likely explanation was that he'd wanted some kind of antidote to Frank and his constant complaining. In any case, she'd adored Granddad Eric ever since she'd been old enough to know who he was, and refusing him would have felt somehow disloyal. Not that her adoration had always been quite so unequivocal. There'd been a long period when he'd suddenly and completely disappeared out of her life, and nobody would tell her why. She'd been thirteen at the time and already too much of a teenager to admit to anyone but herself that she was heartbroken. Angry too that he had betrayed her in much the same way as her father had done when he'd packed his bags and left home for good soon after her fifth birthday.

It was a little over four years before her mother had finally told her the reason for her granddad's sudden disappearance, and after the initial shock, she'd become bitterly resentful — ashamed of herself for putting such unconditional trust in someone who was nothing more than a common crook. But some months after this painful revelation, she'd accidentally come across a cardboard box full of letters and birthday cards he'd sent her from prison, and which her mother had kept hidden. In the letters, he'd explained in great detail about the events that had led to his transformation from respectable teacher to convicted criminal, and gradually her attitude had softened towards him. She started to visit him in prison, and the visits became increasingly regular until she began to see him as more of a lovable rogue than an out-and-out villain, especially when she learned that neither he nor his partners had ever once resorted to violence during any of their robberies. He'd also made it a deal-breaking condition that no-one would carry a gun on any of the jobs he was involved in. Not a real one anyway. But that didn't seem to make any difference as far as the Law was concerned, and that was why he'd got such a long sentence for the jewel robbery even though the guns they'd used were replicas.

A car horn sounded from the street outside, and she put down her mascara brush and crossed the small, sparsely furnished living room to the balcony. She peered over the railing at the blue lamped top of a police car, Pericles leaning against its bonnet with his arms folded across the short-sleeved blue shirt of his uniform. Oh, excellent. Very low profile.

Pericles looked up and waved. '*Kalıméra.*'

'Two minutes,' said Kate. 'Okay?'

'*Oraía.*'

She went back into the bathroom and took her time putting the finishing touches to her makeup.

* * *

Kate stared out of the side window at the slowly passing shops and cafés as Pericles drove between the rows of cars parked bumper-to-bumper on both sides of the town's main street.

'August,' he said when the traffic in front of them came to a standstill once again. 'I hate August.'

'Oh?'

'Most of the year, this place is like the cemetery, but in August, all the *malákkes* come down from Athens to show off their fancy cars and their expensive clothes and their stupid fat kids — and then chaos.'

'Well, you Greeks invented it.'

'What?'

'Chaos. Greek word, isn't it?'

'Ah yes. *Káos. Naı.*'

The traffic began to creep forward again, but within a matter of seconds, Pericles was forced to stop behind a double-parked Audi with its hazard lights flashing.

'This is what I mean,' he said, slapping the steering wheel with the palms of both hands. 'They think because they put on their warning lights they can do what the hell they want.'

Kate didn't really know what to say in response, so she kept quiet and let him fume in silence until he reached across her and opened the glove box.

'But not today, my friend,' he said. 'Not today.'

He took out a pad of what looked like traffic tickets and slammed the glove box shut.

'You going to book him?' said Kate.

'You see the number plate? He is from Athens. If I book a local, for sure they will be family of the mayor or another officer or the Chief of Police, so the fine it never gets paid. — I won't be long.'

So saying, he flicked on his own hazards and got out of the car.

Oh great, thought Kate. Not only a copper, but an overzealous one at that. — Or maybe he's just trying to impress you. — Well, Sergeant Pericles, you'll have to do a damn sight more than giving somebody a parking ticket, that's for sure.

She watched him strut round to the front of the Audi and begin writing out a ticket. Two men of about the same age as Pericles stopped and engaged him in what appeared to be some jovial friendly banter, but Pericles was clearly far too intent on the job in hand to offer more than a few words and the occasional smile in return. The men moved off, laughing, only to be replaced by a fat man in a sleeveless vest and flip-flops. He shouted something at Pericles, who ignored him and poked the completed ticket under a windscreen wiper. The fat man confronted him square on, alternating between planting his hands on his hips and waving them wildly in the air while he spat out words that Kate couldn't make out. Pericles responded in kind with his own version of flailing arms and pointing finger before finally walking away with a dismissive backward wave, pushing his way through the small crowd of spectators that had gathered on the pavement.

'I thought you were off duty,' said Kate when he got back into the car and returned the pad of parking tickets to the glove box.

'For a policeman this is never possible, Kate. Not if I do my job well. Murderers, thieves, rapists, they are never "off duty".'

'Not to mention the illegal parkers,' said Kate and instantly regretted having given voice to what should have been a private thought when Pericles glowered at her, his eyes filled with wounded pride.

'Joke?' she said with what she hoped was a facial shrug of apology.

There was a brief pause while Pericles appeared to be analysing her expression, and then he slapped his thigh and let out an inappropriately explosive guffaw of laughter.

'Ah yes,' he said. 'The English humour. I'd almost forgotten.'

Still chuckling, he switched off his hazard lights and pulled out past the Audi, the owner of which stooped to peer in at him and ostentatiously ripped the parking ticket in two.

19

Milly had given up on chasing airborne insects as a lost cause and had transferred the focus of her hunting instincts to wandering around the edge of the pool and batting at the occasional pond skater that dared to come within range of her paw. Sandra had gone back to reading her magazine, and Herbert was stretched out on one of the other loungers a few feet away from the protection of the sunshade, his pale skin turning redder by the minute.

'Well, that was a bit weird,' said Trevor when he returned from showing their latest two visitors up to Ingleby's bedroom. 'He didn't seem to know them at all.'

'Maybe he's having one of his "episodes",' said Sandra. 'Mrs S says he gets a bit of dementia now and again.'

'Could be,' said Trevor and sat on the vacant lounger next to Sandra's. 'By the way, I was going to cut up some of the watermelon that whatsherface brought. Couldn't find it anywhere.'

'Wasn't it in Ingleby's bedroom?' said Herbert.

Trevor shook his head. 'Nope.'

'Kitchen?' said Sandra.

'Nope.'

'Oh well, I'm sure it'll turn up eventually,' she said.

There was a deep rumbling sound from Trevor's stomach, and he put his hand to it as if to suppress the noise.

'So what's happening with this paella you promised us then, Herbert?' he said.

Herbert leapt to his feet and saluted. '*Mais bien sûr, monsieur*. Coming right up.'

'I suppose there's peas, is there?' said Trevor.

Herbert looked blank.

'You can't make paella without peas,' said Trevor. 'It's an essential ingredient.'

'*Oui, je sais*. I didn't spot any in the freezer though.'

Sandra lowered her magazine. 'There's another freezer in the basement. Mrs S showed me it yesterday when she gave me the grand tour. I'm fairly sure there were some in there, so I'd check it out before you give up on the paella idea.'

'*Mais oui, madame. Tout de suite*,' said Herbert, saluting again and adding a click of the heels before heading off towards the house.

Trevor lay back on the sun lounger and clasped his hands behind his head. Maybe Herbert wasn't so bad after all. If he wasn't so perpetually cheerful and cut out all the talking French crap, he might even be tolerable to have around. But tolerable or not, there was no escaping the fact that he'd still be surplus to requirements in one particularly important respect. One of the main reasons Trevor had finally given in to Sandra's badgering about taking the Greek job was that it was going to be just the two of them — well, three counting Milly of course — and a long leisurely trip in the van followed by a few weeks soaking up the sun would have been the perfect opportunity to... move their relationship on a bit... so to speak. But then along came Herbert like the proverbial third wheel and put the kibosh on that idea before it had even got off the ground.

Not that there hadn't been plenty of opportunities before then to tell Sandra how he felt. They'd known each other for a year and a half now, and although

Trevor had a sneaking suspicion that Sandra had a similar inclination, he couldn't be absolutely certain, and that was more than enough to stop him from making the first move. And if he was brutally honest with himself, he was totally crap when it came to that sort of thing. Even his ex-wife, Imelda, had been the one who'd got things started between them, and as it turned out, that was purely because he suited her purpose at the time. He'd only had a couple of girlfriends before Imelda, and in both cases they'd been the ones with the chat-up lines.

Of course, if Sandra really did feel the same way as he did, she could just as easily have raised the stakes herself. After all, she was certainly no wilting violet and every inch the "modern woman", as the expression goes. — Well, maybe not *every* inch. You still got the occasional glimpse of the traditional about her, so perhaps it was this that had held *her* back from making the first move.

Take the time they went to that wedding in the Cotswolds, for instance. It was five or six months ago, and Sandra had been invited (plus one) but hadn't fancied going on her own, so she'd asked Trevor to tag along for the ride. Their detective agency was still doing reasonably well back then, so they'd decided to lash out on a couple of nights at the hotel where the wedding reception was being held. They hadn't been exactly flush though — and Trevor had been burned before, paying well over the odds for a single room — so they'd booked just the one room but with twin beds. When they arrived, however, they discovered there'd been a mixup, and there was a king-sized bed where two singles should have been. Because of the wedding, all the other rooms in the hotel were occupied, so they'd had no choice but to accept what they'd been given. Trevor had offered to sleep on the floor, but Sandra wouldn't hear of it.

'You'll only moan all day tomorrow about how you

hardly slept a wink and how much your back aches,' Sandra had said. 'We'll just have to make do the best we can.'

Hardly an invitation for a night of passion and rampant sex of course, but Trevor had been mightily relieved she hadn't taken him up on his offer because she'd almost certainly have been right about the sleepless night and the aching back. The moaning all day part had been a bit harsh though.

They'd avoided the rest of the wedding party that evening and gone out on the town for a few drinks and then a meal in a fairly upmarket restaurant. The food had been excellent, and what with the candles and the soft lighting, it would have been the perfect spot for a romantic night out — if that had been the intention. There'd even been a moment when they'd been about to tuck in to their *crème brûlées*, and a young woman had arrived at their table with a wicker basket of single red roses. 'Would sir care to buy a rose for his rose?'

Like a couple of coy teenagers, the pair of them had blushed an even deeper red than the roses themselves, and it was all Trevor could do to blurt out the words 'Er, no thanks. We're fine.'

We're fine? What, as in "No, it's okay, we've got plenty already"?

'Jesus,' Sandra had said when the young woman had moved out of earshot. 'Next thing you know, we'll be getting a gypsy violinist serenading us.'

They'd both laughed, albeit rather unconvincingly, and then lowered their heads while they addressed the business of their desserts in silence. Mercifully, the gypsy violinist never materialised.

It was already late by the time they'd got back to the hotel, so after a quick nightcap from the half bottle of whisky Sandra had brought with her, they'd decided to call it a day. Trevor had let Sandra use the bathroom first, and when she'd reappeared a few minutes later, she was wearing one of the white towelling dressing gowns supplied by the hotel. He'd had no idea what, if anything, she had on underneath, so taking his own turn in the bathroom, he'd erred on the side of caution and stripped down only as far as his T-shirt and underpants.

Back in the bedroom, Sandra had already got herself under the duvet, but only her head was visible, so he still didn't know quite how far she'd gone with the undressing. He'd slipped in beside her, lifting the duvet rather more than was strictly necessary in order to get a quick peek. The faded pink T-shirt was clearly discernible, but what happened lower down remained a mystery.

The bed had been plenty big enough for them to leave a good twelve inch gap between them, especially as they'd both opted to lie as close as they could to the edges without running the risk of actually falling out. Trevor had lain awake for what had seemed like hours, and according to the laws of irony, would very probably have got more sleep if he *had* bedded down on the floor. Ordinarily, if he'd been in his own bed, he'd have tossed and turned until he finally dozed off, but on this occasion he lay flat on his back, rigid as a plank and with his arms welded to his sides, not daring to twitch so much as a muscle. All the while, he'd listened to Sandra's slow, shallow breathing, but he'd been almost certain that she was only pretending to be asleep.

And according to the second law of irony, it was the rhythmic sound of her breathing that had probably been the cause of his eventually dropping off, but he'd woken again with a start soon after dawn. The meerkats he'd been counting in an effort to get to sleep — sheep never seemed to have the desired effect — had now manifested themselves in a dream where they were all wearing faded pink T-shirts and were building what looked like a

Trojan horse but in the shape of an enormous rabbit. Then, as soon as the structure was complete, a trapdoor had opened below the rabbit's tail, and all of the meerkats had beckoned to him to climb inside. And as if this wasn't nightmare enough, the incident that had finally made him sit bolt upright in bed was the sight of the enormous wooden rabbit rearing up above him and threatening to crush him beneath an enormous wooden paw.

Pouring with sweat, Trevor had slipped out of bed and trotted into the bathroom, where he spent the next five minutes splashing his face with cold water and waiting for his heartbeat to return to something approaching a normal pace. When he came back, he'd checked that Sandra really was asleep and then, once again, lifted the duvet a few inches more than was necessary to get underneath it. But this time, his hand froze with the duvet still in the raised position. The faded pink T-shirt had gone.

Mesmerised, he'd watched the rise and fall of Sandra's breasts, focusing now and then on the small pert nipples before slowly lifting the duvet an inch or two more to take in the ever so slight bulge of her stomach. The stirring sensation in his underpants had told him that this might be the perfect opportunity, and that maybe — just maybe — Sandra had stripped off deliberately in order to provoke exactly that reaction...

Hmm. On the other hand, perhaps she'd simply got too hot in the middle of the night and taken off her T-shirt to try and cool herself down.

Reluctantly accepting that this was the far more likely explanation, he'd carefully lowered the duvet and resumed his plank-like position on his own side of the bed.

Their second night at the hotel had proved to be much the same as the first except for one major difference.

Before they'd got into bed, Sandra had made a point of opening both the windows in the room because it had been "hot as hell in here last night".

So that had been that really, and in the months since then, there hadn't been a single tangible indication that Sandra might be… romantically interested in him.

A wasp settled on Trevor's nose, bringing him sharply back to the present, and he swatted it away with the back of his hand. In so doing, his head twisted to the side, and he caught sight of Sandra on her sun lounger just a couple of feet to the side of him. Her magazine lay open across her chest, and although it was hard to tell through the sunglasses, she seemed to be asleep. Propping himself up on one elbow, he stared at her for several minutes, casting his mind back to their first night at the hotel and imagining her now without the magazine and the bikini top beneath it. As on that occasion, he began to feel a stirring inside his swimming shorts and, worried that Sandra might wake up and spot the evidence, was on the point of taking a plunge in the pool when a sudden and highly uncharacteristic flash of self-confidence swept through him.

Right, he thought. This is it. This is the moment. No more pussyfooting around. It's time to *act*. What's the worst that can happen, for God's sake?

And before he could give his brain the chance to come up with a whole list of deeply embarrassing outcomes that he would inevitably regret, he reached across the narrow divide between them and placed his hand lightly on her forearm.

'Sandra?' he said.

'Mmm?' she said in a dreamily relaxed tone.

'Sandra, I've been thinking.'

She took off her sunglasses and turned to face him, her eyes dazzling blue in the late morning sun. 'Oh yes?'

'The thing is…' — *Oh, come on, Trevor. You've*

started now, so just bloody well get on with it.

He took a deep breath, partly to calm his nerves and partly because he wanted to get all his words out in one go without a chink of a pause where she might be able to interrupt.

'The thing is, I've been giving a lot of thought to how things are between us and—'

But he got no further because it was at this precise moment that Herbert came tumbling out through the patio door and staggered towards them. His face was contorted into a grimace of terror, the colour of his skin no longer reddened by the sun but a sickly greyish white. His right arm was held out behind him, pointing stiffly back at the house.

'There's a—' He took a gulp of air and began again. 'There's a—'

Then his eyes rolled back in his head, his knees crumpled, and he sank to the ground in a heap like a punctured inflatable doll.

20

The air in the bedroom was rank with the smell of stale cigarette smoke and urine, so Eric remained close to the open window, leaning his back against the wall. Frank — apparently immune to the stink, or more likely focusing too intently on the business in hand to notice — was sitting on a chair close to the head of the bed, where Ingleby sat upright, bare-chested and with an idiotic grin on his face.

'I'll have the Greek salad with feta, please, and perhaps some tzatziki,' he said.

Frank bent forward, bringing his face to within a few inches of Ingleby's. 'Don't fook about, Marcus. You know bloody well who we are.'

Ingleby studied his features for several seconds until his forehead knotted into a frown. 'I do?'

'Eric and—'

'Ernie?'

'Frank.'

'Ah,' said Ingleby with apparent realisation. 'The singing waiters.— Give us a song then, boys.'

Frank brought his clenched fist up to just below Ingleby's chin. 'I'll give you a f—'

'Perhaps we need to prompt your memory a little,' said Eric, pushing himself away from the wall. 'After all, it was a long time ago. Getting on for sixteen years in fact.'

'Most of which I've spent doin' time because you ratted us out to the cops to save yer own skin, yer little shit,' said Frank.

'As you can see, Frank here is a teensy bit unhappy about the situation and would dearly love to cut off various bits of your anatomy and make you eat them. However, I believe we might be able to avoid any of that kind of unpleasantness in exchange for—'

'Giving — us — our — fooking — share,' said Frank, slowly enunciating each of the words.

'Of course, given the passage of time, it may well be that you have sold the proceeds from that ill-fated day, and if so, we would be perfectly amenable to accepting one third each of the total sum thereby acquired. Alternatively, if the jewellery is still in your possession, then the same apportionment would be equally satisfactory.'

There was a lengthy pause while Eric and Frank waited for Ingleby's response, which came eventually in the form of another frown and a question addressed to Frank: 'Did *you* understand any of that, Ernie?'

Frank's simmering anger finally reached boiling point. His face turned an alarming shade of puce, and he raised his walking stick above his head, ready to strike.

'So help me, if you don't cough up right now, I'll—'

Eric held up a restraining hand. 'You see, Marcus, the very fact that the boys in blue never discovered the whereabouts of the jewellery was — as I'm sure you'll be aware — one of the reasons why Frank and myself received rather longer sentences than would otherwise have been the case. And it was only the expectation that we would one day receive our just deserts that we were able to retain some modicum of sanity throughout all those long years of incarceration.'

'Desserts?' said Ingleby. 'But I haven't even had my starter yet.'

Frank sat back in his chair with a sharp exhalation of air and looked at Eric, his palms spread wide in a gesture of exasperation, but all he got in return was a shrug.

Eric turned away and stared out of the window. He was at a loss where to go from here, and he needed time to think it through. He'd never for one moment expected that Marcus would simply hand over what was due to them with a cheery smile and a "There you are, lads", but this was proving to be even harder than he'd anticipated. He was fairly certain that the whole crazy act was exactly that — an act the old bugger was putting on to try and fob them off. But what did he expect to achieve by it? That they'd just say "Oh right, you're obviously mad as a hatter, so we'll call it quits and clear off then, shall we?"? Ingleby wasn't stupid. — In fact, he used to be quite bright, and the planning of the jewellery job had been mainly down to him. Not that it had turned out well of course, but that was hardly his fault. There'd been nothing wrong with the plan itself, and it would have worked perfectly if it hadn't been for Frank's cockup. And as for Frank's accusation that Ingleby grassed them up to the police, that was all nonsense, and he knew it. All he was doing was trying to shift the blame onto somebody else in a pathetic attempt to divert attention from his own stupidity.

He and Eric had spent four hours in a professional makeup studio on the morning of the robbery so they could waltz into the jeweller's like ordinary customers without having to worry about CCTV cameras and eagle-eyed witnesses. But as well as disguising their physical appearance, they'd also decided that neither of them would speak a single word once they were inside to avoid any possibility that they might be recognised by their voices later on. All communication with the staff would be carried out by means of instructions written on cards which they'd prepared in advance. Unfortunately — and to this day, Eric had no idea why — they'd entrusted the task of writing these cards to Frank, and neither Eric nor Ingleby had taken the precaution of checking his work. So when Eric and Frank had walked into the shop and pulled out their replica guns, Frank had shown the first card to the manager, who'd peered at it and begun to read the words aloud but with obvious difficulty: 'Keep your hands where we can... see them, and don't even thank — *think* about setting off any... aliens — *alarms* or you're— What's this word supposed to be?'

She'd pointed to the word she couldn't make out, and Frank had obliged with a mime of cutting his own throat.

'Ah, "dead",' she'd said and then continued reading aloud. 'Put all the jumblery... *jewellery* into this... barge?'

Frank had handed over an empty canvas holdall.

But Frank's lousy handwriting hadn't been the worst of it. All that had done was delayed the operation by a couple of minutes and had Ingleby starting to get twitchy in the car outside. No, Frank's even bigger — and far more serious — cockup was that he'd dropped one of the cards on the floor without realising, and not surprisingly, one of the first things the police had done was dusted it for fingerprints. Since Frank hadn't bothered to wear gloves when he'd written the cards, it was only a matter of hours before the police had battered in the door to his flat and found not only Frank himself but also the pieces of their latex disguises, which he was supposed to have destroyed. So, thanks to Frank's incompetence and another round of fingerprint matching, Eric was next on their list for an early morning visit.

When Ingleby had heard that Eric and Frank had been arrested, he'd made a run for it and — not unreasonably — taken all the loot with him. The police of course had been well aware that there'd been a third member of the gang, but Eric and Frank had observed the most sacred credo of the criminal fraternity and kept their mouths shut — no doubt having another year or two added to their sentences in the process. Not that Eric had borne Ingleby any ill will even during all those long years in prison. After all, he'd almost certainly have done the same if the boot had been on the other foot.

'Is the calamari good today?'

At the sound of Ingleby's voice, Eric turned away from the window, and at the sight of his insanely grinning face, he felt suddenly very tired.

21

'The calamari it is really excellent today,' said Pericles, lifting another forkful of deep-fried squid to his mouth. 'You should try it.'

'I'm fine with this, thanks,' said Kate, pointing her knife at the plate of Greek salad in front of her.

She'd already explained to him that she was a vegetarian and that, no, this didn't mean she could eat fish or chicken and, yes, lamb was in fact derived from a living creature and therefore off limits as far as she was concerned. Pericles — like most Greeks she'd met on previous visits — seemed to think that abstaining from eating meat or fish must be the result of some form of mental illness, but despite the majority of Greeks being rampant carnivores, hardly any of them had ever given her a hard time about it.

Pericles was clearly not a multi-tasker and was apparently more interested in stuffing his face with calamari than continuing the conversation they'd been having before the food had arrived. Nearly all of it had been little more than smalltalk anyway, so she was quite content to have a break from the chitchat. Putting down her knife and fork, she rested her forearms on the wooden balustrade next to their table and stared down into the clear blue water directly beneath. Every so often, a shoal of tiny silver-coloured fish would dart into view and then be gone again as quickly as they'd arrived, sometimes to be replaced by a much larger solitary fish, which moved through the water with the stealth of a predator — which it very probably was.

She shifted her gaze upwards and took in the view of the little harbour, the fishing boats bobbing gently at anchor, the sunlight glinting off their cabin windows. Here and there, men with rods and lines stood or sat on the edge of the quayside, patiently waiting for a bite, and she smiled to herself when she remembered that someone had once described fishing as an activity where you have a jerk on one end of a line waiting for a jerk on the other. One such jerk on the harbour wall furthest from her was yelling angrily at a small group of children who were jumping into the water and clambering back out, repeating the process over and over again and screaming and shouting with the sheer joy of it all.

Her eyes drifted towards the calmer water at the centre of the harbour where, seconds later, a circular ripple appeared and a small black blob broke the surface.

'Look. What's that?' she said, pointing.

Pericles looked up from what little remained of his calamari. 'Where?'

'There. You see it?'

'Ah yes. Caretta caretta. Giant sea turtle,' he said with about as much enthusiasm as if she'd told him the sky was blue. 'This time of year, they lay their eggs in the sand all along this coast.'

'And do you eat those as well — the turtles?'

'Certainly not,' said Pericles indignantly. 'They are... what is the word? — Protected.'

'Glad to hear it.'

While Pericles polished off the rest of his calamari, she stared at the turtle's head until it disappeared back under the water. Her eyes fixed on the immediate area, she waited for it to reappear, but the surface of the water remained flat and unbroken. A wisp of cigarette smoke drifted past her nose, and she wafted it away with the back of her hand.

124

'I'm sorry,' said Pericles. 'I wasn't thinking.'

'I thought you weren't supposed to do that in public places any more.'

'You're not.'

'Tut tut. And you a policeman too.'

'Policeman or not, no Greek likes being told what he can and cannot do.'

'Like double parking for instance.'

Pericles laughed. 'We are not always logical either.'

'But I thought it was the Greeks who *invented* logic. Aristotle. Plato. The Stoics.'

'How you know all this?'

'I studied philosophy at university — and Greek.'

'Ah,' said Pericles. 'So that explains how you speak so well our language.'

He leaned forward across the table and lightly placed his hand over Kate's. Her instinct was to withdraw it the moment she felt the touch of his skin, but she resisted the urge and held her breath in apprehension of what might be coming next. Apparently encouraged by the fact that she *hadn't* removed her hand, Pericles gave it a gentle squeeze and gazed deep into her eyes.

'Kate,' he said. 'I know it is only a small time we have known each other, but already I am feeling that—'

The strident opening bars of a Greek pop song cut him short.

'Gamóto!' he said, snatching his mobile phone out of the top pocket of his shirt and glancing at the display. 'I'm sorry, Kate. It might be important.'

Kate feigned disappointment but was heartily grateful for the interruption.

'Nαι?' Pericles said into the phone. *'Aléethia? Ápo poión? ... Nαι, katálava. Sto spíti tou kiríou Ingleby. ... Nαι, to xéro. ... Améssos, nαι.'*

He ended the call and returned the mobile to his pocket.

'Problem?' said Kate.

'Kate, please forgive me, but I have to go.'

'Anything juicy?'

Pericles raised an eyebrow. 'Excuse me?'

'Something big. Something, you know…'

She struggled to find a less idiomatic alternative, but his eyebrow had already dropped back to its normal position.

'Possibly,' he said, 'but I can't really— Look, I give you a lift back to your apartment on the way.'

'No, that's okay. I'll finish my lunch first and walk back.'

'You sure?' he said, getting to his feet and picking up his car keys from the table. 'It's very hot today.'

'I'll be fine. It's really not that far.'

'*Lipón*. Well, if you're sure. — And don't worry about the bill. The owner is cousin of mine. Order what else you like and I pay him later.'

'Thank you,' said Kate, smiling sweetly but thinking what a bloody nerve it would be if he'd left her to stump up for the bill.

He hunched his shoulders in apology. 'Kate, I'm so sorry—'

'Pericles, it's fine.'

'Okay. But I will see you again soon?'

'Yes, soon. Of course.'

Pericles hurried away and, pausing only for a brief word with one of the waiters, jumped into his car and sped off up the road, blue light flashing and siren blaring.

As soon as he'd gone, Kate rummaged in her bag for her own mobile.

'Granddad, it's me,' she said when Eric answered. 'You still at Ingleby's? ... And everything's okay? ... Well, listen. I've no idea why, but the police are probably on their way there. ... Pericles, yes. ... Right now, yes. So

126

if I were you I'd— ... Exactly.'

She hung up and put the phone down on the table, then swivelled her chair round to get a better view of the harbour in case the turtle decided to make a reappearance.

22

Herbert was sitting on the edge of the pool, dangling his legs in the water, his face in his hands and rocking gently to and fro.

'And you're absolutely certain?' said Trevor, addressing the remark to Herbert's back.

'Of course I'm certain,' he snapped. 'I think even I know the difference between a packet of peas and a severed bloody head.'

'So whose is it?'

'How the hell should I know? I mean, we didn't exactly introduce ourselves. — "Hello, my name's Herbert." — "Pleased to meet you, Herbert. I'm a severed head and my name is..."'

'I'm only asking if you recognised him.'

'No.'

Sandra crouched beside him and laid a hand on his shoulder. 'It's definitely a man, right?'

Herbert nodded.

'Any idea how long he's been there?' said Trevor.

'It's a freezer,' said Herbert, lowering his hands and turning to face him. 'And I didn't actually check to see if he had a "best before" date stamped on his forehead.'

'It wasn't there yesterday when Mrs S was showing me round,' said Sandra.

'So how did it get there?' said Trevor. 'Ingleby?'

'You seen him go down into the basement since we arrived?'

Trevor shook his head.

'Herbert?'

'What?' said Herbert, whose face was once again hidden in his hands.

'Did you see Ingleby go down into the basement since we got here?'

'No.'

'What about Mrs S and her husband then?' said Trevor. 'Maybe they cut somebody's head off and put it in the freezer before they went off last night.'

Sandra raised an eyebrow. 'In the almost certain knowledge that we'd spot it as soon as we went to fetch a bag of peas or whatever?'

'Well, if it wasn't any of them and it wasn't one of us...?'

'I've no idea,' said Sandra and then carefully prised one of Herbert's hands away from his face. 'What's he look like, Herbert? Young? Old? Any distinguishing features?'

He looked at her through his one open eye. 'No teeth.'

'What?'

'It didn't have any *teeth*.'

'Must be old then. — What about the rest of the face? Did it look old to you?'

Herbert dropped his other hand to reveal the rest of his face. His eyes were rimmed with red and clearly close to tears. 'Listen,' he said, 'if you're so keen, why don't you go and see for yourselves?'

With that, he slid into the water and swam towards the far end of the pool without breaking the surface.

Trevor watched, not daring to meet Sandra's eye for fear of what she might be about to say.

But she said it anyway. 'Perhaps we should.'

'Should what?' said Trevor even though he knew exactly what she meant.

'Go and take a look in the freezer.'

'Well, yes, you're probably right, but I suppose we

don't *both* need to go.'

'You volunteering?'

'Well, I…' Trevor began, desperately trying to think of a valid reason why it made much more sense for Sandra to go than him. 'It's not that I'm—'

'Thanks very much. We'll be off now then.'

Saved by the interruption, Trevor turned to see Eric and Frank stepping out of the patio door.

'So, was he pleased to see you?' said Sandra.

'Oh, yes indeed,' said Eric as he and Frank almost broke into a run to get to the side of the house. 'We'll drop by again some time. Maybe this evening. Bye.'

Then they were gone.

'Why's everybody in such a hurry today?' said Trevor.

Sandra held up her hand to silence him. 'Shush! Listen.'

Trevor listened, but all he could hear was the incessant chattering of crickets and Milly snoring from where she lay curled up on one of the sun loungers. A few seconds later, however, and he picked up the sound that Sandra was presumably referring to. A two-tone siren which was rapidly getting louder.

'Police?' he said.

Sandra shrugged.

'You don't think…?' Trevor began but didn't bother to finish the question. It was perfectly obvious what they were both thinking.

'Dunno,' said Sandra. 'But it definitely seems to be coming this way, and there aren't that many houses round here.'

'Maybe it's an ambulance or a fire engine,' said Trevor. 'Or if it *is* the police, maybe they're just chasing somebody for speeding.'

'Could be. But I don't think we should take any chances.'

'How d'you mean?'

Sandra gave him one of her "are you completely stupid?" looks. 'You want them to find a head in the freezer?'

'Why on earth would they—?'

'I've no idea, Trev, but why take the risk? — I'll get Herbert out of the pool and send him up to keep an eye on Ingleby and keep him out of the way. We don't want the old boy knowing anything about the head just yet. You go down to the basement and do something with it.'

'It?'

'The head.'

'What do you mean "*do* something"?'

'I don't know. Hide it somewhere.'

'Oh right. Of course,' Trevor said with heavy sarcasm. 'It's in a bloody freezer already. Where else am I supposed to hide it?'

'Just go, will you?'

Trevor hesitated. The very thought of playing hide and seek with a severed head turned his stomach, but he couldn't see any way out of it. Sandra's tone had already hit eleven on the pissy scale, and he know from experience there was little point in arguing with her once she'd reached that stage. Still, it was worth a shot. 'So how come I get to do it?'

'Because I'll be much better at keeping them talking than you.'

She was absolutely right of course. Trevor's dealings with authority figures — particularly ones in uniform — always brought on an attack of the shakes, a bright red face and a high-pitched wobbliness in his voice that made him sound like Joe Pasquale on helium. This was why, on the very rare occasions he travelled by plane, it was always him who got pulled over to have his bags searched at Customs.

He set off towards the house, bracing himself for the

horror that awaited him in the basement.

* * *

Dressed only in khaki knee-length shorts, Marcus Ingleby stood by the open bedroom window, staring down at the scene that was being played out by the swimming pool. The blonde woman — Sandra — was talking to two uniformed coppers, but from this distance it was impossible to hear what any of them were saying.

'What the bloody hell do they want?' he said.

'I don't know exactly,' said Herbert, who had stayed well away from the window in the middle of the room.

'So do you know *approximately*?'

Herbert shuffled his feet. 'Sorry. They just kind of... arrived.'

'Yeah? Well, they can just kind of fuck off then, can't they?' said Ingleby, and before Herbert could stop him, he'd brushed past him and was out of the door.

Herbert was undecided whether to follow or not. Sandra had been more than clear in her instructions to keep Ingleby out of the way, but the old man wasn't somebody you could argue with once he'd made up his mind to do something. He'd already witnessed the unpleasant consequences when Sandra had tried to tell Ingleby he shouldn't drink so much, although that didn't mean she wouldn't still be narked with Herbert for disobeying orders.

Oh, sod it, he thought and headed for the open doorway. May as well be hung for a *mouton* as a... *mouton*.

* * *

Sandra's face muscles were beginning to ache from keeping up the fixed smile, but the hardly-pausing-for-

132

breath waffling seemed to be doing the trick of keeping the two policemen at bay for the time being at least.

'It's really not up to me, I'm afraid. We're not the owners, you see, and Mr Ingleby — he's the real owner — he's in bed, you see, and he's not at all well and the thing is—'

'But as I have told you,' said the one with the sergeant's stripes, who'd been doing most of the talking, 'this is a very serious matter and I insist that—'

'Insist what?' Ingleby interrupted when he was still only half way between the house and where the three of them were standing.

The sergeant opened his mouth to speak, but Sandra got in first. 'They want to search the house.'

'Search the house?' said Ingleby. 'What in God's name for?'

'As I have already explained to the *kyría* here,' said the sergeant with a pained expression and the tone of a man on the brink of despair, 'we have received informations that a serious crime has been committed and—'

'Crime? What sort of crime?'

'I'm sorry, *kírie*, but I really cannot—'

'You got a warrant?'

The sergeant's forehead creased into a frown of incomprehension.

'A warr - ant,' said Ingleby. 'Piece of paper giving you permission to search the place.'

'No,' said the sergeant, 'but as I said before, this is a—'

'Well, fuck off then and don't come back till you've got one.'

The sergeant stiffened. 'We must also look inside the *máxi* at the front of house.'

'The what?'

'The camping van.'

133

'Yeah?' said Ingleby with a contemptuous sneer. 'So that means you're gonna need *two* search warrants, don't it?'

While the two men glowered at each other in bristling silence, Sandra wondered what reason the police could have for wanting to search the van as well as the house. The only plausible explanation was that it had something to do with the head in the freezer, but was it really the head they were here for at all? Perhaps they were looking for something else entirely, although she was forced to admit that this seemed highly unlikely in the circumstances.

'So what's it to be?' said Ingleby. 'You gonna leave or do you want me to set the dog on you?'

The sergeant and his constable followed the direction of his pointing finger to where Milly lay stretched out on a nearby sun lounger and snoring peacefully.

'Oh, don't let appearances deceive you,' Ingleby added. 'One word from me and...'

He drew his thumb swiftly across his throat in a cutting motion, and the two policemen returned their gaze to the dog, presumably trying to weigh up whether the old man was having them on or not.

'Very well, *kírie*,' said the sergeant, having apparently come to the conclusion that it wasn't worth the risk of doubting him. 'But I shall come back immediately when—'

'Sabre!' Ingleby yelled.

Rudely awoken from her slumber, Milly stirred and looked all around her for the source of the sudden disturbance.

The two policemen eyed her briefly and took a step backwards.

'We will return,' said the sergeant, and Milly's head swivelled slowly as she watched every step that he and the constable took towards the side of the house. They in turn kept their eyes fixed on her, their pace increasing as they went.

'I'd go with 'em if I was you,' said Ingleby. 'Unless you want 'em takin' a sneaky peek inside your van, that is.'

But Sandra was already on her way, partly because she also suspected they might be tempted to take a sneaky peek inside the van, but also because she wanted to check it out for herself. If there was anything in there that was even remotely associated with the severed head, she wanted to be the first to know about it.

23

Donna adjusted the focusing ring on the binoculars to get a sharper image of the front of Ingleby's villa in the vain hope that her eyes had deceived her. — No, it was true. The two uniformed cops had got into their car and were driving away.

'That's ridiculous,' she said.

'What is?' said Eddie as he came to join her at the edge of the terrace.

'The cops. There's no way they'd have gone off so soon if they'd found anything.'

'You told them where to look, I s'pose?'

'Course I did,' Donna snapped. 'Freezer in the basement and the rest of the stuff in the camper van.'

'I thought you were gonna put everything in the van.'

'I was,' said Donna, lowering the binoculars. 'But then I thought the head might start giving off a stink if I left it in the van in this heat, and I didn't want any of them finding it and getting rid of it before the cops got there.'

'Didn't the cops search the van then?'

'Walked straight past it. — Well, not quite *straight* past. They stopped to have a look in through the window, but then that Sandra woman came round the corner and they buggered off.'

'So what do we do now?'

It wasn't an easy question to answer. If everything had gone according to plan, Trevor Hawkins and Sandra Gray would have been on their way to the local police

136

station by now and facing a very long stretch in a Greek prison. But for some reason or other, the cops had screwed up, and Donna's entire plan seemed doomed to fail unless she could somehow get it back on track again. Easier said than done of course, but she'd invested far too much time and effort to simply give up now. One way or the other, Hawkins and Gray were going to have to pay the price for what had happened to her Harry.

'I'll go round there later,' she said. 'See if I can find out what's going on.'

Eddie pulled a face. 'You sure that's a good idea, Mrs V?'

'Maybe not. But I need to know the score before I can work out what to do next.'

'Never say die, eh?'

'Something like that,' said Donna, and she set off back towards the house. What she really needed right now was a very large drink and a lie down in a darkened room.

* * *

Sandra had searched through every one of the van's overstuffed cupboards, the glove box, the oven, the fridge and even the grill compartment, but had found nothing out of the ordinary. The only item of any note so far had been a well-thumbed copy of *Playboy* under the foam mattress on the back seat, which she presumed belonged to Herbert. At least, she sincerely hoped it belonged to Herbert and not Trevor. She'd have words with her nephew later, but for now, there were far more pressing matters demanding her attention.

She dropped to her knees and tentatively slid her hand into the gap between the floor and the bottom of the driver's seat. Nothing. Repeating the operation beneath the passenger seat, her fingertips came into contact with some kind of soft material. It felt damp to the touch, and reluctant to take hold of whatever it was and pull it out in case it was something unpleasant Herbert had shoved under there, she pressed the side of her face against the floor and peered into the gap. But the light was too dim to make out any more than what appeared to be a small bundle of cloth, so she took a deep breath and eased it out into the open.

Still on her knees, she pinched a loose end of the fabric between her forefinger and thumb and lifted it slowly to unravel the bundle — a pair of blue and white checked swimming shorts. Almost half of their surface area was stained with a vivid red, and as the shorts unfurled, something fell out and clattered to the floor. Sandra dropped the shorts and sprang upright.

'Jesus,' she said, staring down at the enormous blade of a butcher's cleaver between her feet. It too was heavily stained with the same vivid red as the swimming shorts — a vivid red that glistened brightly in the early afternoon sunlight.

She stood frozen to the spot for several seconds, unable to avert her gaze from the cleaver and the shorts. Blood pounded in her ears as her mind swirled with one half-formed theory after another and spiralled into a chaotic whirlpool of confusion.

'You seen Trevor?'

Sandra spun round at the sound of the voice. It was Herbert, standing outside the open doorway of the van.

'What?' she said.

But Herbert didn't repeat his question. His eyes were popping at the sight of the swimming shorts and the meat cleaver. 'Blimey. Where'd they come from?'

'Dunno yet. — What were you saying about Trevor?'

'I've been trying to find him and tell him the coast's clear. I thought you might have seen him.'

'Hang on a minute and I'll come with you,' said

Sandra and took a plastic carrier bag from the cupboard over the sink. With her hand inside the bag to avoid any direct contact, she picked up the meat cleaver by the handle and dropped it onto the swimming shorts. Then she loosely rolled up the shorts and pulled them into the bag, turning it inside out with her other hand. 'Right. Let's go.'

Back inside the house, there was no response when they called out Trevor's name, and after a quick search of the basement, Sandra tried the door of the downstairs bathroom. It was locked.

'Trevor?'

'What?' came the barely audible but definitely grumpy reply.

'Are you decent?'

Sandra heard the sound of the door being unlocked, and she pushed it open to find Trevor sat on the toilet, his shorts round his ankles.

He looked up at her sheepishly. 'Have they gone?'

'Don't tell me...' said Sandra, pointing at the toilet bowl beneath him.

'Well, what else was I supposed to do? Paint it orange and pretend it was Halloween?'

24

The fierce heat of the day had begun to subside, and an occasional light breeze floated past the balcony, bringing its own additional relief. Kate loved the summer evenings in Greece, and this one would have been almost perfect if it hadn't been for the brainless fat pisshead on the other side of the table. She watched Frank pour himself yet another generous measure of ouzo and add a dash of water before swilling nearly half of it down his throat in one go. Not that she gave a toss that he was performing his normal evening ritual of steadily drinking himself into unconsciousness. In fact, it was always a blessing when he eventually did keel over because it was only then that she and Eric were able to have a sensible conversation in peace. Until then, they both had to endure Frank's drunken ramblings, which were often incoherent, usually bitter and always loud. Try as they might, Kate and her granddad found it impossible to ignore him completely, and tonight was no exception.

'Bastard knew exactly who we were. Bloody sure he did,' Frank was saying while Eric was trying to find out how Kate's lunch date had gone and particularly the reason for Pericles's sudden departure.

'He had a call on his mobile,' said Kate. 'From the police station, I guess. Said he had to go and left.'

'He didn't *tell* you he was going to Ingleby's?' said Eric.

'I worked it out from what he said on the phone.'

'It's a bit of a coincidence if it wasn't something to do

with us being there.'

Frank belched. 'Need to get 'eavy with 'im next time. *Make* the bugger tell us.'

'There was one thing, now I think about it,' said Kate.

'Yes?'

'When he was on the phone, he said "from who?".'

'Ah, you mean he should have said "from *whom*?",' said Eric and winked at her.

'Ha ha, very funny. Especially as he was speaking Greek.'

'Sorry, sweetheart. Couldn't resist. Do go on.'

'I don't know,' said Kate. 'It's a bit two plus two equals ninety-seven, but it could've been they'd had a tipoff.'

'About what?'

Kate shrugged.

'Fifteen bloody years I did because of that little arsehole. Fifteen bloody years,' Frank said to his almost empty glass.

Eric sat back in his chair and clasped his hands behind his head. 'So if you're right about the tipoff, maybe the police coming to Ingleby's didn't have anything to do with us after all. Maybe it *was* just a coincidence. I mean, who else knows we're even here?'

Kate realised the question was rhetorical so didn't bother to answer.

'When are you seeing Pericles again?' said Eric after a moment's thought.

'Dunno.'

Her granddad leaned forward and took her hand in his. 'You want to give him a call? Get together with him again and see what you can find out?'

Kate had been expecting this from the very beginning of their conversation. Truth be told, she'd been expecting it ever since Pericles had left the restaurant in such a hurry. Even so, she still hadn't made up her mind whether she could face another date with Sergeant Parking-ticket.

Eric gave her hand a squeeze and stuck out his lower lip in an exaggerated pout, a mournful look in his eyes.

She laughed, fully aware that refusing his request had never been an option. 'You know, I didn't think the role of a granddad included pimping out their granddaughters.'

'My dear girl,' said Eric, feigning a horrified expression. 'Perish the thought that I would ever be the one to subject my favourite granddaughter to the lustful inclinations of a virtual stranger against her will.'

He clapped his hand over his heart, and the horrified expression morphed into one of wounded pride, aided and abetted by the protruding lower lip once again. As his *only* granddaughter, Kate stuck her tongue out at him and smiled as she fished in her bag for her mobile phone.

'No, Marcus fooking Ingleby owes me big time. Big fooking time, I tell yer,' said Frank, his voice having by now reached such a volume that it was utterly impossible to ignore him.

'Shut up, Frank,' Eric and Kate chorused.

Frank stuck up two fingers in their general direction and poured himself another ouzo.

25

The basement of Ingleby's villa was about the same size as the other two floors and almost as well ordered. Close to the bottom of the concrete steps which led down from the kitchen was the large chest freezer containing the severed head. On the opposite wall was a long row of plastic tool cupboards, a pair of mountain bikes and two canoes. A couple of impressively stacked wine racks and a stainless steel vat of olive oil stood against the third wall as well as a variety of neatly arranged cardboard boxes. In the centre stood a full-sized snooker table and two armchairs, one of which was occupied by Trevor and the other by Sandra. Herbert was perched on the edge of the snooker table, and all three were leaning forward and staring at the open carrier bag on the floor between them.

'You sure it's blood?' said Trevor, eyeing the red stain on the blue and white checked material inside the bag.

'Well, I haven't exactly carried out a chemical analysis,' said Sandra, 'but I'd be very surprised if it wasn't.'

'So how did it get into the van?'

'At a rough guess, I'd say whoever put the head in the freezer also put this stuff in the van.'

'But that's insane. It's almost as if somebody's trying to...'

'Frame us?' said Sandra.

'No,' said Trevor, sitting back with his palms planted squarely on the arms of the chair. 'The whole idea's just too ridiculous for words.'

'You got a better explanation?'

Trevor's silence was evidence enough that he hadn't, but if the deep furrowing of his brow was anything to go by, he was desperately trying to come up with one. The possibility that someone wanted to frame them for murder — let alone a beheading — made no more sense to Sandra than it did to Trevor, but in the short time she'd had to think about it, an alternative interpretation of events had so far failed to present itself.

That there was no connection between the severed head, the shorts and the meat cleaver clearly stretched the bounds of coincidence to well beyond breaking point, so whoever had put the head in the freezer must also have planted the stuff in the van. But who was this "whoever"? They'd already established that Ingleby hadn't been in the basement since they'd arrived, and it was even less likely that he'd been out to the van without them noticing. So who else had had the opportunity? There was Donna of course, but they'd only just met the woman, so what possible reason could she have for wanting to frame them? What about the two old guys who'd come to visit Ingleby? The shorter one had definitely been on the shifty side, and they could certainly have stopped off at the van, either on their way in or their way out, but when did they go down into the basement? Herbert had found the head while they were still up in Ingleby's bedroom, and Trevor had been with them all the time when he'd shown them up there. — Or maybe they and Donna were in on it together. But that didn't make much sense either. As far as Sandra was aware, they had no more motive for framing them than Donna did.

'So what do we tell Ingleby?' said Herbert.

'Nothing,' said Sandra. 'Since I found the stuff in the van, it seems fairly obvious that it's us that's supposed to be on the receiving end of all this and nothing to do with Ingleby.'

'He told me he wanted to know what the police said to you when they turned up. What exactly it was they were looking for.'

'No problem. I tell him the truth.'

'Which is?'

'That they wouldn't tell me anything except that it was a very serious matter, that they'd had a phone call and that they needed to search the place.'

'You don't think he has a right to know what's been going on?' said Trevor. 'It is his house after all.'

'You *want* him to have a heart attack?' said Sandra. 'He's got high blood pressure and a heart condition, and the last thing Mrs S said to me before she left was to make sure he didn't get over-excited about anything. I don't know about you, but I'd say that might include telling him there was a severed head in his freezer.'

Trevor and Herbert nodded their subdued agreement, and at the very same moment there was a shout from somewhere on the floor above. The words were indistinct, but the voice was recognisably Ingleby's.

Sandra leapt to her feet and snatched up the carrier bag. 'Quick, Herbert. Get up there and see what he wants before he comes poking his nose in.'

'What are we going to do with that?' said Trevor as Herbert hurried towards the steps.

Sandra looked down at the bag. 'Stick it in the freezer. We'll have to figure out what to do with it later.'

'And the head?'

'That'll have to stay there too,' said Sandra, lifting the lid of the freezer while attempting to avert her eyes from the rictus grin of the head in question.

26

The one-piece blue overalls were a couple of sizes too small, and the heavy seam at the crotch chafed like hell when he walked. Still, it wasn't as if he'd be covering any great distance, and they were the best he could get hold of in the short time available. The plastic toolbox — complete with enough tools to look the business — had cost him a small fortune, though, but it was a small price to pay compared to what he hoped to gain in return.

Reynolds rang the doorbell for a second time and waited, his other hand fingering his lucky coin in his pocket. He checked his watch — the very one given to him as part of his retirement present.

Christ almighty, he thought. Surely they can't still be having siestas at this time of the evening. — Or maybe they are. That's what's wrong with all these bloody countries who go cap in hand for a bailout every time their economies go tits up. A bit less kipping in the afternoon and a bit more elbow grease would soon sort 'em out. Lazy buggers.

Again he rang the bell, his finger lingering on the button for far longer than was entirely necessary. The moment he released it, the door opened, and a young lad in a blue and white striped T-shirt and a gormless expression stood gawping at him.

'*Bonjour*,' said the lad.

Oh great, thought Reynolds. First Greek and now I've got bloody French to contend with. 'Er, you speaky English?'

'Of course I do. Can I help you?'

Reynolds cocked an eyebrow. Not a bad accent for a Frenchy.

'I'm here to service the aircon,' he said and held up the toolbox as if in proof.

'The what?'

'Aircon. — Air conditioning.'

'Oh,' said the lad but made not the slightest move to step aside and let him in.

'Perhaps I could... come in?'

But the lad didn't answer. Just stood there like a lemon with his mouth open, apparently trying to figure out whether it was a trick question. Not only a Frog but a bloody halfwit to boot.

'Who is it, Herbert?'

It was a woman's voice from somewhere inside the house.

'Somebody come to service the hair conditioning.'

'*Air* conditioning,' Reynolds corrected.

A woman with blonde hair — which actually looked like it *was* in need of some serious conditioning — appeared at the lad's shoulder.

Reynolds felt himself involuntarily touch the peak of his baseball cap. 'Evening, madam. Annual aircon service,' he said and then added, 'Air conditioning?'

'Yes, I do know what aircon means,' said the woman.

Ouch. Tread carefully, Bruce. Looks like we've got a feisty one here.

Still there was no invitation to step inside the house.

'Who is it, Sandra?'

Jesus wept. What *is* this? The Waltons?

It was a man's voice this time, and it was followed by his arrival behind the other two.

'I've come to—' Reynolds began, but the woman cut him short.

'He's come to service the air conditioning.'

The second man looked him up and down but seemed just as unlikely as the other two to let him in, so Reynolds decided that a bit of flannel might nudge them along.

'I do all the expats round here,' he said with what he hoped was a reassuring smile. 'They seem to appreciate someone who speaks English doing this sort of thing. Someone a bit older they feel they can trust.'

During the pause that followed, he thought back to the dozens of interrogations he'd conducted with some of the biggest villains on the planet and how they'd been a damn sight easier to crack than these three goons.

'Half an hour tops,' he said and waited for them to stop exchanging shall-we-shan't-we glances.

'The thing is,' the woman said at last, 'we're not the owners, you see, and Mr Ingleby's gone for a lie down.'

Reynolds clocked the name but didn't immediately recognise it. 'Oh, that's no problem,' he said. 'I spoke to Mr Ingleby on the phone earlier, and he said it was absolutely fine.'

This time, he didn't wait for them to finish their glance exchanging but took a step forward, and they parted obediently to let him through.

'I'm not even sure where the aircon is,' said the woman as he carried on along the corridor.

Nor was Reynolds, but he'd once been to a big house in England to investigate a burglary, and while he was interviewing the owners, a heating engineer had turned up and they'd sent him down to the basement. It was as good a guess as any.

'House this size, the main gubbins is usually in the basement,' he said and was almost certain he heard a sharp intake of breath and an "Oh hell" from behind him.

* * *

Herbert stopped when he reached the bottom of the concrete steps.

'This is the basement,' he said, realising the pointlessness of the statement and making a determined effort to prevent his eyes drifting towards the large chest freezer on his left.

The air conditioning man scanned the area and then headed for the far corner beyond the freezer.

'Here it is,' he said and slapped his palm against an enormous steel duct that disappeared up into the floor above. He put down his toolbox and opened the lid. 'You can leave me to get on with it now if you like.'

'That's okay,' said Herbert and, as if in a trance, sidled over to the chest freezer without any awareness of the direction he was taking. 'I've got nothing else to do.'

Finding himself next to the freezer, he decided that it would probably attract more attention if he now moved away from it, so he stayed put and tried to look casual, his backside leaning against it and his arms folded.

Why me? he thought as he watched Aircon Man take a screwdriver from his box and start to remove a mesh grill from the side of the duct. Trevor or Sandra could have kept an eye on the guy just as easily as me, and after all, it was them that had put the head back in the bloody freezer.

'So how is Mr Ingleby then?' said Aircon Man, grunting with the effort of loosening a stubborn screw.

'Er, okay, I guess.'

'Must be knocking on a bit now.'

'Yes.'

'What, early seventies, would you say?'

'About that.'

Good grief, can't he just get on with what he's doing and stop asking all these questions?

'Lived here a few years, has he?'

'Not sure.'

For the next couple of minutes, Aircon Man busied himself with whatever he was supposed to be doing in silence, apart from the occasional cursing when he dropped something or couldn't get something to budge. Herbert was grateful that the interrogation was over, however temporarily it might be, and couldn't have cared less what the man was actually working on. All he *did* care about was that he'd finish the job as soon as possible and clear off out of it. Thirty minutes tops, he'd said. Herbert prayed he wouldn't find some problem that needed fixing, which would mean he'd have to outstay his welcome even more than he had already.

But no sooner had the possibility entered his brain than Aircon Man took a step back from the air conditioning unit, removed his baseball cap, scratched his head and made a "Hmm" sound.

Oh hell, thought Herbert. He's found a problem. 'Problem?' he said.

Aircon Man wheeled round. 'What? — Oh no, not at all. It's just that I forgot to bring any water, and I'm gasping. I don't suppose there's any chance you could…?'

He didn't finish the sentence, but it was blindingly obvious what he was after. "Don't leave him on his own for even a second," Sandra had said, so now what was he supposed to do? Tell the guy the water had been turned off and that they'd run out of the bottled stuff? Oh yeah, he's bound to believe that, isn't he?

'Er, right,' he said. 'I'll go and er…' Then a flash of inspiration hit him, and he went to the bottom of the steps. 'Trevor? Sandra?'

He waited for a response, and when none came, he called out again. Where the hell were they? It was all very well getting him to go down into the basement to keep an eye on Aircon Man, but they might at least have stayed within earshot.

Bugger it. I'll just have to fetch it myself, and if anything goes wrong, they can hardly blame *me*, can they? In any case, the kitchen's right at the top of the steps, so how long's it actually going to take? Ten, fifteen seconds at most. And what's Aircon Man gonna be able to do in that time?

* * *

Reynolds watched the lad take the steps two at a time and set to work even before he'd disappeared from view. He knew he might only have a few seconds, and this could be the only opportunity he was going to get.

Opening the nearest tool cupboard, he rooted through rolls of duct tape, masking tape, waterproof sealing tape and balls of string but failed to find anything of interest. Not that he really expected to, but he was sure one of the three weirdos had muttered "Oh hell" when he'd said about going into the basement, so maybe there was something down here they didn't want him to see. Either way, it was certainly worth getting rid of the lad so he could have a quick rummage.

He closed the door of the cupboard and went on to the next. Cans of paint, varnish, wood preservative, plastic containers of white spirit, thinners and brush cleaner. The third cupboard yielded nothing more than half a dozen light bulbs, a roll of electrical cable, a couple of plugs, some chewed-up fragments of plastic and what looked suspiciously like a generous scattering of rat shit.

'Waste of time,' he said to himself, then shut the door and leaned his back against it.

It was like searching for the proverbial needle in a haystack but with the added complication of not knowing what the needle looked like or even whether there was a needle at all. The likelihood that the loot was hidden somewhere down here in the basement was slim to the point of non-existent. It probably wasn't even in the house at all.

His main objective in tricking his way into the house had been to check out who it was that Phelan and Emerson had come to see and find out if it really was the man he'd been after for all those years. It definitely wasn't any of the three weirdos. Witnesses to the robbery had been very vague about the identity of the getaway driver, but one thing they'd all agreed on was that he was male and aged between forty and sixty. This Ingleby bloke sounded a distinct possibility, though, and the French lad — if he really was French — had been more than a little reticent when he'd asked about him. And why else had Phelan and Emerson come all this way to see him the moment Phelan had got out of prison?

He was about to head back over to the air conditioning unit when he heard the lad coming back down the steps. Reynolds was on the opposite side of the basement, and he couldn't have covered the distance without the lad seeing him, but he'd already foreseen this eventuality, and he took three strides to where two mountain bikes were leaning against the wall and grabbed one by the handlebars.

'Nice bike,' he said when he heard the footsteps approaching from behind him.

The lad didn't answer, so he turned to face him. 'Yours, is it?'

'No. Here's your water.'

Reynolds took the plastic bottle from him and began to unscrew the cap. As he did so, he noticed the lad take what could only be described as a furtive glance at the chest freezer against the far wall. Come to think of it, he'd been paying it quite a lot of attention the whole time he'd been down here.

'I don't suppose you happened to bring a glass, did you?' he said.

'Sorry, no.'

'My fault,' said Reynolds, slapping his forehead with the palm of his hand. 'It's just that I've got this condition, you see. I won't bore you with the details. It's rather unpleasant actually, but the upshot is I'm not supposed to drink straight from the bottle — and especially not if someone else is going to use it after me.'

He snorted a laugh, but the lad merely stared at him.

'So if you wouldn't mind...' he said, dangling the water bottle in front of him by the neck.

The lad continued to stare as if he was trying to make sense of what he was being asked to do, and Reynolds scoured his memory for the French word for "glass".

'*Une tasse*?' he said.

He wasn't at all sure if this was right or not, but the lad seemed to get the message and trotted off back to the steps.

What the hell, thought Reynolds as he hurried over to the freezer. If he gets back and catches me, I'll say I had a headache and was looking for a bag of peas or something to ease the pain.

27

'He's not dead, is he?' said Herbert.

He glanced at Trevor and then Sandra, but there was no reaction. They were staring down at the prone body of Aircon Man, who was lying face down next to the freezer, a large bag of frozen peas beside him.

Herbert stooped to get a closer look. 'No, I'm pretty sure he's still breathing.'

'Why?' said Trevor.

'Because his back seems to be moving up and down a bit.'

'No, you idiot. I mean why did you have to go and hit him?'

'He wanted some water, and neither of you two were around — like you said you'd be — so I had to fetch it myself. Then he wanted a glass, and when I came back, he had his head inside the freezer.'

'*His* head?'

'Looking inside. — No way he couldn't have seen it. The head. The one with no body attached. I panicked, I guess. I didn't have time to think. So I hit him.'

'With a bag of peas.'

'It was the first thing that came to hand.'

'Brilliant.'

'What else was I supposed to do? Would you have preferred it if I'd whacked him with a frozen chicken or a... a buy-three-get-one-free four-pack of stoneground luxury pizzas with extra topping?'

Trevor rounded on him. 'I'm not questioning your

culinary choice of weapon here, Herbert. What I *am* questioning is why you knocked him out cold in the first place.'

'I already told you I—'

'Will the pair of you *please* stop bickering for two seconds and let me think,' Sandra interrupted.

She crouched down beside the body and placed two fingers against the side of the neck. 'Definitely not dead, thank God.'

'Another thing I don't understand,' said Trevor, 'is how you can knock somebody out with a bag of peas.'

'He's no spring chicken, is he?' said Sandra. 'And if you happen to hit exactly the right spot... Anyway, there's no point analysing it. Help me turn him over.'

Trevor bent down beside her, and they eased the body onto its side and then onto its back. The eyes were closed, but the rise and fall of the chest was definitely more visible now. Sandra was right. The guy was certainly knocking on a bit. Late sixties by the look of him. Odd that he was still doing this kind of work then, but maybe that's how it was over here. Move abroad to live your dream in the sun when you retire and pick up some pin money here and there to supplement your pension. Perfectly plausible of course, but Trevor couldn't help thinking there was something iffy about the guy. The overalls were way too small for him for a start, and there was also the phone conversation he'd said he'd had with Ingleby earlier in the day.

'Either of you know of any phone calls Ingleby's had today?' he said.

The others shook their heads.

Trevor looked up at Herbert. 'Did he actually do anything with the air conditioning while he was down here?'

'Seemed to,' said Herbert. 'But I wasn't really paying too much attention to be honest. — Asked quite a lot of questions though.'

'Oh?' said Sandra. 'What about?'

'Ingleby mostly. How old was he. How long had he lived here. That kind of thing.'

Trevor went over to the air conditioning unit and cast his eyes over it, but he'd no idea what he was looking for, so he turned his attention instead to the toolbox on the floor. The top tray contained an assortment of screwdrivers, pliers and spanners, but when he lifted it, the main compartment of the box was empty.

'I reckon we should search him,' he said.

'I was just thinking the same thing,' said Sandra and began to unzip the man's overalls.

Underneath, he was wearing a short-sleeved shirt and lightweight cotton trousers. There was nothing in the top pocket of the shirt, so she put her hand inside one of the trouser pockets.

'What exactly are we looking for?' said Herbert.

'Some kind of ID,' said Sandra.

'Find out who he really is,' Trevor added.

'You mean you don't think he's—'

'Bingo,' said Sandra, pulling out a thick leather wallet. The contents were all neatly ordered with euros and pounds kept separately and a variety of plastic cards, each with its own slot. She randomly selected one of these and read out the name. 'Bruce Reynolds.'

'Wasn't he one of the Great Train Robbers?' said Trevor.

'I doubt this is the same one,' said Sandra. 'I'm not even sure he's still alive, and if he is, he'd be a lot older than this guy.'

'Doesn't really help us much then.'

'Hang on a minute. What's this?' Tucked into the same compartment as the euros was a folded piece of paper. She took it out and opened it up. 'Oh. My. God.'

Trevor and Herbert peered over her shoulder at a

newspaper clipping that was beginning to yellow with age. Under the headline "DCI Bruce Reynolds Retires" was a photograph of the man himself in full uniform and with a chestful of medals.

'Bloody Nora,' said Trevor. 'You've only gone and knocked out a cop.'

'*Retired* cop,' said Herbert.

'What's the difference?' said Trevor and began to skim the article, but he got no further than "rose through the ranks", "long and faithful service" and "impressive conviction rate" before a loud groaning sound interrupted him.

'I think he's coming round,' said Sandra.

'So now what do we do?' said Trevor.

'I suppose I could always apologise,' said Herbert.

Trevor glared at him. 'Oh yes? And what about the little matter of the head in the freezer?'

'Herbert,' said Sandra. 'Get some rope or something to tie him up with.'

Herbert hurried over to the row of tool cupboards.

'Tie him up?' said Trevor. 'Are you out of your mind?'

'We need to buy ourselves time to think. We've no idea whose head it is yet or how it got here, but this guy's obviously seen it, and he's an ex-cop. You think he's just gonna forget all about it?'

Trevor didn't know how to answer. Tying the guy up and effectively keeping him prisoner was utterly insane, but Sandra was right. Until they had more information about the head in the freezer, they were sitting ducks. Who else were the police going to suspect? An old man with a catheter who was on more medication than Michael Jackson and Elvis Presley combined? And then there were the swimming shorts and the meat cleaver in the van. Sandra had removed them, but there were still bound to be traces.

157

Herbert returned with a bundle of rope and a roll of silver duct tape, and the three of them set about tying Reynolds's hands and feet. They worked quickly as he was groaning even more now, and his eyelids were beginning to flutter. When they'd finished, they carried him over to one of the armchairs and sat him down. Sandra tore off a length of duct tape and fixed it across his mouth.

'In case he starts yelling,' she said.

Reynolds's eyes flicked open, and there was a pause of several seconds while he appeared to be taking stock of where he was and what had happened to him. He looked from Herbert to Trevor and Trevor to Sandra, and the duct tape stretched tighter across his mouth as he tried to speak. At the same moment, he tried to move, and his eyes widened in horror when he realised his hands and feet were tied.

'What's Milly barking at?' said Herbert.

Trevor was so used to Milly's barking for reasons which were only known to herself that he'd long ago learned to blot out the sound, but this was different. This was a particular kind of bark, in both volume and pitch. This was her "real and present danger" bark and not to be taken lightly.

'Shit,' he said. 'There must be someone coming.'

He'd made it to the bottom of the steps when he heard a woman's voice calling from somewhere upstairs. 'Hello? Anyone home?'

When he was three steps from the top, Donna poked her head through the doorway.

'Oh, there you are,' she said. 'I thought maybe you'd done a runner.'

Trevor wasn't sure whether he was supposed to take the remark seriously, but he kept going, and Donna had no choice but to take a step backwards when he reached the doorway. She made no attempt to disguise the fact that she was trying to look over his shoulder and down into the basement, but fortunately the armchair that Reynolds was trussed up in was well outside her line of sight. As an extra precaution, however, Trevor shut the door behind him.

'Good game?' said Donna with a nod towards the now closed door.

'Pardon?'

'Thought you must be playing snooker. — Not much other reason to be down there, is there?'

'Oh, right,' said Trevor, concentrating hard on stifling a blush even though he knew this would probably turn his face all the redder. 'Snooker. Yes.'

Without being fully conscious he was doing it until it was too late, he found himself running an imaginary cue back and forth between his forefinger and thumb and then playing a shot, making a "click" noise with his tongue. He realised it was a bit of an odd thing to do, and judging by her expression and the brief silence that followed, so did Donna.

'Look,' she said, rallying a smile, 'I'm sorry to barge in unannounced — again — and I know you'll think it's a bit strange, but I was wondering if you had any peas I could borrow.'

'Peas?' The very mention of the word made his insides churn.

Donna gave a little laugh that was almost coquettish and far too young for her. 'It's just that I had this sudden mad craving for paella, but I've run out of peas, and everybody knows you can't make paella without peas.'

In any other circumstance, Trevor would have told her how she was a woman after his own heart, but as things stood, his mind was awhirl with potential excuses, none of which were likely to be in the least convincing until he hit on the most obvious one of all. But he'd just opened his mouth to say "I'm sorry, but we don't have any either" when the basement door opened behind him.

'Oh, hi, Donna,' said Sandra. 'Anything wrong?'

'No, not at all. I only—'

'She wants to know if we've got any peas,' Trevor blurted.

'Peas?' said Sandra, closing the door.

Once again, Donna did her coquettish giggle. 'Silly, I know but—'

'She's making paella,' said Trevor and made a mental note to try and stop gabbling his words and speaking with the voice of someone who was being slowly strangled to death.

'No problem,' said Sandra, cool as you like. 'I'm fairly sure there's some tinned ones in the cupboard.'

She started to move past Donna into the kitchen, but Donna held up her hand.

'Oh God, no,' she said. 'I don't want to be fussy, but I really can't *bear* those processed things. You don't have any frozen ones, do you?'

Sandra gave her an apologetic shrug. 'We're fresh out, I'm afraid.'

'Oh, that's a shame,' said Donna, pouting slightly, but then she suddenly brightened. 'By the way, did I see the police round here earlier? Not been burgled or anything, have you?'

'No, nothing like that,' said Sandra. 'Just some routine stuff about the van.'

'Oh?'

'Came to tell us we'd have to register it if we were planning on staying in Greece for more than three months.'

'I see,' said Donna, fixing Sandra with a narrow-eyed stare as if she knew she was lying but couldn't outright accuse her of it.

'Anyway,' said Sandra, cutting through the awkward silence. 'Sorry about the peas, but we really need to—'

'You know, it's just occurred to me,' said Donna. 'There might be some in the freezer down in the basement. Mind if I take a look?'

She'd taken only two paces towards the door before Trevor edged sideways to block her path.

'Sorry,' said Sandra, 'but that's where we got the last packet from.'

Donna frowned. 'Are you sure about that? I could have sworn I saw some this morning when—' She broke off abruptly, and this time it was her turn to blush. 'Oh well, never mind. I guess I'll have to make do without. Either that or an omelette — again.'

The coquettish laugh was even less convincing than before, but she kept it going till she was almost at the patio door.

'Well,' whispered Sandra. 'I reckon that answers *one* of our questions, don't you?'

28

Once they were certain Donna had left, Trevor went to the fridge and took out two cans of beer.

'I don't know about you,' he said, 'but I could do with a drink after all that.'

He gave one of the cans to Sandra, and they both popped the ringpulls and glugged.

'But why would she do it?' said Sandra.

Trevor wiped his mouth with the back of his hand. 'I suppose we're sure it *was* Donna?'

'Who else could it have been? First she turns up with a heavy carrier bag and says it's a watermelon for Ingleby. Then she leaves with an empty bag and there's no sign of a watermelon. And not two minutes ago she near as dammit admits she was down in the basement rooting around in the freezer.'

She put her drink down on the breakfast bar and hoisted herself up next to it.

'But why would she put a severed head in Ingleby's freezer?' said Trevor.

'Maybe her own was full.'

Trevor was about to tell her how ridiculous that was when he spotted the twinkle in her eye. 'Yeah, okay, I get it.'

'Seriously though,' said Sandra, 'she could easily have planted the shorts and the meat cleaver in the van as well, and if that's the case, she's obviously trying to frame us.'

'But we hardly know the woman. Why would she—?'

'And what about the police turning up out of the blue like that?'

'You mean she tipped them off?'

'Bit of a coincidence, don't you think?'

Trevor didn't answer. He was too busy trying to think up an alternative explanation, and preferably one that didn't involve being arrested for cutting some bloke's head off. But nothing else seemed to fit.

'So what are we going to do about it?' he said. 'Go to the police and give them our side of the story before they come back with a search warrant?'

'And what makes you think they'd believe us?' said Sandra. 'No, I reckon our only option is to go and see Donna and have it out with her. Try and find out what she thinks she's playing at. Maybe even record what she says in case she gives herself away.'

'You think that's likely?'

'You got a better idea?'

'Well, there is one other possibility,' said Trevor. 'We pack up the van and get the hell out of here — *tout de suite*, as Herbert would say.'

'Oh, and that wouldn't look at all suspicious, would it?' said Sandra. 'And what about Ingleby? We just leave him here on his own and—?'

'Did I hear my name being taken in vain?'

They spun round to see Ingleby almost at the bottom of the stairs which led up to the first floor. He was clutching an empty whisky bottle and was distinctly unsteady on his feet as he crossed the living room floor.

Trevor couldn't think of a quick answer to the old man's question and apparently nor could Sandra.

'It's like Piccadilly bloody Circus round 'ere today,' said Ingleby. 'Who was the bloke in the overalls and the baseball cap?'

'Er,' Sandra faltered. 'He came to service the air conditioning.'

163

'Not the bloke who usually does it. And anyway, we 'ad it done less than a fortnight ago.'

When Trevor and Sandra failed to respond, he added, 'Still 'ere is he?'

'Um, how d'you mean?' said Trevor.

'Christ almighty, son, it's a perfectly simple question. I've been sat at me bedroom window for the past hour or so watchin' all the comings and goings, and he came but he didn't go. I mean, I might be knockin' on a bit, but I ain't blind and I'm certainly not bloody stupid.'

Well, if that's the case, then why did you ask the question in the first place? Trevor wanted to say, but instead — and in the absence of any input from Sandra — the best he could come up with was 'He went out the back way.'

'Back way? Back way? There is no fucking back way, you moron. — So where the fuck is he?'

'I think what Trevor meant to say,' said Sandra, 'was that he's down in the basement.'

'Thank you,' said Ingleby with blatant sarcasm and patted Trevor a couple of times on the cheek. 'You see? It wasn't that 'ard, now was it? — So one of you go and tell 'im I want a word before he clears off, and while you're at it, you can fetch me another one o' these.'

He waved the empty whisky bottle at them, and Trevor took it from him. It was bad enough that they had a retired senior police officer tied up in the basement, but now they'd also have to figure out how to deal with Ingleby's insistence on seeing the guy.

Ingleby headed for his favourite armchair and called back over his shoulder, 'And what did that Donna woman want?'

'She wanted to borrow some peas,' said Sandra.

'Peas? — Woman's a bloody idiot.' He slumped down in the chair and lit a cigarette. 'Oh yeah, and one of you do something about them rubbish bins out there, will yer? There's a right old pen and ink comin' up into me bedroom window.'

As if we haven't got enough on our plate already, Trevor thought, but the immediate priority was to fetch Ingleby his whisky and keep him quiet for a while. With a bit of luck, the old bugger would drink himself senseless and forget he'd ever even seen Reynolds.

* * *

There were several reasons why Eric wanted this whole business over and done with as soon as possible, not least of which was that he could be shot of Frank and his incessant inane ranting.

'I still reckon the only way we'll get a result is by beating it out of 'im' was his latest offering, to which Eric responded by opening the car door and saying, 'I need to get some air.'

The whole point of driving back out to Ingleby's and parking up close to the entrance to his driveway was that Eric had had a vague notion that proximity might spark an idea as to how to get him to hand over their share of the loot. But so far, he'd drawn a blank, and his concentration wasn't helped by Frank's constant yabbering.

He strolled off along the road, breathing in the warm scent of wild sage, and thought about what Kate had told him on the phone a few minutes earlier. Not that there was much to think about because all she'd got from her quick drink with Pericles was that he was waiting for a warrant to search Ingleby's villa.

The significance of even this scrap of information wasn't lost on Eric, however, and it heaped still more pressure on him to come up with a strategy fast before the cops started swarming all over the place. He still had no idea what it was the police were actually expecting to find, but even if they weren't looking for the jewellery, what if they stumbled across it by chance? And if Ingleby had sold it, there was no way he'd have banked the money, so there must be a hefty pile of cash somewhere around. Okay, Ingleby wasn't stupid, so he probably hadn't stashed it in the house, and even if he had, he'd certainly have shifted it once he knew the police were about to search the place. So where was it? And how the hell were they ever going to get Ingleby to give them their share?

Damn it, he thought. I'm just going round in circles here. May as well get off back to the flat and have an early night.

He turned and walked back towards the car, wondering if a good night's sleep might be all he needed to freshen up his brain and come up with a solution. Besides, he'd heard enough about Greece and its convoluted bureaucratic processes to hope that the issuing of search warrants would take a lot longer than just a few hours.

Comforting himself with this tiny glimmer of hope, he was almost level with the back bumper of the car when a figure emerged from the driveway. There were no street lamps, but there was a sufficiently full moon for him to recognise the youngest of the three people they'd met when they'd been to visit Ingleby earlier in the day. He was carrying two bulging black bin liners and was heading for the steel rubbish container halfway between their car and the entrance to the drive.

Finally, inspiration struck. It probably wasn't the greatest idea he'd ever had, but it would have to do in the circumstances. He opened the car door and leaned in. Frank was fast asleep, his head back and snoring loudly.

'Frank. Wake up.'

Frank didn't stir, so he shook him roughly by the shoulder, and he jolted awake.

'Wha—? Who—? Whassamatter?'

'Those three people by the pool this morning. Anybody say who they were?'

'Don't think so.'

'You reckon they're family?'

Frank yawned. 'How the fook should I know?'

Eric didn't know either, but it had to be worth the gamble.

'You still have that gun with you?' he said.

Frank grinned and tapped the bumbag strapped under his belly.

'Is it loaded?' said Eric.

'You told me to keep it empty,' said Frank with not a little indignation.

'Good. Let's go.'

29

What was it Sandra had said when she was trying to persuade him to take this job? "Money for old rope" was one of the expressions. Oh yes, and after they'd got here, something about not being the kind of place where you were likely to be beaten to a pulp by a deranged heavyweight boxer. Well, he had to admit she'd been right about that part so far, but as he stood looking down at the bound and gagged cop who was sitting only a few short feet away from a freezer containing an unexplained severed head, Trevor began to wonder if being beaten to a pulp might actually be the preferable option right now.

'Money for old rope,' he said. 'Quite ironic really when you think about it.'

'What?' said Sandra.

'Him being tied up like that. — I told you it was a mistake bringing Herbert along.'

'Oh, don't start that again, Trev. We need to work out what we're going to do.'

'Well, my vote would be we untie him and let him go.'

DCI Reynolds nodded his head vigorously and made some grunting noises through the silver duct tape across his mouth.

'And then what?' said Sandra. 'He goes straight to the police and tells them about the head in the freezer.'

This time, the vigorous head movement was in a side-to-side direction, but the grunting sounded very similar.

'Yes, but we had nothing to do with that,' said Trevor,

'and maybe the cops will believe us. Either way, we can hardly plead innocence when it comes to this guy, can we? — Assaulting a police officer...'

A single, slow nod from Reynolds.

'...kidnapping...'

Two nods and a grunt.

'...and probably false imprisonment as well.'

More energetic nodding and some sustained grunting.

'He seems to agree with you,' said Sandra.

'So what's the alternative? Do him in and ditch the body somewhere?'

Reynolds's eyes looked as if they were about to explode out of his head.

There was a pause while Trevor and Sandra stared down at him, each mirroring the other with arms folded and lips pursed. It was Sandra who finally broke the silence.

'Maybe we should hear what he has to say for himself before we do anything rash.'

Trevor turned to face her. 'I wasn't serious about doing him in, you know.'

'Yes, I do realise that,' said Sandra.

Reynolds's eyes retreated into their sockets, and Trevor bent forward and took hold of a corner of the tape across his mouth.

'No shouting, okay?' he said.

Reynolds nodded, and Trevor slowly peeled the tape away in an ultimately futile attempt to cause as little pain as possible.

'Christ, lad, have you never taken a plaster off?' said Reynolds. 'Quick and sharp. Don't prolong the agony, eh?'

'Sorry,' said Trevor and immediately felt foolish for apologising to a man who was essentially their prisoner, so added, 'I'll try and remember next time' and hoped he sounded a little more *Goodfellas* and a lot less *Mary*

169

Poppins.

Reynolds stretched his mouth in a variety of directions to ease the stiffness in the muscles.

'So you're not actually a service engineer then,' said Trevor.

'Hah,' Reynolds snorted. 'And I thought *I* was the detective.'

'*Ex* detective apparently,' said Sandra.

'I prefer "retired". No such thing as an ex cop, love.'

Trevor checked the newspaper clipping they'd taken from his wallet. 'Bruce Reynolds. Odd name for a policeman.'

'Yes, I know. I thought of changing it to Ronnie Kray or John Dillinger but—'

'And you're here because...?' Sandra interrupted.

Reynolds held up his wrists, presumably to indicate he wasn't going to say anything until they untied him.

'Explanation first, I think,' said Sandra.

He held her gaze for several seconds, then sighed and launched into a story about how he'd led the investigation into a jewellery shop robbery nearly sixteen years ago, how they'd caught two of the robbers almost immediately and how there must have been a third, but he'd slipped through the net. In fact, they'd never even been able to discover who he was, never mind where he'd skipped to, but whoever he was and wherever he'd gone, he must have taken the jewellery with him because none of it had ever been found. Reynolds had eventually been ordered to drop the case, but he'd already become obsessed with finding not just the third member of the gang but the loot as well. "Obsessed" was putting it mildly though. He'd used every spare moment he'd had to pursue even the most tenuous of leads, but every one of them had ended in disappointment. Lack of sleep and sheer frustration at the constant string of failures eventually drove him to the edge of a nervous breakdown. His wife left him and his kids stopped talking to him, and even his closest friends drifted away, presumably sick to death of his one and only topic of conversation.

'But that still doesn't explain what you're doing *here*,' said Sandra.

Reynolds held up his wrists once again. 'You sure we can't do without the ropes now, love?'

'Positive,' said Sandra. 'And you call me "love" once more and the gag goes straight back on as well.'

He rolled his eyes and took a deep breath. 'Okay, so a few months after the wife leaves me, I get up one morning and I'm brushing my teeth when I catch sight of myself in the mirror. And what I saw scared the shit out of me. You know the Oscar Wilde story about *The Portrait of Dorian Gray*? Well, that was me, and it wasn't a pretty sight, I can tell you.'

He paused briefly as if recalling the image in his mind's eye.

'Anyway,' he went on, 'that's when I realised I needed to get a serious grip on my life before it was too late. So I quit the job, and instead of chasing one dead end after another, I took a bit more of a back seat and waited for things to happen.'

Trevor glanced at his watch. It was getting late in the evening, and the last thing they wanted was for Ingleby to make an appearance, demanding to know where his dinner was. Still, Herbert was supposed to have that under control, so maybe there wasn't any need to panic just yet.

Reynolds had probably spotted Trevor checking his watch because he suddenly started speaking more quickly as if he himself was in a hurry to get the story finished.

'All I had to do — or so I reckoned — was wait for the other two members of the gang to get released. Sure as hell, the first thing they'd do was head straight for the third man to get their share of the loot. But when Emerson got out six years ago, nothing happened. I couldn't be certain of course because although I still had contacts in the Force and I even paid the occasional private detective out of my own pocket, it was impossible to keep tabs on him all the time. Anyway, my guess was that Emerson was waiting for Phelan's release so they could make their move together.'

'And?' said Trevor, still struggling to understand what all this had to do with Reynolds turning up at Ingleby's villa pretending to be an air conditioning engineer.

'Haven't you met them already?' said Reynolds.

'Who?'

'Emerson and Phelan. They were here this morning. About lunchtime. Fat bloke with a red face and a walking stick and a taller, smarter-looking one.'

'You mean Eric and…?' Trevor searched his memory for the other name.

'Frank,' said Sandra.

'And you think Ingleby…' Trevor began.

'…is the third man?' Sandra finished.

'Well, I wouldn't stake my life on it,' said Reynolds, 'but I'd be bloody surprised if he wasn't.'

Trevor looked at Sandra to see how she'd taken this bombshell of news, and judging by her wide eyes and half open mouth, she was as stunned as he was. Just when he'd thought things couldn't get any worse, they find out that the old guy they're babysitting is a big-time jewel thief on the run from the police. Once more, Sandra's remark about "money for old rope" flashed through his mind, and he was about to remind her of it again when there was a shout from the top of the basement steps.

'What the bloody hell are you doin' down there?' It was Ingleby himself. 'Are we ever gonna eat tonight or you plannin' on starvin' me to death?'

Trevor was at the foot of the steps before Ingleby had finished the second question and was almost at the top before he could come down far enough to get a sight of Reynolds.

'Sorry, Mr Ingleby. I thought Herbert was sorting dinner out.'

Ingleby craned his neck to peer over Trevor's shoulder. 'That aircon bloke still 'ere, is he?'

'Er, just finished, I think,' said Trevor, and he took Ingleby by the arm and steered him back through the basement doorway and into the kitchen.

'Well, don't forget I want a word with 'im before he goes, okay?'

* * *

When Sandra came into the living room, closely followed by Reynolds and his toolbox, Ingleby was ensconced in his armchair, a cigarette in one hand and a tumbler of whisky in the other and stroking Milly's upturned belly with the sole of his foot.

''Bout bloody time,' he said. 'And you needn't think you're gettin' paid either. Once a year it needs servicing. Not every bloody fortnight.'

Reynolds took off his baseball cap and scratched his head. 'Yes, I'm sorry about that. Must have been an admin error. I'll have a word next time I'm in the office.'

'Well, make sure you do. Just 'cos I'm knockin' on, don't think you can put one over on me, okay?'

'Course not, sir,' Reynolds said with an ingratiating smile, and he put his cap back on and headed for the front door.

''Ang on a minute,' said Ingleby.

Reynolds stopped and turned.

'Don't I know you from somewhere?'

173

'I don't think so,' said Reynolds. 'It's the first time I've been here to service—'

Ingleby scowled and dismissed the comment with a flap of his hand. 'No, not now. I'm talkin' about years back. — Come over 'ere so I can get a proper look.'

Reynolds put down his tool box, and as he approached Ingleby's chair, Milly leapt up and went to meet him, sniffing energetically at the legs of his overalls.

Ingleby squinted up at him. 'Take the cap off again.'

He did as he was told, and Ingleby tilted his head from side to side while he studied Reynolds's face. 'What's yer name?'

'Barry Clark,' said Reynolds.

Ingleby took a deep drag on his cigarette and stared up at him for several more seconds, then shook his head and said, 'Nope, name doesn't ring any bells, but the boatrace definitely does. — Still, it'll come to me, I expect.'

He stubbed out his cigarette and drank down a finger of the whisky. 'All right, you can piss off now.'

Trevor and Sandra went with Reynolds to the front door, and as soon as he'd gone, Trevor asked her why she'd let him go.

'I'll tell you later,' she said. 'Where's Herbert?'

'Haven't seen him,' said Trevor. 'He was supposed to be cooking dinner, and Ingleby's doing his nut.'

'Okay,' said Sandra, 'I'll go and find Herbert and you get dinner going, yeah?'

Before Trevor had time to suggest a reversal of the roles, Sandra was out of the door and away, so he trudged back though the living room and into the kitchen area, ignoring Ingleby's comment about how his stomach thought his throat had been cut. When it came to the culinary arts, Trevor was certainly no Jamie Oliver. Not only that, but he hadn't been listening when Sandra and Herbert had been discussing the menu earlier, so he had no idea what he was supposed to be cooking.

Maybe there's something quick and easy in the freezer, he thought, but dismissed the idea the instant it entered his mind.

30

Although it was still quite early in the morning, the heat was becoming even more intense than the day before. After her initial — and completely accidental — plunge into the swimming pool, Milly had apparently decided that being almost fully immersed in water brought refreshingly welcome relief, so she was taking full advantage and flailing around in a loose approximation of a doggie-paddle. Side by side on one of the sun loungers, Trevor and Sandra sat watching her in almost complete silence apart from the constant clinking of Sandra's teaspoon against the inside of her coffee mug as she repeatedly stirred the now tepid contents. Neither of them had had more than a couple of hours' sleep, and even those had been little better than fitful. Every sound had brought with it the possibility that Herbert might have returned from wherever he'd got to, but each time it had been a false alarm.

After they'd finished dinner, Sandra had stayed behind to look after Ingleby while Trevor had taken the van into town and scoured the streets in the hope of spotting him, but the search had been in vain. Back at the villa, he'd asked Sandra about Reynolds and why she'd decided to release him, and she'd told him they hadn't had much of an option. For one thing, Ingleby had insisted on seeing him before he left the house, and for another, she hadn't thought that kidnapping someone — especially a retired police officer — was such a great idea, particularly on top of everything else they were involved in already.

Trevor had asked her what Reynolds was going to do about the head in the freezer, but Sandra said he'd assured her that he couldn't have cared less about it. All he was interested in was the so-called "third man" and the missing jewellery, and besides, she'd done a deal with him that if he kept his mouth shut about the head, they'd keep him informed about any developments on the Ingleby front.

It had also come as a surprise to Trevor — not to mention a huge relief — that Reynolds had been prepared to accept Sandra's explanation that knocking him unconscious and tying him up were merely the result of an unfortunate misunderstanding and the fact that Herbert was a bit "touched in the head". So at least the potentially dire consequences of *that* disaster had been averted. As for the plan to go and confront Donna about the severed head and the stuff in the van, that would have to wait. There was currently the more pressing matter of Herbert's unexplained disappearance.

Trevor shifted his head slightly to take in Sandra's profile. Her eyes remained fixed on Milly splashing about in the pool, but it was clear that her focus was somewhere else altogether. He reached out a hand and took Sandra gently but firmly by the wrist to bring an abrupt halt to the incessant stirring of her coffee. She turned to face him, the tears only an eyelash away from brimming over.

'I'm sure he'll turn up sooner or later,' he said and instantly regretted the lameness of the platitude, but Sandra gave him a half smile. It was barely more than a flicker, though, and her features collapsed once again into an expression of gloomy despondency.

'There is one thing we haven't tried yet,' she said.

He raised an eyebrow and waited for her to continue.

'Checked with the local hospital.'

Trevor felt his heart pumping against the inside of his

ribcage. The thought had certainly crossed his mind, but it was a thought he hadn't wanted to entertain, much less voice aloud.

'You think?' he said, letting go of her wrist and staring down at his knees.

'We've covered every other possibility.'

'I s'pose.'

Silence descended again, now without the clinking of Sandra's teaspoon, although it was interrupted soon afterwards by the arrival of Milly at the edge of the pool, barking for assistance. Trevor got up and helped her clamber out, jumping back as soon as he did so to avoid the inevitable drenching when she shook herself dry.

On his way back to the sun lounger, he noticed that Sandra was still staring at the same spot where Milly had been thrashing about a few moments earlier.

'You want another coffee?' he said. 'That one must be stone cold by now.'

By way of an answer, Sandra held her mug out to him and smiled. It was rather more than a flicker this time, and as Trevor took the mug from her, she grasped his other hand in hers.

'Thank you,' she said.

'That's okay,' said Trevor. 'It's my turn anyway.'

'I wasn't talking about the coffee. I meant... you know... stuff.'

She gave his hand a squeeze and then let go, her cheeks a less than delicate shade of pink. Trevor wasn't exactly sure what she meant by "stuff", but he felt his own face begin to flush, so he turned quickly and walked towards the house.

* * *

For some reason, the kettle seemed to be taking longer than ever to boil, and while he waited, Trevor gazed out

178

of the window to where Sandra still sat on the sun lounger, stroking Milly's head. But the action was almost mechanical, as if she was going through the motions without even realising what she was doing. Not that this was at all surprising of course. The whereabouts of her missing nephew was all her mind could cope with right now. For her part, Milly seemed to understand that something was wrong, staring up at Sandra with her ears pricked and now and again tilting her head first to one side and then the other.

Hearing the faint click of the kettle switching itself off, Trevor turned away from the window, but as he did so, his peripheral vision registered a sudden and unexpected movement. He looked back out of the window to see two people crossing the terrace towards Sandra. Even from behind, they were immediately recognisable as the two men who had come to see Ingleby the day before. Eric and Frank. And considering what Reynolds had told them, there was no way he was going to leave Sandra to deal with them on her own.

'It's absolutely imperative that we speak to him straight away,' the taller one — Eric — was saying when Trevor came within earshot.

Sandra was on her feet now and standing between the two men and the house with her hands on her hips, which was a sure sign she wasn't going to back down, whatever crap they threw at her.

'And as I just told you,' she said, 'Mr Ingleby is still asleep and doesn't want to be disturbed.'

The fat one with the walking stick — Frank — rolled his shoulders like he was getting ready to throw a punch. 'Listen, flower…'

Uh-oh, thought Trevor. "Flower" is definitely not going to win you any favours.

'…What you don't seem to understand is that what we 'ave to say to 'im is as much in his interest as it is ours.

179

So if you don't mind…'

He took a diagonal step forward to move past her, but Sandra shifted a pace to the side to block his path.

Before Frank could say or do anything else, Eric grabbed him by the arm. 'Come now, Frank. There's no need for any unpleasantness. I suggest we all calm down and—'

'What in the name of Christ's goin' on down there?'

All four of them looked up at the house to see Ingleby leaning out of his bedroom window, both hands planted firmly on the sill.

'Good morning, Marcus,' said Eric with a cheery wave. 'And how are we today?'

'Oh, it's you, is it?' said Ingleby. 'What do you want?'

'We need to discuss a matter of some urgency,' Eric shouted back.

'Like what?'

'Something which could be to our mutual advantage.'

There was a pause while Ingleby appeared to be considering his options.

'Shall we come up?' said Eric.

'No,' Ingleby snapped. 'You stay where you are and I'll come down. — Sandra, I need a hand with me bag and stuff.'

He disappeared from view, and after a quick exchange of glances with Trevor, Sandra set off towards the house.

'This your dog?' said Eric, who was making a big thing of stroking Milly even though she was far more interested in sniffing at Frank's feet.

'Go on, piss off, yer mangy mutt,' said Frank, aiming a none too gentle kick at Milly's chest and raising his walking stick above her head.

But before he had time to strike, Trevor shot out a hand and grabbed hold of the stick, wrenching it out of Frank's grasp and tossing it into the middle of the

180

swimming pool.

'You ever touch my dog again and you'll be going in with it,' he said, somewhat surprised at his own words and the force with which they were delivered.

Frank fixed him with bloodshot eyes. 'You get my stick back right now or I'll bloody clatter you.'

Trevor laughed. 'Oh yeah? Now that I'd like to see.'

If Frank's face had got any redder, his cheeks would have exploded with the sudden inrush of extra blood. He drew back his fist, and Trevor dodged his head to the side to avoid the blow, but Eric intervened with a firm grip on Frank's arm.

'Do try and behave yourself, Frank,' he said. 'There's a good chap.'

With almost glacial slowness, Frank lowered his fist, but the bright crimson of his complexion showed no sign of abating. Trevor unclenched his own fists, a little taken aback when he realised they'd been clenched in the first place. Nevertheless, he felt a fleeting glow of pride at having stood up to the guy. Fleeting, not only because of his awareness of the man's advancing years, but also because he'd just heard Milly's muffled attempt at a bark, and he'd turned to see her at the edge of the pool with Frank's walking stick clamped triumphantly between her teeth. And despite this encumbrance, she managed to scramble out of the water unaided, then trotted across the terrace and dropped the stick at Frank's feet.

A timely distraction from this rather embarrassing conclusion to Trevor's display of bravado came in the shape of Ingleby coming out of the house with Sandra close behind him.

'You've got five minutes,' Ingleby said.

'Should be plenty,' said Eric with a broad smile and offering his hand to Ingleby.

Ingleby ignored the gesture and eased himself down

onto one of the sun loungers, his face contorting with the effort.

'Glad to see you seem to be feeling better today,' said Eric. 'You didn't seem to know who we were yesterday.'

'Course I bloody did. I'm not senile yet, you know.'

'Told you,' said Frank with a grin of self-satisfied smugness.

'Perhaps we should have our little chat... in camera?' said Eric with a nod in Sandra and Trevor's direction.

'You wanna take photos?'

Eric's chuckle was thin and unconvincing. 'Always the joker, eh, Marcus? — No, I mean what we have to tell you might better be said in private?'

Ingleby waved a dismissive hand. 'Just get on with it, will yer?'

'Very well then. — It will no doubt have come to your attention by now that one of your number is missing.'

Trevor felt Sandra's grip on his forearm. 'Herbert?' she said.

'I believe that is his name, yes,' said Eric. 'And to come straight to the point, Marcus, he will be safely returned to the bosom of his family as soon as you have given us what is rightly ours.'

'You've kidnapped him?' said Sandra, releasing her grasp on Trevor's arm.

'Let's just say he's currently our guest.'

Ingleby pulled a packet of cigarettes and a lighter from the pocket of his shorts. 'And what's that got to do with me exactly?'

Eric's expression was one of genuine surprise. 'But, Marcus, surely even you couldn't bear such a callous disregard for the safety and wellbeing of a member of your own family?'

'Family?' said Ingleby, almost choking on a lungful of cigarette smoke. 'What the fuck are you talking about?'

'But I thought he was your... grandson or something,'

182

said Eric, firing an accusing look at Frank.

Ingleby nearly choked again, but this time on a burst of laughter. 'Dear oh dear. You really 'ave cocked up, 'aven't you, Eric. Grandson? He's the sodding hired help, that's what he is.'

Eric shot another glare at Frank, who shrugged and said, 'Hey, don't blame me. It were you reckoned he were family.'

Sandra stepped forward and jabbed a finger into Eric's chest. 'Listen, you. Herbert may not be Ingleby's grandson, but he *is* my nephew, and if you so much as—'

Eric raised his hands in mock surrender. 'I assure you that no harm will come to the boy as long as we get what we want.'

'But if we ain't back there in half an hour,' said Frank, 'there's a certain pal of ours who's got instructions to—'

'Yes, thank you, Frank,' said Eric. 'I think they get the picture. — So then, Marcus. Twenty-four hours. That's how long you have to reach your decision.'

Ingleby groaned. 'Like I told you before, the kid's got nothing to do with me.'

'We'll see,' said Eric. 'And incidentally, we happen to have a contact in the local constabulary, so we'll know about it if you so much as *think* about getting them involved.'

'Eric, you're starting to bore me now. Why don't you piss off and take hopalong with you, eh?'

'Until tomorrow then,' said Eric, tipping the brim of an imaginary hat.

'Mr Ingleby, I—' Sandra began even before Eric and Frank had disappeared from view round the side of the house, but Ingleby interrupted her.

'Don't worry. It's all bullshit. Eric Emerson's as soft as they come. Wouldn't 'urt a fly, that one.'

'You couldn't just... you know... give them whatever

it is they want?'

Ingleby looked up at her with a wry grin. 'If you want my advice, I'd follow 'em and find out where they're keepin' the lad. — Don't use the van though. Too conspicuous. Same goes for Jackie's motor. It's one o' them bloody great Chelsea tractors the colour of a neon canary. But there's an old Vespa in the garage if you can get it goin'. My idiot son-in-law used it the other day, so it should be all right.'

As it turned out, the scooter's engine burst into life at only the third time of asking, and Trevor felt a twinge of nostalgia at being back astride a Vespa once again.

31

Herbert sat on a pile of old hessian sacks with his back against the corrugated iron wall of the large shed, his legs stretched out in front of him, tied at the ankles with a length of old rope, and his hands in his lap, also tied. For the past hour, his eyes had been glued to the ceaseless activity of two columns of ants — one moving in the opposite direction to the other — as they went about their business of building a nest in the earth floor less than a couple of yards from where he was sitting. Some of the ants who were returning from their scavenging underneath the shed door were carrying pieces of dried grass and slivers of wood that were several times bigger than themselves and were clearly struggling under the weight. Others had strayed from the columns and were wandering here, there and everywhere, trying to find their way back.

The ants' industry and tirelessness were fascinating to watch, and Herbert was grateful for the distraction. If it wasn't for the ants, his mind would have been awash with dark thoughts of the fate which might be awaiting him. He hadn't a clue why Eric and Frank had kidnapped him and very little idea as to where they'd taken him. They'd forced him at gunpoint to get into the boot of their car the night before, and then they'd driven for fifteen minutes or so and parked up outside what sounded like a busy taverna. Ten minutes later and they were off again. From what he'd been able to make out, they'd picked up a third man, who spoke only Greek and shouted a lot. It had been difficult to hear exactly what was being said, but Eric — or maybe Frank — had mentioned money on at least three occasions, starting with twenty euros, then thirty and then fifty. Herbert had panicked that they might have abducted him to sell him into slavery, and he still couldn't be sure that wasn't the case.

The temperature and lack of air inside the boot of the car had become unbearable, and by the time they'd reached their destination, he'd been almost at the point of losing consciousness. Even in the moonlight, it had been impossible to see much when they'd opened the boot and let him out, and they'd immediately blindfolded him before marching him into the shed. Once inside, they'd removed the blindfold, and he'd pleaded with them to let him go, but Frank had just laughed. While Frank tied his hands and feet, he'd asked them why they'd kidnapped him, and Eric had said something about not needing to worry as long as he behaved himself. Another man in a checked woollen shirt and dark baggy trousers had stood watching from the doorway. He was a similar age to the other two — perhaps a little older — and had jabbered on in Greek, frequently flailing his arms around and pointing at Herbert. He was presumably the man they'd picked up from the taverna, and judging by his manner and the way he'd snatched the cash that Eric had held out to him, was very probably the owner of the shed.

As soon as Frank had finished tying him up, they'd all left the shed, slamming the steel double doors behind them but without turning off the single bare light bulb that hung down from the centre of the roof. Either they'd been concerned he might be afraid of the dark, or infinitely more likely, they'd forgotten to switch it off. The unmistakable sharp click of a padlock was followed a few minutes later by the sound of a car being driven off. After that, there was silence apart from the occasional barking of two or three dogs, and every so often he'd thought he could hear the bleating of sheep. Some time around dawn, a cockerel had crowed, and if any more evidence were needed that he was being held on a farm, the shed itself was full of tools and equipment that would have been out of place anywhere else.

Not that knowing he was being held on a farm was going to do him any good. For a start, they'd searched him thoroughly and taken away his mobile, and even if he'd still had his phone, what would he have told Sandra? "I've been kidnapped by Eric and Frank, and I'm locked in a shed on some farm or other." — "Where's the farm?" — "I have absolutely no idea".

One of the ants Herbert had been keeping a particular eye on — and one of those which seemed to have a poorly developed sense of direction — had strayed even further from the columns than the rest of its wayward pals and was getting worryingly close to his leg. He shifted his position slightly by bracing his back against the corrugated iron wall, and at the same moment, he heard the rattling of the padlock and the sound of voices outside. The double doors flew open, and framed against the bright sunlight was the old Greek guy from the night before. He was wearing a much grubbier version of the checked shirt and dark baggy trousers but this time with the addition of a shabby flat cap. The only other difference was that he was now holding a double-barrelled shotgun, and it was pointing directly at Herbert's head.

Keeping the gun trained on Herbert, he came into the shed and then stepped to the side to reveal a woman of about half his age, who was carrying a chipped white plate and a plastic bottle of water. Her shoulder-length hair was yellowish blonde in colour apart from an inch or so of black on either side of the centre parting. The dark eyebrows were arched high on her forehead, giving the impression that she was perpetually alarmed, but it was an impression contradicted by the warmth of the smile beneath. Shuffling rather than walking across the earth floor, she bent down and laid the plate of bread and cheese on the ground close to Herbert's bound hands. As she did so, it was impossible not to notice the generous curve of her breasts above the low neckline of her cotton dress, and Herbert detected the scent of stale perfume and garlic.

She said something to him in Greek and unscrewed the lid of the water bottle, taking her time as if performing an unusual form of striptease. Placing the bottle on his lap so he could grasp it between both hands, she ran the tip of her finger slowly around the rim of the neck a couple of times before putting the finger in her mouth and easing it back and forth with a faint sucking sound. Despite his relative inexperience in such matters, Herbert was left in little doubt as to the significance of the gesture, and to mask his embarrassment, he snatched up the bottle and drank deeply. Perhaps taking this as a sign of encouragement, the woman's already broad smile spread wider still, and she reached out and began to stroke the side of the bottle in a lingering up and down motion.

The old man barked something at her, and the woman's smile faded instantly but not completely. She withdrew her hand from the bottle and clenched it into a fist, pushing the knuckles into the earth floor to force herself upright. She brushed imaginary dust from the front of her dress, paying particular attention to the upper area, and kept her eyes fixed on Herbert's while the tip of her tongue caressed her lower lip.

'Despina!'

At the sound of the old man's voice, she gave Herbert a vastly exaggerated wink and left the shed with an equally extravagant gyration of her hips, pausing briefly in the doorway to turn and flutter her fingers at him in a coy wave of farewell. The old man followed her, backing out of the shed with his gun still aimed at Herbert, and closed the double doors with his foot. Herbert waited to hear the click of the padlock, but instead he heard a car arriving and then the old man shouting something in Greek. A few seconds later and one of the steel doors opened. In walked Eric and Frank, the former with a grin that was almost affable and the latter with an expression that was somewhere between a leer and a scowl.

'I see Thanassis has been looking after you,' said Eric, nodding at the so far untouched plate of food beside Herbert.

'You letting me go?' said Herbert, more in hope than expectation.

Eric shook his head. 'I'm afraid not. Our friend Mr Ingleby has decided not to play ball just yet.'

'He's got twenty-four hours,' said Frank. 'Otherwise it's…'

He mimed cutting off his little finger with a pair of scissors or some similar implement, and Herbert had to fight back an overwhelming urge to be physically sick.

'Yes, Frank,' said Eric. 'I don't think there's any call for that kind of talk just yet.'

The addition of the "just yet" at the end of the sentence did nothing to alleviate Herbert's fear.

'So then,' Eric went on with a jovial clap of his hands. 'We'll leave you to eat your breakfast in peace. We won't be far away though. Thanassis — or rather, his delightful daughter — has invited us into the house to sample their hospitality. — At least, I think that's what they were saying.'

He glanced at Frank, who merely shrugged in response.

Once they had gone, Herbert's nausea began to subside, and he realised he was ravenously hungry. He was about to manoeuvre himself into a position where he could pick up the plate of food when he noticed that a dozen or so ants were already crawling over the bread with a similar number swarming over the feta cheese. A breakaway offshoot from the main columns had also formed, and hundreds of ants were now scurrying to join the feast.

32

The basement of Donna's villa was almost identical to Ingleby's and was similarly stocked except there were no armchairs or snooker table in the middle of the room. Instead, there was an industrial-sized workbench covered with a sheet of thick transparent plastic, which was heavily stained with blood. The same kind of plastic sheeting had been spread out over a substantial area of the floor around the workbench, and this too was heavily streaked with blood. Eddie, almost unrecognisable beneath the goggles and the once-white hooded overalls, was vigorously rubbing at the blade of a bench-mounted circular saw with a scarlet-sodden rag, which he occasionally wrung out into a bucket by his feet.

'How's it going, Eddie?' said Donna, who had stopped to take in the scene when she was halfway down the basement steps.

'Almost done, Mrs V. Just havin' a bit of a cleanup.'

Donna slowly descended the rest of the steps and walked over to a large maroon suitcase which was laid flat on the floor just off the edge of the plastic sheeting. She prodded it tentatively with her toe.

'All in, is it?' she said.

'Yeah,' said Eddie. 'I had to do quite a lot of cuttin' though.'

'Better get rid of it soon as you're finished. Don't want the police round here poking their noses in.'

'You think that's likely?'

Donna pursed her lips and thought about it for a

moment. 'Like I said before, I think Ingleby's nannies might have rumbled me when I was round there yesterday. I shouldn't have gone at all really, but I had to find out what was going on. — Curiosity killed the cat, eh?'

Eddie gave the saw blade a final wipe and dropped the rag into the bucket. 'I'll give it another go with bleach later on. Just to be on the safe side.'

'Oh yes, that reminds me,' said Donna. 'D'you think you could give the pool a bit of a skim when we get back? I couldn't even face getting in this morning with all the dead insects and stuff floating around.'

'Will do, Mrs V.'

Eddie took off his goggles and wiped his brow with the sleeve of his overalls, leaving a smear of blood on his forehead.

* * *

Without a four-by-four, they would have struggled to make it up the dirt track into the hills. More than once, Donna's head had smacked against the side window as the Cherokee bounced over yet another patch of rocks or lurched into a pothole the size of a small crater, but the ordeal was nearing its end. Rounding a sharp uphill bend, they spotted what looked like a small waterfall tumbling down an almost sheer drop. As they got closer, the waterfall revealed itself to be composed, not of water, but a cascade of discarded cookers, fridges, metal bedsteads, builders' rubble, broken furniture and a whole range of assorted carrier bags and bin liners that had burst open to spew their contents down the hillside.

'The perfect spot,' said Donna as Eddie braked sharply to negotiate a particularly deep hole in the road.

He parked the car at the top of the avalanche of debris and rusting white goods, next to a metal sign which had been peppered with shotgun pellets. So numerous and widespread were the holes that it was almost impossible to read what was printed on it, although Donna guessed it was something to do with the penalty for fly-tipping.

Great sense of irony, these Greeks, she thought as she got out of the car and went to the back to help Eddie with the suitcase. It was heavy even without the extra ten pounds or so the head would have added, and in the intense heat of the morning, Donna was already sweating when they set the case down at the edge of the slope.

'On three?' said Eddie.

Donna composed herself for a moment, and then they bent down and each took hold of an end of the suitcase. Swinging it back and forth three times, they let go and launched it down the hillside. The difference in their strengths meant that the case didn't fly flat but twisted in the air before bouncing on one corner and then another, finally coming to rest right-side-up against a broken toilet bowl about fifteen feet below them. There was the briefest of pauses, and then the lid sprang open, the slight upward tilt of the case making its contents clearly visible to Donna and Eddie as they stood staring down at it from the edge of the track.

'You didn't lock it then?' Donna said eventually, trying not to sound too accusatory.

'No key,' said Eddie.

Several seconds passed before Donna spoke again. 'We can't leave it like that. It'll be spotted soon as somebody comes by.'

Eddie shrugged. 'There's wild boar round here. Stray dogs. All sorts. Them lot'll deal with it in no time.'

It was evident from the tone of his voice that he wasn't convincing anyone, least of all himself, that this was a satisfactory solution to their problem, and when Donna failed to respond, he began his descent to the suitcase. First with his back to the slope and then turning to face into it, he clambered slowly over and around the variety of discarded junk, taking care to watch out for broken shards of glass and sharp pieces of twisted metal as he went. Once, when he was nearly halfway down to the suitcase, a heavy iron fire grate slithered away from under his foot, and it was only by grabbing hold of the end of a rusted metal fencepost that he stopped himself from hurtling all the way to the rocky bottom of the ravine fifty feet below.

A minute or so later, he was within reach of the suitcase, and he pushed himself up into a crouching position and took hold of the lid. But as he did so, his foot lost its purchase on a pile of loose rubble, and for a second time he flung out an arm to clutch at the nearest piece of debris that might prevent him from falling further. On this occasion, it was the rim of the broken toilet bowl, but it shifted under his weight, and he overbalanced sideways, rolling down the steep slope until his body slammed into the back of an ancient-looking washing machine. Only then did he release his grip on the suitcase, which had flipped over as he'd fallen and scattered its contents in every direction. A leg here. An arm there. A large chunk of torso tumbling end over end and gathering pace as it pinballed off outcrops of rock on its way to the bottom of the ravine.

He sat up and leaned against the washing machine, each gasp for breath sending a sharp burst of pain across his chest.

'You okay?' Donna called out from the top of the slope.

'Think so,' Eddie shouted back. 'Might have bruised a rib or two though.'

'Can you make it back up all right?'

'What about all this lot?' Eddie waved his arm in the general direction of the various body parts strewn around him.

'It'd take too long, and you're in no fit state by the look of you. Let the wildlife take care of it like you said.'

* * *

Donna had driven on the way back to the villa while Eddie sat in the passenger seat, clutching his chest and wincing with pain every time the car hit yet another pothole or a particularly rocky stretch of the track. On his lap was a plastic freezer bag, and every so often he'd taken something from it and thrown it out of the window.

'Litter lout,' Donna had said after the third time.

'Fingertips,' Eddie had explained. 'And...' He'd tapped one of his front teeth with his fingernail.

Donna had thought it strange how someone who didn't appear to have any great qualms about cutting a body into pieces seemed so squeamish when it came to talking about removing their teeth.

'Very efficient,' she'd said.

'I learned from one of the best.'

'*The* best, I think you mean.'

Eddie had smiled and nodded his agreement, then sent another fingertip arcing through the air.

Glad to be home at last — and relieved to have got Manolis's body out of the house — Donna turned into the driveway but had to brake suddenly to avoid a head-on collision with a blue and white Citroën with a bank of blue lights on its roof.

'Shit,' she said, and the image flashed into her mind of Manolis's head in Ingleby's freezer.

The driver of the police car stayed where he was while the other got out and walked towards them. As he came closer, Donna spotted the three stripes on his shirt and was fairly sure he was one of the two cops she'd seen through the binoculars at Ingleby's the day before. She opened the window and he leaned in, all smiles.

'*Kalıméra.*'

'*Kalıméra,*' said Donna, smiling back at him. 'Is there a problem, Sergeant?'

He tilted his head back and clicked his tongue. Greek for "no". 'It is the routine only, *kyría*. A young man is missing, and I think is someone you know.'

'Oh?'

'Manolis Stathopoulos. I have a picture.'

He handed her a photograph, and she concentrated on keeping her hand from shaking as she pretended to study the grinning features of her ex-employee.

'Yes of course,' she said. 'Manolis. He cleans my pool. Other jobs too sometimes.'

'And when did you see him the last time?'

Donna turned to look at Eddie. 'Couple of days ago, wasn't it?'

'Monday, yeah.'

'What time did he leave?'

'I can't remember exactly. Late afternoon, I think. Four? Five maybe?'

'And you don't see him after that?' said the sergeant.

She shook her head. 'I thought it was a bit odd when he didn't turn up yesterday. He's supposed to do the pool every day this time of year. But you know what these young people are like.'

'Yes, I notice the *pisína* is a little... not clean. — Manolis, he seemed okay to you when he left on Monday?'

Donna pursed her lips to give the impression she was giving the question some serious consideration. 'Seemed fine to me. Quite upbeat as far as I recall.'

'Upbeat?'

'Sorry, yes. Happy. Cheerful sort of thing.'

'I see.'

'You don't think something bad's happened to him,

do you?' said Donna, blurting out the words as if the idea had only just occurred to her but careful not to overdo the look of concern.

'Who knows?' said the cop. 'Perhaps it is as you say that he is young and wild and gone to some place with his friends for a few days. We still have other people to talk to, but it seems you were maybe the last one who has seen him.'

Oh great, thought Donna. And I bet you've seen all those cop shows on TV where the last person to have seen the victim alive is always the one what done 'em in.

'I'm only sorry I can't be of more help, Sergeant,' she said.

'It is possible we will want to talk to you again, *kyría* Vincent, but if you think of something that might help, please to call me at the police station.'

'Of course.'

'And ask to speak to me in person. Sergeant Stathopoulos. Pericles Stathopoulos.'

Donna's mind did a doubletake. A lot of Greek names sounded much the same to her, but wasn't that the name—?

'Yes, *kyría*. Manolis is my cousin,' said the sergeant.

'Oh fuck,' said Eddie as Donna backed out of the driveway to let the police car through.

'I couldn't have put it better myself,' she said.

33

Trevor wasn't entirely without experience when it came to tailing someone who didn't want to be tailed. He'd lost count of the number of times he'd had to follow a wayward spouse since he'd started working with Sandra at her detective agency, and under her tuition, he'd got much better at not being spotted. This was different though. Most husbands and wives who stray from the marital bed aren't actually expecting to be followed, but Eric and Frank almost certainly were. Fortunately, the Vespa was a lot less conspicuous than a car — and definitely less so than a camper van — so it hadn't been too difficult to keep up with them even despite the lack of other vehicles to hide behind once they were out in the open countryside. The last couple of kilometres had been on dirt track and the easiest of all for Trevor to keep his distance, the clouds of dust kicked up by their car providing a clear and lingering indication of the direction they were heading in.

By the time the dust cloud came to a halt and gradually began to dissipate, he was three or four hundred metres behind, and he dismounted immediately to avoid his own cloud of dust giving him away. Parking the scooter just off the edge of the track, he covered the rest of the distance on foot until he had a clear view of where Eric and Frank's Toyota had ended up. It was at the top of a steep sidetrack which led off at a right-angle from the main one, but from his low vantage point it was impossible to see anything else. Between him and the top of the rise, the land was filled with evenly spaced rows of olive trees which had been planted so long ago their trunks were thick enough to conceal someone twice Trevor's size with room to spare. On the negative side, the dense tinder-dry undergrowth probably harboured any number of venomous snakes, ready to strike as soon as he came within range. But this was no time for snake phobias. He was on a rescue mission. Not exactly a damsel in distress of course, but Herbert was Sandra's nephew, so there was a kind of vicarious similarity.

Taking a diagonal route up the slope, he paused briefly at every second tree and peered round its trunk to check for any sign of life before continuing on. When he reached Eric and Frank's car at the top, the land levelled out into a small yard where a dozen or so hens and a couple of roosters were strutting around and pecking at the sun-baked earth. On the far side of the yard stood a large corrugated iron shed with a flat roof and double doors. One of these was open, and standing just outside with his back to Trevor was a man in a flat cap and baggy trousers, who was holding something that looked a lot like a double-barrelled shotgun.

Trevor ducked back behind the last of the olive trees at the edge of the yard and pinned his back against its trunk, feeling the rough bark through his sweat-sodden T-shirt and wondering why it had never occurred to him that guns might be involved. There was something disturbingly familiar about the group of Japanese taiko drummers who seemed to have started warming up inside his chest, and he took several deep breaths to try and quieten them down.

At the sound of voices, he turned back to face the tree trunk and craned his neck so he could see the doorway of the shed without making himself any more visible than he had to. Eric and Frank were deep in conversation, while the man with the shotgun was fumbling with the door. When he'd done, the other two followed him towards a single storey building about forty metres to Trevor's right — presumably the farmhouse. He waited until they'd disappeared inside and then skirted the bottom edge of the yard, keeping just below the top of the slope so he couldn't be spotted from the house. Creeping up to the side of the shed, he tapped on the corrugated iron and, as loudly as he dared, called out Herbert's name.

'Who's that?' The voice was muffled but unmistakably Herbert's.

'It's me. Trevor. You okay?'

'Yeah, having a great time. You gonna get me out of here or what?'

'That's the general idea.'

'You got any explosives?'

'Shit, no, I left them back at the house. — Of course I haven't got any explosives.'

'Well, I don't know how you're going to get me out then. The door's padlocked and my hands and feet are tied.'

Trevor went to the corner of the shed to get a look at the door. Herbert was right about the padlock, and it was a heavy duty one at that. Even if he had a hacksaw, it would take forever to cut through it, and they'd probably hear him up at the house long before he'd finished. It would help if Herbert could at least get himself free.

'What did they tie you up with?' he said.

'Couple of bits of rope.'

'Can you move around at all?'

'I can shuffle about a bit.'

'Okay, is there anything in there you can cut the rope with? Anything you can reach?'

There was a pause before Herbert answered. 'There's loads of tools and stuff... Oh yeah, and an old scythe thing.'

'Can you get to it?'

'Think so. Might take me a while though.'

'Quick as you can then. They might be back any minute.'

Trevor pressed the side of his head against the wall of the shed to try and gauge what progress Herbert was making but withdrew it instantly when his ear came into contact with the sun-scorched metal. Returning to the corner, he kept a lookout for anyone who might be approaching from the farmhouse, and at the same moment, he heard what sounded like a pile of paint cans being knocked over inside the shed.

'Keep it down, will you?' he hissed. 'Somebody might hear.'

'For God's sake, Trevor. It's not easy doing this, you know.'

'You got to the scythe yet?'

'Almost.'

While he waited, Trevor examined the corrugated iron panels the shed was constructed from and realised that each one was held in place with large screws or possibly bolts.

'Are there any nuts on the inside?' he said.

'Not as far as I know, but there's some bread and cheese.'

'No, not those kind of nuts. Nuts-and-bolts nuts the wall panels are fixed with.'

'Yeah... Kind of... wooden frame,' said Herbert through a series of grunts, which Trevor presumed were the result of his efforts to cut himself free.

'Okay, see if you can find a spanner when you get loose.'

Five minutes later, Trevor listened to the "clonk clonk" of spanner against metal and wished Herbert would try a bit harder to keep the noise down. Two minutes after that, he felt a hand on his shoulder, and the taiko drummers abruptly stopped their pounding. He couldn't actually *feel* the muzzle of a shotgun, but he had little doubt it was pointing directly at the middle of his back, so he did the only sensible thing he could think of in the circumstances and slowly raised his hands in surrender.

'Look, it's not what you think,' he gabbled. 'I was just out for a ride on my Vespa, you know, thought I'd have a look round — not here obviously, no, not the shed as such, the countryside I mean, but then it was getting hot and I needed to—'

'God almighty, will you stop your babbling and put your bloody hands down?'

Trevor recognised the voice, and he turned his head inch by inch to check he was right.

'Bloody hell,' said Trevor, lowering his hands and waiting for his heartbeat to return. 'Do you have to creep up like that?'

'So what's happening?' said Reynolds.

'They've got Herbert. — Eric and Frank.'

'Yes, I know.'

'You do?'

'Your girlfriend called me.'

Trevor stifled a blush. 'She did?'

'Uh-huh.'

'But how did you know where to come?'

'I put a lump on their car.'

'A what?'

'Tracking device. — So what's all the racket in there?'

Trevor became aware once again of the metallic clonking sound from inside the shed. 'It's Herbert. He's taking one of the wall panels off.'

Reynolds nodded his approval. 'Good thinking. — So where are the bad guys?'

'Up at the house.'

Reynolds put his head close to the side of the shed. 'How's it going, son?'

The clonking sound stopped. 'Who's that?'

'The man you knocked out with a bag of frozen peas. Remember?'

There was a moment's silence before Herbert said, 'Oh yeah. Sorry.'

'Keep at it then. I don't know how long we've got.'

The clonking sound resumed.

'How many nuts you got off so far?' said Reynolds.

'This one's the third. They're all rusted up though.'

Trevor counted the number of bolt heads on the outside of the panel. Twelve. He looked at Reynolds, who merely shrugged and then sidled to the corner of the shed and poked his head round, pulling it back again as soon as he'd done so.

'Shit,' he said. 'Somebody's coming. And he's got a shotgun.'

He tapped on the side of the shed and told Herbert to stop what he was doing. Then he flattened his back against the wall, and Trevor was about to follow suit when he heard the snap of a twig from behind him.

'Glad you could join us,' said Eric.

'More the merrier,' said Frank, flicking the safety catch of his semi-automatic.

34

Sandra was as sure as she could be that this was the place Reynolds had described when he'd called her, but she drove past the entrance and parked the camper van near the top of a small hill overlooking the farm. She'd asked him to phone her again when he had any more news, but that had been more than two hours ago, and she'd heard nothing since. Not the type to sit at home and fret, she'd made sure that Ingleby was fed and medicated and set off to find out what was happening for herself.

Apart from a few chickens wandering around in the yard, the whole area was deserted. Even Eric and Frank's silver Toyota that Reynolds had told her about was no longer there. So where were Reynolds and Trevor?

She'd have to get a closer look. The corrugated iron shed seemed to be the most likely place that Herbert was being kept, so she crept down the slope towards it, pausing every few steps behind the trunk of a massive olive tree to check the coast was still clear. When she got to the last of the trees, about ten or twelve feet from the shed, she held her breath and listened. There were raised voices coming from inside. One of them was definitely Trevor's, but she couldn't be sure about the others. Maybe one of them was Eric or Frank. Even though their car wasn't there, it didn't mean one of them hadn't driven off and left the other behind.

There wasn't much she could do until she found out

for certain, so she hurried across the open space between the olive tree and the shed and put her ear close to the wall. But all had gone quiet. Edging along to the corner, she peered round it and saw that the double doors were held fast with a heavy steel padlock.

Unlikely that Eric or Frank are inside then, she thought, and rapped her knuckles against the corrugated iron. 'Trevor? You in there?'

'Sandra?' There was evident surprise in Trevor's tone.

'The very same. — Herbert and Reynolds in there too?'

'Yeah, but they tied us all up.'

'Any idea if Eric and Frank are still here?'

'Sounded like they went off in their car, but there's an old Greek guy with a shotgun probably still around.'

'And his daughter.' This was Herbert's voice, and it had a strangely apprehensive edge to it.

'Okay, I'll try and work something out,' said Sandra, the outline of a plan already beginning to take shape in her mind.

Back at the top of the hill, she climbed into the van and manoeuvred it until it was pointing down the slope. Once it had started to roll, she switched off the engine and coasted down between two rows of olive trees. There was only just enough room for the width of the van, and the branches of the trees scraped along its roof, leaving indelible scratches in the fibreglass. — Trevor would *not* be pleased, but this was hardly the time to be picky about a bit of cosmetic damage to his precious van. — By the time the ground levelled out, the van had gathered enough momentum to veer past the shed and come to a halt close to the centre of the yard, scattering chickens in every direction. Sandra jumped out and, keeping a careful eye on the farmhouse forty metres away, flung open the tailgate and took out a towrope with a large metal hook at each end. Crouching low, she scurried over to the shed and fixed one of the hooks through the shank of the padlock.

'Sandra, is that you?'

'Yes. Are any of you near the door?'

'No. What are you up to?'

'I'm going to pull the bleedin' doors off,' said Sandra. 'If it works, you'll need to be ready sharpish 'cos it's going to make quite a din. See if there's a knife or something I can cut you loose with.'

Still watching for any sign of activity from the farmhouse, she raced back to the van and climbed in behind the steering wheel. She turned the key in the ignition and, with as low revs as possible, backed up to the nearer end of the towrope and hitched it to the bracket beneath the van's rear bumper. Inching forward in first gear to take up the slack in the rope, she began to accelerate. Too much. The back wheels spun in the dirt with a high-pitched whining noise that was bound to be heard from the house. She eased off the throttle and tried again, one eye on the shed door in the rear-view mirror and the other on the farmhouse. This time, there was the harsh grating sound of twisting metal, and the van shot forward. Slamming it into reverse, she skidded to a halt a few feet in front of the shed and, pausing only to grab something from the glove compartment, jumped down from the cab.

A quick glance towards the house told her that a man with a flat cap and a shotgun was already on his way, and a glance towards the shed told her that one of the double doors was now hanging from one hinge and the towrope had wrenched off the padlock, hasp and all. The bottom corner of the busted door had wedged itself in the earth, so she threw open the other one and stepped inside. Trevor, Herbert and Reynolds were all sitting along the far side of the shed with their hands tied behind upright wooden supports that held the wall panels in place.

'Over there, on the floor by the workbench,' said Trevor, nodding to Sandra's left. 'Some sort of saw.'

It had a curved blade of about nine inches long and was a little on the rusty side, but it would probably do the job, so she snatched it up and reached behind Trevor's back to get at the rope. She worked as quickly as she dared but carefully enough to avoid taking a chunk out of his wrist. There was a shout from outside. Something in Greek. Presumably the guy with the shotgun. No more than twenty feet away now. She pushed down harder with the saw blade and quickened the strokes. Six more and the rope came apart. Dropping the saw onto Trevor's lap, she scampered back to the other side of the shed and pressed her back against the wall, obscured from the outside by the open door.

Less than a second later, the barrel of a shotgun nosed its way through the doorway, advancing inch by inch, and then abruptly stopped. More shouting in Greek, and the muzzle suddenly dipped, pointing directly at Trevor, who was crouching down and sawing at Herbert's rope. Another shout, and Trevor raised his hands in surrender, kneeling on the earth and staring up at the shotgun.

Sandra realised that the man on the other end of it wasn't about to come in far enough for her to exercise Plan A, and she shot a glance to her side in search of a Plan B. She spotted it straight away in the shape of a long-handled spade leaning up against the wall beside her and, grasping it in both hands, snapped it upwards under the barrel of the gun. A booming explosion reverberated around the metal walls of the shed and blew a hole in the roof the size of a tennis ball. Sandra dropped the spade and whipped the small canister of pepper spray from her pocket. The burst of gas hit the old man full in the face, and he dropped the gun, his hands clutching at the searing pain in his eyes. Trevor launched himself forward and grabbed the shotgun, aiming it at the man's chest as he collapsed to his knees.

Sandra raised an eyebrow. 'You know how to use that thing?'

'Not a clue,' said Trevor. 'But he doesn't know that, does he?'

While he kept the old man covered, Sandra finished cutting through Herbert's rope and then handed him the saw so he could do the same for Reynolds.

'Handy stuff that pepper spray,' said Trevor.

Sandra grinned. 'Wouldn't be without it, Trev. You know me.'

35

Milly hurtled out through the patio door, across the terrace, round the side of the house and slithered to a halt on the gravel driveway before Trevor had even switched off the Vespa's engine. She jumped up with both her front paws on his thigh, and he had to react quickly to stop the scooter from overbalancing.

'Hey, Milly, did you miss me then?' he said, cradling her head in his hands and rocking it gently from side to side.

The camper van pulled up behind him, and Sandra and Herbert climbed down from the cab.

'Food. Shower. Sleep,' said Herbert as he swept past on his way to the house.

'He okay?' said Trevor.

'Bit traumatised, I think,' said Sandra. 'Needs a sleep more than anything.'

'Not surprising really.'

'Actually, he seemed more freaked out by some woman at the farm than the kidnapping business.'

'Oh?'

'Farmer's daughter, I think, but that's all he'd tell me.'

How odd, thought Trevor, and decided he'd quiz Herbert about the mystery woman as soon as he got the chance.

'What about Reynolds?' he said.

'Gone back to his place,' said Sandra.

'So how come he was helping us?'

'Not out of the goodness of his heart, that's for sure.

Probably keeping us sweet so we keep him informed of what Ingleby's up to. Plus, he's got that tracker thing on Eric and Frank's car and seems to want to follow them wherever they go.'

'Funny they didn't seem to recognise him.'

'It's been a long time, I suppose. And they wouldn't have been expecting to see him out here either. — Anyway, we'd better check on Ingleby. Make sure he's still in the land of the living.'

Marcus Ingleby was never one for smalltalk, and this was no exception.

'Start packing,' he said, the moment Trevor and Sandra stepped into the living room.

'Packing?' said Trevor.

'We're going on a little trip.'

'We?'

Ingleby cocked an eyebrow at him and then looked at Sandra. 'Parrot belong to you, does he?'

'Sorry,' said Trevor, 'but we've all just been through quite a traumatic experience and—'

'And that, me old sunshine, is precisely why we need to hit the road. — As soon as bloody possible.'

'I don't understand. Where are we going exactly?'

'Packing first. Explanations later.'

* * *

Eddie dipped the long-handled net into the pool and scooped up another batch of dead and dying insects. He flipped them over the wall and then wiped the sweat from his face with the tail of his unbuttoned Hawaiian shirt.

Donna laughed. 'Sorry, Eddie. I'll get a replacement for Manolis soon, I promise.'

'Maybe I'll do the rest later when it's cooled down a bit.'

'Aw,' said Donna with an exaggerated pout. 'I was kind of hoping I'd get a swim in after lunch.'

'Not good for the digestion, that. Swimming on a full stomach.'

'I wasn't exactly planning on a pig-out, Eddie. Bit of salad or something, that's all.'

'Fair enough,' said Eddie and plunged the net back into the water, paying particular attention to a floundering bee that was in imminent danger of drowning.

Donna raised the binoculars from where they hung on a strap round her neck and resumed her surveillance of the front of Ingleby's villa. Half an hour earlier, the young lad — Herbert — had opened the sliding door on the side of the camper van and tossed some kind of holdall inside. Then he'd disappeared back round the side of the house, reappearing soon afterwards with a heavy-looking cardboard box, which he'd also put in the van. Since then, there'd been no activity whatsoever.

Five more minutes and then lunch, she decided, but no sooner had the thought entered her mind than Trevor and Sandra came out to the van, one carrying another holdall and the other a small rucksack.

'Looks like they might be leaving,' said Donna, leaning forward slightly as if this would give her a better view.

'Who?'

'The three of them who are supposed to be looking after Ingleby.'

Eddie laid his net down beside the pool and went to join her at the edge of the terrace. 'Maybe he sacked 'em.'

'Could be,' said Donna, who considered this to be a distinct possibility, knowing as she did what a cantankerous old bugger Ingleby was.

Talk of the devil, the old man himself came into view,

clutching a small suitcase and followed by Herbert with a pickaxe in one hand and a shovel in the other. Trevor opened the tailgate of the van, and in went the suitcase, the pick and the shovel.

What the hell do they want those for? thought Donna, beginning to suspect there was more to this than Ingleby downsizing his care staff.

Trevor set off back towards the house, and Ingleby shouted something after him. A minute or so later, the dog came bounding out, barking her head off, and leapt inside the van. Trevor was hot on her heels and was carrying what appeared to be a large coolbag cradled in his arms, which he put into the back of the van with the pick and shovel and closed the tailgate. Then, after a brief conversation between him and Ingleby, all four of them climbed inside the van, and it set off up the driveway.

Donna lowered her binoculars. 'Eddie. Get the car.'

36

Trevor glanced in the rear-view mirror. Herbert was sound asleep on the back seat with his arms folded and his head lolled forward onto his chest. Ingleby was gazing out of the side window, and Milly was sitting between the two of them, her ears pricked and staring straight ahead. They'd been on the road for nearly two hours now, and Ingleby still hadn't told them where they were going.

'All in good time,' he'd said. 'Just keep driving and I'll let you know when you need to turn.'

He'd totally ignored Sandra's question about the need for a pickaxe and shovel, but he'd at least been rather more forthcoming about the urgency for the trip, which he'd claimed was as much for their benefit as his. 'Eric and Frank are after something they think belongs to them. Something they think I have. And if they're prepared to kidnap young 'Erbert 'ere, I don't know what else they might get up to now you've made a bollocks of that little scheme.'

'I thought you said Eric was harmless,' Sandra had said.

'Used to be. Maybe he's changed. No telling what a few years in chokey might've done to 'im. And in any case, it's Frankie Phelan's the one you wanna worry about. That little bastard's capable of damn near anything if you get in his way or stop 'im from gettin' what he wants.'

Sandra had asked him if that was where they were

going — to get whatever it was that Eric and Frank were after — but he'd simply turned away and gone back to staring out of the window.

That was nearly half an hour ago, and since then, nobody had spoken until Ingleby broke the silence and said, 'I reckon someone in this van is in serious need of a dump.'

His voice sounded strangely nasal, and Trevor checked the rear-view mirror again to see that Ingleby had one hand clasped over his nose and was pointing at Milly with the thumb of the other.

'Course, I might be doin' 'er a disservice,' Ingleby added. 'Might be mon-*sewer* 'Erbert who dropped one.'

It was the first time that Trevor had heard Ingleby laugh with anything other than sarcasm.

'I'll pull over soon as it's safe,' he said. 'I could do with a bit of a break myself.'

'Five minutes,' said Ingleby, suddenly serious again. 'We're not on a Sunday School bloody outing.'

A couple of kilometres further on, Trevor steered the van onto a dirt track which forked off to the right from the main road and parked up on the edge of a field that was unusually free of olive trees. Milly covered the distance between the back seat and his lap in two bounds, and he opened the driver's door to let her out.

'Don't go far,' he called after her. 'And watch out for snakes.'

Herbert woke with a start. 'Wha—? No. Get those things out of my face.' He shook his head vigorously to clear it of whatever — or whoever — he'd been dreaming about and slowly took in the reality of his surroundings. 'Where are we?'

'Greece,' said Sandra.

'Ah,' said Herbert, the sound developing into an extended yawn. 'I need a pee.'

So saying, he slid open the side door of the van and

214

wandered off in search of the nearest bush. Trevor decided to stretch his legs in the little time Ingleby had allocated, so he climbed down from his seat and strolled up the dirt track in the opposite direction to the main road. After a dozen or so paces, he turned and walked back again. Sandra came to meet him and fell into step as they went back and forth along the short distance of track.

'Magical mystery tour, eh?' she said.

'And we still haven't had a chance to talk to Donna,' said Trevor.

'But at least the police won't find anything now if they go back and search Ingleby's place while we're away.'

'I know, but I'll feel a lot happier when we've got rid of the— Hang on. What's he—?'

They were within a few yards of the van on the inbound leg of their stroll when Trevor glanced in through the open side door and spotted Ingleby reaching over the back seat and lifting the coolbag onto his lap.

Trevor quickened his pace. 'Wait!' he shouted. 'Don't open that.'

'Anything to drink in 'ere?' said Ingleby, the toggle of the zip between his finger and thumb.

'No. There's some in the—'

But it was too late. The lid of the coolbag was already open, and Ingleby was staring down at its contents.

'What the fuck...?'

'It's not ours,' Trevor blurted. 'We found it. In the freezer in your basement. The head, that is. Not the shorts and the meat cleaver. They were in the van.'

'You found a *head* in *my* basement?'

'That one, yes. In the freezer.'

'So whose is it?'

'We don't know. Quite young by the look of him though.'

215

'I don't mean whose *head* is it,' Ingleby sneered. 'I mean who the fuck put it there?'

'We're not sure but—'

'Did Donna bring you up a watermelon yesterday?' Sandra interrupted.

'Donna? 'Aven't seen her for a couple o' days or more. Not to speak to anyway.'

'So she didn't come up to your room at all?'

Ingleby narrowed his eyes at her. 'What did I just say?'

'She had something in a bag when she arrived,' said Trevor. 'Something heavy. Said it was a watermelon. For you.'

'I fuckin' hate watermelon. All them pips and tastes like a wet bloody sponge.'

'Well, in that case—' Sandra began, but she broke off when Milly came hurtling into the van, leapt up on the seat beside Ingleby and started frantically sniffing at the inside of the coolbag.

'Milly!' Trevor chased in after her and grabbed her by the collar, having to use not inconsiderable effort to extract her nose from out of the bag.

'I think you can close it now, Mr Ingleby,' said Sandra.

Ingleby zipped the bag shut. 'So you reckon it was Donna put it there?'

'It's probably what the police were looking for. We reckon she must have planted it and then tipped them off. That's why she put the shorts and the meat cleaver in the van — to try and frame us.'

'Frame you?' Ingleby couldn't have looked more surprised if Sandra had told him she was expecting his lovechild. 'What the 'ell for?'

'I've no idea,' said Sandra. 'None of us had even laid eyes on her till yesterday.'

'You don't think she's a bit... you know...?' said Trevor, tapping the side of his head instead of finishing the sentence.

'A nutjob?' Ingleby pursed his lips while he considered the possibility. 'Well, she's always been kind of on the loopy side, I s'pose, but now you come to mention it, Jackie says she's been actin' a bit weird ever since 'Arry snuffed it.'

'Harry?' said Sandra.

''Arry Vincent. Her 'usband. Died about eighteen months ago. Least, that's what they say. Never found the body though.' He let out a snort of laughter. 'Course, I wouldn't be a bit surprised if the old bugger turned up large as life one o' these days. It wouldn't be the first time he'd faked his own death.'

While Ingleby had been speaking, Trevor's insides had begun to turn cartwheels and he had to remember to make himself breathe. Cogs had suddenly started to slot into place in his brain. Harry Vincent. Donna's husband? Until that moment, they hadn't even known her surname was Vincent, let alone made any connection between her and Harry. So was that the reason she'd been trying to frame them? Revenge for Harry's death? But that was absurd. They'd been involved with Harry, yes, but it had very definitely been by accident rather than design. In fact, they'd done their level best to keep as well out of his way as possible, and if he really was dead, it had nothing to do with him and Sandra. But maybe Donna had been fed some dodgy information that made it look like they *were* responsible in some way. Either that or — and probably more likely — she'd found out that MI5 had killed him, and since there was no chance she'd ever get her revenge on any of those guys, she'd decided that he and Sandra were the next best thing.

'What's up with you two?' said Ingleby.

Trevor looked round at Sandra. Her mouth was frozen in a half open position, and her complexion had turned a peculiar shade of grey.

* * *

When they'd seen the camper van pull off the main road, Eddie had driven past the turning and parked the Cherokee behind a derelict stone cottage on the opposite side of the road. From here, they had a clear view of the van about a hundred metres away but without being spotted themselves. Donna had been watching the various comings and goings through her binoculars, but there had been nothing out of the ordinary until Trevor opened the tailgate of the van and took out the pick and shovel she'd seen them put on board at Ingleby's villa. Then Sandra emerged through the side door with a coolbag, and she and Trevor set off across the field with Herbert bringing up the rear. The dog trotted along at Sandra's heel, repeatedly leaping up at the coolbag with evident excitement.

'So that's their little game, is it?' said Donna.

'What's happening?' said Eddie, needing confirmation of what he thought he could make out with the naked eye.

Donna didn't answer straight away but waited until she saw them stop at the far edge of the field next to an area of dense woodland. 'Looks a lot like they're burying something,' she said as Trevor and Herbert began hacking at the ground with the pick and shovel. 'And I've got a pretty good idea what that might be.'

She continued watching for a couple more minutes, then lowered the binoculars and reached inside the car for her mobile phone. 'Time to do our public duty again, I think.'

But she'd only got as far as tapping in the first of the

three digits when Eddie put his hand on her arm.

'Hold up a minute,' he said. 'I don't think you need to bother.'

Donna looked up from her phone to see a police car easing to a halt close to the turning where the camper van was parked. She snatched up the binoculars again and focused in on two uniformed officers as they got out of the car and sauntered up the track towards the van.

'Well, well, I must be psychic,' she said and swung the binoculars back in the direction of the hole-digging party. All three of them were now lying down side by side on the ground, the coolbag next to them and the dog dancing round it and alternately barking and thrusting at it with her snout.

37

Kate couldn't be sure whether Pericles genuinely believed it was the best restaurant in town or whether he was a tightarse and got a discount because his cousin owned it, but here they were again at the same quayside taverna they'd had lunch at the day before. The only difference was that it was now the middle of the afternoon, so there was no food on the table, just his Greek coffee and her tall glass of iced cappuccino. And however much she'd prodded and probed, Pericles had been as reticent as ever to tell her anything much about what he was after Ingleby for or why he wanted to search his villa. One thing he *had* let slip was that he still hadn't got his search warrant and that it was probably too late anyway. Ingleby would have got rid of "the items" or moved them somewhere else as soon as he knew the police would be coming back to look for them.

She stirred the frothy contents of her glass with the straw, thinking there wasn't much point hanging on here if that was all she was going to get out of him, when her mobile rang. It was her granddad. He and Frank had been round to Ingleby's place, but there was no sign of anyone. The camper van had gone too.

'*Looks like he's done a runner,*' Eric said. '*Are you with Pericles?*'

'Yes.'

'*Does he know Ingleby's gone?*'

'Don't think so, no.'

'*Okay, tell him and hopefully he'll want to find out*

where Ingleby's got to as well. Then all you have to do is stick close to him until we find out where he is.'

'Oh, is *that* all?'

'*All in a good cause, sweetheart. All in a good cause,*' he said and hung up.

Kate stared at the display of her mobile for several seconds while she waited for Pericles to take the bait.

'All okay?' he said at last.

'My granddad,' she said, giving him a half smile. 'He's just a bit upset, that's all.'

'Oh?'

'It's nothing really. Only that he went to visit an old friend that happens to live in the area, but he wasn't in.'

'Perhaps his friend has gone to the beach or for shopping and will come back soon.'

Kate shook her head. 'The house is all shut up and a neighbour said he'd seen Granddad's friend drive off in a camper van with some other people. Such a shame. Granddad was so looking forward to seeing him after all these years. In fact, he hardly stopped talking about him for the whole trip over. Marcus Ingleby this. Marcus Ingleby that.'

Pericles's coffee cup was almost at his lips, but he lowered it again without taking a sip. 'What? Did you say *Ingleby*?'

'Yes. Do you know him then?'

'And your grandfather says he is not at home?'

'Whole place is deserted apparently.'

Pericles swore and grabbed his mobile phone. He rang the police station and gave a description of the van and its likely occupants, demanding to be informed the moment it was spotted.

'Is something wrong?' Kate asked as soon as he'd put down the phone.

'Your *papóose* — your grandfather,' said Pericles. 'He knows this Ingleby well?'

'Known each other for donkey's years.'

'Excuse me?'

'Sorry,' said Kate. 'A very long time. But they hadn't been in touch for quite a while until now. Why do you ask?'

Pericles shrugged. 'Perhaps I should speak to your grandfather. Try to find out more about Ingleby and if he is the kind of man who could...'

'Could what?'

He took a deep breath. 'The thing is this. We had a telephone call — a woman who did not say her name — and she said that there was a...'

Once again, he left the sentence hanging, and Kate leaned forward across the table and placed her hand on his arm. 'Yes?'

'I'm sorry, Kate. I should not tell you this, I think.'

'But I might even be able to help. I know Ingleby quite well myself,' she lied.

'You do?'

She gave his arm a gentle squeeze. 'Pericles, I wish you could learn to trust me a little.'

He placed his hand on top of hers and gazed into her eyes. Windows to the soul or not, Kate had little difficulty in seeing the turmoil that was going on inside his head. Time to play her trump card.

'After all,' she said. 'We're almost...'

She lowered her head and forced a flush of colour into her cheeks to add a touch of finesse to her pretence of coquettish embarrassment.

'Almost?' said Pericles with undisguised eagerness. 'Almost what?'

Kate looked up and met his eyes. Christ almighty, the man was almost panting.

'I think you know what I mean,' she said and reached her other hand across the table towards his.

38

Ingleby was still contemplating the bizarre story that Sandra and Trevor had told him about their involvement with Harry Vincent when he spotted a police car pull up near the end of the track. He got up from the back seat of the van and sat in the open doorway, his feet planted on the earth and his eyes fixed on the two cops as they walked towards him.

'*Kalıméra, kírıe,*' said the older and much fatter of the two. '*Aftó eínaı to óchıma sas*?'

'What?'

The cop scowled with the realisation that this wasn't going to be an easy conversation. '*Deutsch*?'

'Eh?'

'You are German?'

'Course I'm not fucking German.'

'The car, it is Volkswagen,' said the cop. 'German, yes?'

'Yeah, and I've got a Swiss watch, but it doesn't mean I can fucking yodel, does it?'

The younger cop nudged his partner. '*Tı eínaı* "yodel"?'

Fat Cop waved him to silence. 'This is your car?'

'Kind of, yeah.'

'The camping here is *verboten*.'

'Fir what?'

Fat Cop tutted and said something in Greek to the other cop, who shrugged and said, 'Penalty?'

Fat Cop looked doubtful, and his voice was hesitant

223

when he turned back to Ingleby. 'It is penalty the camping here.'

Ingleby knew exactly what he meant, but he was beginning to enjoy winding the guy up as well as appreciating the need to stall for time, so he spread his palms wide in an I've-no-idea-what-you're-on-about gesture. It seemed to have the desired effect because the cop took off his cap, slapped a palm to his forehead and gazed up at the sky before eyeballing Ingleby again and almost shouting the words 'Not. Here. The. Camping.'

'Well, that's okay because I'm not bloody camping, am I?' said Ingleby and opened the tap at the bottom of his catheter bag.

The two cops watched in silence as the stream of urine spattered onto the earth, and both took a step backwards to avoid any of it splashing up onto their boots. During this brief period of no-one speaking, Milly's barking from the far side of the field became even more apparent, and Fat Cop seemed to be aware of it for the first time.

'You are not alone here?' he said.

Ingleby closed the tap on his now empty catheter bag. 'Just me and my dog.'

The cops went to the front of the van, paused momentarily to identify the location of the barking dog and then set off across the field.

* * *

Milly was so preoccupied with the coolbag that she failed to notice the cops approaching until they were less than ten feet away, at which point she instantly switched the focus of her barking from the bag to the new arrivals. Clearly, neither of them welcomed this attention, and each jockeyed for position to try and manoeuvre his partner between himself and the dog. Whilst this jostling continued, they both looked down at the three people lying side by side on the ground.

'You speak Greek?' said Fat Cop.

'Sorry,' said Sandra. 'Only English.'

'And French,' added Herbert, sounding rather put out by Sandra's oversight.

Fat Cop groaned. 'What you do there?'

'Stargazing,' said Sandra.

'What?'

Sandra pointed up at the sky. 'We're looking at the stars.'

The two cops followed the direction of her finger.

'*Astéria*?' said Fat Cop.

'Possibly.'

'But it is afternoon.'

'Patience is a virtue, they say,' said Herbert.

Fat Cop frowned at him, took off his cap and scratched his head. 'But why are—? Can you shut up this dog?'

Milly hadn't stopped barking at them from the moment they'd arrived, and totally out of character though it was, she actually stopped when Trevor shouted at her and then resumed her enthusiastic inspection of the coolbag.

'What is in bag?' said Fat Cop.

All three answered in unison.

'Picnic,' said Sandra.

'Food,' said Trevor.

'Nothing,' said Herbert.

There then followed a brief discussion between the cops, and judging by their gestures and body language, it was centred on the coolbag and its possible contents, and from what Trevor could make out, involved words which sounded a lot like "bomb" and "narcotics".

'Please open him,' said Fat Cop.

'Pardon?' said Sandra.

'The bag. Open him.'

Trevor felt the taiko drummers begin to beat out an up-tempo rhythm inside his chest again as Sandra, who was lying next to the coolbag, slowly began to raise herself into a sitting position. But she'd scarcely achieved more than two inches from the horizontal when Ingleby interrupted her.

'Stay where you are,' he said and, groaning with the effort, crouched down over the bag and took hold of the zip toggle. He looked up at the two cops. 'But you're gonna look bloody silly when you find all that's in here is a few sandwiches and some fruit.'

The cops exchanged glances of bewildered incomprehension, and by the time they returned their attention to the coolbag, Milly had gripped the carrying strap between her teeth and was dragging the bag away at an impressive speed, considering the weight of its contents. Also reacting with impressive speed, Fat Cop's partner whipped out his pistol from the holster on his hip and aimed it at the hastily departing Milly. But before he could get off a shot, Fat Cop grabbed his gun arm and forced it downwards.

'What the bloody hell do you think you're doing?' he yelled at him — or at least that appeared to be the gist of it.

Gun Cop shouted something back at him, and a full scale row then developed with the accompaniment of some wild arm waving and a lot of pointing at Milly and each other. Trevor interpreted this as a heated debate about which one of them should chase after Milly and retrieve the coolbag — which neither of them seemed at all keen to do. Eventually, a consensus seemed to be reached — which was apparently to do nothing at all — and Fat Cop's partner sulkily holstered his weapon.

Fat Cop wagged a finger at Ingleby. 'I say you before

that the camping is *verboten* and you must go immediate.'

'Certainly, officer. No problem,' said Sandra, smiling up at him from her prone position on the ground.

'And if you still here when we return back, I will...'

He clicked his fingers at his partner for help with the word he was searching for.

'Kill you?' said the partner.

'Arrest you,' said Fat Cop.

'*Bien sûr, mon capitaine*,' said Herbert.

Fat Cop stared down at him and opened his mouth to say something, but changed his mind and wearily shook his head instead.

'*Ella*,' he said to his partner, and they traipsed off back to their car, stopping on the way to make a note of the van's registration number.

'Okay, I think you can get up now,' said Ingleby.

Trevor, Sandra and Herbert levered themselves upright, each of them reaching behind their backs to try and massage away the pain caused by lying on top of the pick, the shovel and a half dug hole.

* * *

The two police officers got back into their car and drove off.

Donna lowered her binoculars. 'Unbelievable,' she said and ducked back behind the partially collapsed wall of the derelict cottage as the police car went past. 'I mean, what is it with these Greek cops?'

'Maybe they took a bribe,' said Eddie. 'Or maybe cutting off someone's head isn't illegal out 'ere.'

Eddie wasn't always the sharpest knife in the drawer, and Donna couldn't tell whether this was meant as a joke or not, but even if it was, she'd never felt less like laughing in her life. If revenge was a dish best served cold, then this one was beginning to develop several layers of frost.

39

The whining noise from the van's engine didn't sound at all promising. Trevor turned the key in the ignition once again, but as on the previous four attempts, the engine failed to start.

'What's the problem?' said Ingleby from the back seat.

'Er, how about it won't start?' said Trevor.

'Don't smartarse *me*, sunshine. I mean *why* won't it start?'

Trevor looked across at Sandra in the passenger seat beside him with an expression of murderous intent.

'Stupid question, but I suppose there's petrol?' she said.

'Plenty.'

'Well, don't just sit there,' said Ingleby. 'Go and 'ave a butchers and see if you can fix it.'

Trevor closed his eyes and counted to five. He was fully aware of his own limitations when it came to the workings of the internal combustion engine — or almost any task which involved the use of spanners, screwdrivers or similar implements — but he also knew that he'd have to at least pretend, if only to keep the old man quiet.

Sandra and Herbert joined him at the back of the van and helped him unload the boxes, holdalls, pickaxe and shovel so he could remove the lid of the engine compartment. They all peered inside, but Trevor was fairly sure the others had no better idea of what they were looking for than he did.

'Everything's so plastered in oil and grease, it's hard to tell what's what,' said Herbert.

Trevor grunted. 'Says the guy who can't even drive.'

'Doesn't stop me from knowing about engines though, does it?'

'Oh well, in that case, please do enlighten us, Mr Henry Ford.'

Herbert leaned forward to get a closer look, occasionally tilting his head to get a better view of some component or other and poking at it with a twig he'd picked up off the ground. Thirty seconds later, he straightened up and tossed the twig over his shoulder.

'Try it now,' he said.

'But you haven't done anything,' said Trevor.

'Yes, but you never know. It might've sorted itself out by now.'

Trevor was very rarely driven to even the contemplation of inflicting violence on others, never mind actually carrying it out, but this was the second time in a couple of minutes that the compulsion to throttle another human being was almost overwhelming.

Ingleby's face loomed over the back seat of the van. 'Well?'

'I think we'll have to get somebody out,' said Sandra.

'Oh, that's bloody marvellous, that is.'

'We could always try *le bump-start*,' said Herbert.

* * *

'Doesn't look like they're going anywhere soon,' said Eddie, lowering the binoculars and looking round at Donna, who was sitting in a camp chair in the shade of a nearby olive tree and fanning herself with a magazine.

'Why? What's happening?' she said.

'Three of 'em pokin' round at the back of the van.'

'What for?'

'It's where the engine is.'

'Ah.'

Donna got up from her chair and went to stand at Eddie's shoulder. 'Won't it start then?'

'Seems that way.'

'Perhaps we should go and offer them a tow.'

'I don't think that'd be a good idea, Mrs V. I mean, we—'

'Joke, Eddie,' she said, shielding her eyes from the sun and squinting at the activity around the van. 'Is that Ingleby getting out?'

Eddie raised the binoculars again. 'Yeah, but he's getting in the driver's seat now.'

'I thought you said it wouldn't start.'

'Looks like they're gonna try and bump-start it.'

Donna exhaled with a low whistle. 'Good luck with that in this heat.'

They continued watching, Eddie through the binoculars and Donna with the naked eye, while Trevor, Sandra and Herbert put their shoulders to the back of the van while the dog danced around them, barking excitedly. The van began to move, but the ground was rough and almost exactly level, so there seemed to be little chance of achieving any real momentum.

Sure enough, after five minutes of heaving and straining, the van had travelled less than twenty metres and had barely exceeded walking speed. The three who'd been pushing slid down the back of the van like lava oozing down a mountainside and collapsed onto the earth while the driver's door flew open, and Ingleby stomped over to them. Even at this distance, Donna could hear that he was yelling his head off, and although she couldn't catch any of the words, it was perfectly clear that a full-scale bollocking was in progress.

'What now then?' said Eddie.

Donna took the binoculars from him and focused in on the patch of dirt on the far edge of the field where she'd watched them bury the coolbag after the police had left. Then she traced a route back through the woodland to where it petered out on the opposite side of the road from where she now stood.

'We got anything to dig with in the car?' she said.

40

Another whiff of cigarette smoke and another impulse to move to a different table, but there was a part of him — a big part — that couldn't tear himself away from the vicarious pleasure he was getting from inhaling the secondhand smoke. Of all the people sitting on the terrace of the little café overlooking the harbour, well over half were smokers, and of the rest, at least a third were probably under the age of twelve.

Reynolds worked his lucky coin back and forth across his knuckles and tried to focus on what was happening down by the quayside without letting his eyes stray yet again towards the tobacco-stuffed kiosk twenty metres to his left. No easy task since there was nothing of interest to hold his attention and no activity whatsoever apart from Frank Phelan's constant pacing.

For want of something else to occupy his nicotine obsessed mind, he read Sandra's text message again. At least he had somebody on the inside now. Somebody who had a perfectly valid reason for sticking close to Ingleby and who could keep him up to speed with whatever the old bugger was up to. Whether she'd actually tell him if Ingleby did go and fetch the loot was another matter altogether, which was why he'd given serious consideration to leaving Phelan and Emerson to their own devices so he could keep tabs on Ingleby himself. On the other hand, there was still the issue of the head in the freezer. Sandra and her pals were obviously terrified that he'd report it to the local police, so it ought to be a fairly safe bet that they wouldn't hold anything back. No, better to trust to that and keep his eye on Eric and Frank in case they knew something nobody else did and led him to his Holy Grail themselves.

Reynolds took a long drink from the bottle of water on the table in front of him and only vaguely registered the overladen moped whizzing along the quayside below.

* * *

The soft chugging of a fishing boat was momentarily obliterated by the shriek of a moped speeding past them on the quayside, its engine straining under the burden of two adults and three small children. Frank took a step to the side as smartly as his arthritis-ridden knee would allow and almost lost his balance. Only by thrusting out his walking stick and hooking it round a conveniently nearby lamppost did he prevent himself from toppling headlong into the water.

'Fookin' idiot!' he yelled, waving his stick at the rapidly disappearing moped as soon as he'd recovered his equilibrium.

Eric and Kate were sitting on a wooden bench parallel to the edge of the quay, and solidly constructed though it was, she could still feel the vibration from her granddad's half-hearted attempt to suppress his laughter. She herself had no such qualms, however, and let go with gusto.

'Yeah, very bloody funny,' said Frank, carving an arc through the air with the tip of his walking stick and prodding it in her direction. 'Laughed yer bloody socks off if I'd fallen in and drowned, wouldn't yer?'

'Course not,' said Kate, barely able to get the words out. 'I mean, where would we be if we were so tragically deprived of your scintillating company and intelligent conversation?'

Frank muttered something unintelligible and returned to his pacing. For the past quarter of an hour or so, it had been like watching an absurdly slow tennis match as Kate's eyes had followed him taking a dozen paces in one direction and then turning and retracing his steps. Back and forth. Back and forth. Over and over again, his head bowed and his lips moving silently as he walked, the metal tip of his stick tap-tapping on the concrete with irritating monotony. Ever since Pericles had had to go back to work and she'd met up with Frank and her granddad on the quayside, Frank had been banging on about one of the men they'd grabbed at the farm. He'd got some bee in his bonnet about how the guy had seemed somehow familiar but couldn't remember where he might have known him from. Eric had been adamant that he'd never seen the man before in his life, and he and Kate had left Frank to his pacing while they discussed what they considered to be the far more pressing matter of finding Marcus Ingleby.

'You've done amazingly well, Kate, I must say,' said Eric when she'd finished filling him in on the details of her conversation with Pericles. 'Getting him to agree to taking you along when they track down the camper van was a stroke of pure genius.'

'Let's just say I had to use all my powers of persuasion,' she said,

Eric raised an eyebrow, and Kate laughed.

'No, not yet,' she said. 'But I'm pretty sure he reckons he's on a promise now.'

Eric's eyebrow dropped back to its normal position and then joined its neighbour in producing a heavy frown. 'Katie dear, I know you're a grown woman and all that, and I know I said it was really important that we... The thing is, Kate, I really can't condone you having to... I mean, I'm kind of *in loco parentis* here and I—'

'Should be looking after my moral well-being? — Bit late for that, I'm afraid, Granddad.'

'Even so, I... I...'

It was one of those rare occasions that she'd known him to be lost for words. The truth was, though, she had absolutely no intention of sleeping with Pericles, but she was rather enjoying the novelty of teasing her granddad. The teaser teased for once.

'Don't worry,' she said. 'I know all about the birds and bees.'

'Well, yes, but—'

'Got it!' Frank had suddenly stopped his pacing almost directly in front of where they were sitting, and he turned to face them, triumphantly brandishing his walking stick. 'I told you we knew 'im.'

'And I told you I've never seen the man before in my life,' said Eric.

'You 'ave, you know,' said Frank with the smug grin of someone revelling in their superior knowledge. 'Long time ago, mind, but people don't change their spots that much, do they?'

'If you say so, Frank.'

'He's Old Bill, that's who he is.'

'Old Bill. Old Bill,' said Eric, stroking his chin as if struggling to recall the name. 'Hmm. The name's certainly familiar, but I can't quite—'

'Yeah, yeah, very comical. Well, 'ere's summat that's not quite so funny. Perhaps you remember a certain detective chief inspector by the name of Bruce Reynolds?'

When Eric didn't respond, Kate turned her head to the side and took in the wide eyes and the twitching jaw muscle.

'You okay, Granddad?' she said.

No answer.

'Granddad?'

Eric shook his head as if he were trying to free his mind of some unwelcome image. 'Sorry, sweetheart. Bad memories, that's all.'

'About this Reynolds guy?'

'He was the one who nicked us for the jewel robbery.'

'And what I'd like to know,' said Frank, 'is what the bloody hell he's doin' here.'

'Well, I think we can safely rule out coincidence,' said Eric. 'But we've done our time, so it can't be us he's after. Which leaves what? Ingleby?'

'Nah. Not after all this time. Anyway, Reynolds must've retired years ago.'

'So if it's not a coincidence and it's not us and it's not Ingleby, what other possible reason could there be for—?'

He broke off and looked up at Frank, who seemed to have had the same thought at exactly the same moment.

'Oh shit,' said Frank and slumped down onto the bench beside them.

41

The hard ground, Milly's snoring, the constant anxiety that the police might come back, and an almost pathological fear of snakes meant that Trevor had had very little sleep. By the time the roadside rescue truck had arrived, it was already dark, and although it had taken the mechanic less than fifteen minutes to get the van started, they'd decided to camp for the night and set off again the next morning. Not that it had been a unanimous decision. Ingleby had ranted and raved about the urgent need to get to their destination as quickly as possible, but Trevor had lied about the van's headlights not working, and Ingleby had eventually capitulated — on the condition that he slept in the van while the others dossed down outside in their sleeping bags.

Trevor was already wide awake when the side door of the van slid open and Ingleby stepped out, squinting in the early morning sunlight. He stretched, yawned, scratched each armpit in turn and then bent down to empty his catheter bag.

'Surprisingly comfortable, that bed,' he said.

'Slept well, did you?' said Trevor, making no attempt to conceal the bitterness in his tone.

'Best I've 'ad in a long while.'

'Good for you.'

Ingleby wandered over and gave Herbert a less than gentle prod with his foot. 'Come on, sleepyhead. Rise and shine.'

Herbert groaned and turned onto his side while Sandra

unzipped her sleeping bag and eased herself up onto her elbows.

'What time is it?' she said.

'Late,' said Ingleby and gave Herbert another jab with his foot.

'Stop bloody kicking me,' came the muffled response.

Sandra reached across and shook him by the shoulder. 'Come on, Herbert. We have to get going.'

'What about *le petit déjeuner*?'

'The what?' said Ingleby.

'Breakfast,' said Sandra.

The upper half of Herbert's face emerged over the top of his sleeping bag. 'I said we should've brought more food with us. We ate everything we had last night if you remember.'

'And who scoffed most of that?' said Trevor, but Herbert ignored him.

Ingleby rolled his eyes and grunted. 'We'll pick up something on the way. Just get a move on, okay?'

He headed off back to the van, and Trevor and Sandra wriggled themselves out of their sleeping bags.

'I bet we won't, you know,' said Herbert.

'Won't what?' said Trevor.

'Stop for breakfast. And I'm *faim comme une vache*.'

'Some time today would be good,' Ingleby shouted from inside the van.

* * *

When it had become apparent that Ingleby and his crew were going to camp for the night, Donna and Eddie had driven the Cherokee into a clearing in the woodland which afforded a perfect view of the van, whilst the trees provided more than adequate cover against being spotted themselves. Donna had been up and about since shortly after dawn, keeping a careful watch for any sign of activity, and as soon as she spotted Ingleby getting out of the van, she went back to the car to rouse Eddie. He was sound asleep behind the wheel, the seat tilted back as far as it would go.

'Wake up, Eddie,' she said. 'Looks like they might be on the move.'

Eddie slowly opened his eyes and turned his head to face her, wincing as he did so and clutching at his neck. 'Ow. Jesus.'

'What's up?'

'Bloody neck locked up.'

'Which is what the Famous Five over there should've been by now. — You want me to drive?'

'Nah, I'll be all right in a minute. I could murder a coffee though.'

He started raising his seat into a more upright position, and Donna glanced at the coolbag on the seat behind him.

'Maybe we should stick that in the boot out of sight for now,' she said. 'And it's going to stink like hell once the sun gets going. It's not exactly Coco Chanel as it is.'

* * *

Kate very rarely suffered from travel sickness, but she'd never before been in the back seat of a police car that was hurtling along at Mach 3 and overtaking other vehicles on blind bends. The constant wailing of the siren wasn't helping either.

She leaned forward and tapped Pericles on the shoulder. 'Do you think we still need the siren? It's starting to give me a headache.'

'Of course,' he said, then spoke to the driver in Greek. 'I think we can kill the siren, Dimitris.'

'I thought we were in a hurry,' said Dimitris.

'We are, but we're in open country now, and there's

240

hardly another car on the road.'

'What about sheep?'

'What about them?'

'There might be some in the road — or goats. You wouldn't want us to run them over, would you? I mean, two of my uncles are sheep farmers, and there was this lorry once which—'

'Just turn the damn thing off, will you? — You can keep the flashing lights on if you must.'

Dimitris grunted like a teenager who'd just been told he was grounded for a week, but he flicked a switch on the dashboard and the siren was no more.

'I don't think sheep'll take much notice of flashing lights,' he muttered.

Kate sat back, grateful that the assault on her eardrums was finally over, and stared out of the side window at the speed-blurred image of olive groves and vineyards, interspersed every now and again with the occasional field of citrus trees. From the information Pericles had received, it was going to be a good couple of hours or so before they caught up with Ingleby and the camper van even at this speed. Pericles had gone all official on her from the moment they'd set off — presumably for the benefit of Constable Dimitris — so there'd been very little in the way of chit-chat to help pass the time. Not that she minded very much because at least he wasn't blathering on about his two favourite topics — his job or, worse still, their so-called relationship.

For want of something better to alleviate her boredom, she took out her mobile phone and began scrolling through the inbox, deleting unwanted messages. It was hardly a task that required her full concentration, so part of her brain was left free to translate the conversation which Dimitris then struck up with Pericles.

'It's because of her, isn't it?'

'What is?'

'Why I had to turn the siren off.'

'For God's sake, Dimitris, you're not still—'

'I can't see why we had to bring her along in the first place.'

'I told you before,' said Pericles with the tone of a schoolteacher speaking to a particularly dim pupil. 'She's helping us with our enquiries.'

'That's usually another way of saying she's been nicked.'

'Well, she hasn't, and this time it means exactly what it says.'

There was a brief pause before Dimitris said what had probably been on his mind all along — or started to anyway. 'So it's not because you're... you know...'

'What?'

'You know...'

The car swerved slightly, and Pericles yelled at Dimitris to keep his hands on the wheel. Kate looked up from her phone a fraction of a second too late to see whatever gesture the constable had made which required both hands — but it wasn't hard to imagine. Pericles twisted round in his seat to see if she'd spotted it, but she decided to keep the peace with an expression of quizzical incomprehension, and he smiled at her and turned back to Dimitris.

'You do realise that the young lady speaks excellent Greek,' he said.

'Oh,' said Dimitris.

'Yes, "oh". — Now perhaps you could concentrate on your driving and don't speak again unless you have something sensible to say.'

Kate grinned to herself and went back to her text-deleting. Seconds later, the phone chirruped the arrival of a new message.

* * *

Eric took his eyes off the road for a moment to glance across at Frank, who was sitting in the passenger seat of the Toyota and prodding at the keys of Eric's mobile phone.

'Haven't you sent it yet?' he said.

'Give us a chance, will yer?' Frank snapped.

'Ten minutes to send a simple text message.'

'It might 'elp if you kept the bloody car a bit steadier.'

'Oh, and I suppose it's my fault that Greek roads have bends in them.'

Frank stabbed at the delete key. 'Jesus. Why can't they make these sodding buttons bigger?'

'Because if they made them big enough for a hamfisted buffoon like you, the phone would be the size of a breezeblock.'

A minute later, Eric heard the "diddly-dee" sound of the text being sent, and Frank slumped back in his seat like he'd just reached the summit of Everest.

'There. Done,' he said, then opened his window a couple of inches and put his ear to the gap. 'Christ knows where they are. I can't even hear the bloody siren now.'

'Kate'll get back to us any second. — Always assuming of course that what you just sent her wasn't complete gobbledygook.'

'I told you you should've let me drive. My granny drove quicker than you.'

'Frank, they only had horse and carts when your granny was alive.'

'That's what I mean.'

'Look, I really don't think you could do any better. I'm already going as fast as I can.'

Frank grunted. 'Bloody Toyota. Piece of Jap crap. We should've 'ad the other one like I said. That red seat thing.'

'Say-at,' said Eric. 'It's pronounced "Say-at".'

'I bet it's a damn sight quicker than this, whatever the fook it's called.'

He wasn't going to admit it to Frank, but Eric wasn't really pushing the car at all. Nowhere near. The fact was that even though he'd been totally innocent, his hit-and-run conviction had put him off driving for life. For nearly thirty years, he'd relied almost entirely on public transport to get him from A to B and, more recently, on Kate's generosity as his occasional chauffeur. Here in Greece, however, Kate had usually been otherwise engaged with Pericles whenever they needed to go anywhere, and letting Frank loose behind the wheel was a recipe for instant death. Not only was he off his face on booze most of the time, but Eric couldn't even be sure that he'd stick to driving on the right on the grounds that it was "a lot of bloody foreign nonsense, and I can't be doin' with it".

Eric changed down a gear to negotiate a particularly potholed stretch of road and checked the rear-view mirror as he'd been doing every few seconds since they'd left the apartment. So far, there'd been nothing untoward, but now they knew Reynolds was sniffing around, it was more than likely he wouldn't be far behind.

* * *

Reynolds pulled over to the side of the road and propped the tablet computer against the steering wheel. The red dot on the map had stopped again for the third time in less than an hour. The route which Emerson and Phelan had been following was tortuous to say the least, so either they weren't entirely sure where they were going or they knew he was on their tail and were trying to give him the slip. The latter explanation seemed unlikely because the tracking device meant that he'd no need to keep them in sight, and he'd been careful to keep his distance. And even if they suspected someone was tailing them, it was highly doubtful they would think it was him. They'd shown no sign of recognising him when they'd trussed him up at the farm, but they'd presumably been too busy with their ropework to pay him much attention.

The red dot on the tablet screen began to move again.

'Oh shit,' he said when he realised it was heading back towards him.

The last turning he'd passed was too far behind to make it in time, and there were no side roads ahead that he could see, so he grabbed the newspaper from the seat beside him and opened it in front of his face.

42

'Are we nearly there yet?' said Herbert, who seemed to lose all interest in speaking French at times of extreme stress and intense hunger. He'd been right about not being allowed to stop for breakfast, Ingleby having claimed that it was only about another hour or so and they'd eat when they got there.

'Cough 'n' a spit,' Ingleby answered.

Trevor guessed this was meant to convey that their destination was very close, although he'd already learned not to trust Ingleby's estimates of distances. On this occasion, however, it appeared that the old man was telling the truth for once because no sooner had he spoken than the road met the sea and then ran northwards, high up above the beach. About a kilometre ahead, a small island appeared, barely five hundred metres long and shaped like a spearhead with a lighthouse at its seaward tip. It was little more than three or four metres above sea level at its highest point and was linked to the mainland by some kind of causeway.

'That's it,' said Ingleby.

Trevor eyeballed him in the rear-view mirror. 'The island?'

'That's the one.'

The concrete causeway jutted out at ninety degrees to the main road with the open sea to the right and a variety of brightly painted fishing boats moored along its left. It was barely wide enough for the van, so Trevor covered the couple of hundred metres as quickly as possible, hoping to get to the end before anything started coming from the opposite direction. On the nearest point of the island was a little cluster of buildings, which, as Herbert enthusiastically pointed out, included a restaurant that was clearly open for business. Ingleby ignored him and told Trevor to keep following the track, which then turned inland past a substantial-looking chapel and continued on through a thicket of pine trees, opening out into a clearing near the middle of the island. On the left was a square, castle-like tower about three storeys high and attached to a long, pitch-roofed building of about half the height.

'Go round the back and park up,' said Ingleby.

Trevor chose a spot that was at least partially in shade and switched off the engine. Milly, who had been working herself up into a frenzy of excitement ever since they'd turned off the main road, was alternately whining and barking, staring fixedly at the side door of the van as if willing it to open with telekinetic energy. When the door failed to respond and Herbert obligingly got up from the back seat and opened it for her, she shot out of the van like a canine cannonball.

'Right then,' said Ingleby. 'Let's get to work.'

'Work?' said Sandra. 'What do you mean, "work"?'

'Herbert, you fetch the pick and shovel.'

'Pick and...?' Herbert faltered. 'What about breakfast?'

'Christ, will you ever stop whingeing about your bloody breakfast?' said Ingleby.

'At this rate, it'll be lunchtime before I *get* any breakfast, and I really don't think I can—'

Ingleby held up his hands in mock surrender. 'Okay, okay. If you promise to shut the fuck up, you can nip back to that caff we passed and get something for all of us. — But don't dick about. I want you back 'ere pronto to do your share of the diggin'.'

247

'Digging?' said Trevor, simultaneously registering the rapidly increasing heat of the day and the prospect of what sounded like serious hard labour.

'Jesus wept, is there an echo in 'ere or what?' said Ingleby, heaving himself to his feet. 'Sooner we start, sooner it's done, okay?'

Once Sandra had given Herbert some money and he'd set off on his hunter-gathering expedition, Trevor retrieved the pick and shovel from the back of the van and awaited further instructions. Ingleby took a folded sheet of paper from his pocket and studied it briefly before heading towards the pine trees at the far edge of the parking area.

'Come on,' he called out over his shoulder. 'There's work to be done.'

Sandra took the shovel from Trevor, and he slung the pick over his shoulder as they followed Ingleby into the wood.

'Maybe we should be singing a couple of verses of "Hi-ho, hi-ho, it's off to work we go",' said Trevor, who hardly ever felt like singing and least of all at that particular moment.

'He's got some kind of map,' Sandra whispered. 'I only caught a glimpse of it, but it's a kind of rough sketch with a big X on it.'

'What, like a treasure map, you mean?'

'That's what it looked like.'

'Ooh,' said Trevor, heavy on the sarcasm. 'How frightfully jolly.'

About ten metres into the wood, Ingleby struck off at a thirty degree angle to the sea, then turned right and followed the narrow strip of land between the rocky shoreline and the wood. A couple of minutes later, the gap between sea and trees suddenly widened into a small glade, and after checking his map, he made directly for a pine tree which stood slightly apart from its neighbours and was considerably taller. Then, with his back pressed up against its trunk, he appeared to take a sighting from the lighthouse a hundred metres away at the far end of the island.

'Perhaps "Yo-ho-ho and a bottle of rum" might be more appropriate,' said Trevor as he and Sandra watched him take ten long strides towards the lighthouse and then stop.

'Here,' said Ingleby, using his foot to mark out a cross in the thick layer of pine needles.

'Here be dragons?' said Trevor, and Sandra tried not to giggle.

Ingleby glowered at her. 'Maybe you won't find it so bloody funny after you've been diggin' for half an hour.'

'Half an hour?' said Sandra. 'So how deep do we have to go then?'

'More to the point, what exactly is it we're digging *for*?' said Trevor.

'Never mind all the questions. Just get on with it, will yer?'

Ingleby retreated to a nearby tree stump and perched himself while Trevor rammed the blade of the shovel into the earth. The recoil sent jarring shudders up both of his arms, and the shovel almost bounced out of his grasp.

'Ground's probably a bit 'ard this time o' year,' said Ingleby with a mischievous smirk. 'Good thing I thought to bring the pick, innit?'

'Very considerate of you,' Trevor muttered, dropping the shovel and taking hold of the pick.

43

Herbert's phrasebook didn't have the Greek word for croissant, so he might have to settle for toast, which was apparently the same word as in English but without the "a" and pronounced "tossed". The Greek for "may I have some…" was a little trickier, however, and he practised it aloud as he walked.

'*Borró na écho… Borró na écho…*'

Hang on a minute though, he thought. Isn't "borro" some kind of donkey? Do they eat donkeys in Greece? — Oh hell, I really don't want to end up with some kind of donkey-burger by mistake. Maybe I'll just forget about the polite bit and go straight for "tossed". As long as I stick a "please" on the end, they can hardly think I'm being rude.

Realising he'd forgotten the Greek for "please", he flicked through the phrasebook, keeping half an eye on the track ahead in the unlikely event that a car might be coming towards him.

'Ah, here we are — "*parra-ka-lów*".'

By the time he'd repeated the word four times, the unlikely event occurred, and a black Cherokee Jeep appeared, bearing down on him at speed. He jumped to the side of the track to avoid being run over and got a fleeting glimpse of the woman in the passenger seat as the car went past, leaving him squinting into the cloud of dust it left in its wake. Despite — or perhaps because of — the enormous sunglasses and the floppy straw hat, he recognised her immediately. But what was Donna doing *here*? It was way beyond the realms of coincidence, so the only possible explanation was that she'd been following them.

Herbert peered through the dust as the Jeep slowed almost to a halt near the castle tower and then picked up speed again, heading towards the far end of the island. She wouldn't have been able to see the van from there, but it was pretty certain she'd be back to take a closer look as soon as she'd drawn a blank on the rest of the island — unless she spotted Sandra and the others first of course.

All thoughts of breakfast reluctantly suspended, Herbert cut back through the pine trees and stopped at the edge of the wood, where he had a clear view of the parking area. Five minutes later, the black Cherokee nosed its way round the far end of the building and rolled up within a few feet of the van. A well-built man in a Hawaiian shirt got out and, one by one, tried each of the van's doors. Then he looked back at Donna and shook his head, saying something to her which Herbert couldn't make out. Her reply was equally inaudible, but she went to the back of the Jeep and took out what appeared to be a long metal blade.

It was difficult to see what happened next because the man had his back to him, but Herbert had seen people breaking into cars enough times on the TV to figure out what he was up to. Sure enough, he had the driver's door open within a matter of seconds, and Donna gave him a hearty pat on the back before returning to the Jeep and coming back with— No, it couldn't be.

Herbert whipped out his phone and used the camera function to zoom in. There was no doubt about it. The very same coolbag they'd buried the day before. The very same coolbag with the severed head inside it, and which Hawaiian Shirt Guy was now taking with him as he climbed inside the van.

"And if some god should strike me, out on the wine-dark sea, I will endure it."

Kate couldn't remember much of the Homer she'd read at university, but his description of the sea as "wine-dark" had always puzzled her, and it came into her mind now as she gazed out of the side window of the car at the gently rolling waves. Turquoise certainly and even azure at a pinch but "wine-dark"? Either the guy had been colourblind or the Ancient Greeks used to drink wine that was more like the colour of Curaçao than a Burgundy or a Merlot. Still, whatever colour you called it, the sea looked a far more inviting alternative to sitting in the back of a police car with Pericles and Constable Dimitris arguing their heads off at an ever-increasing volume. Each blamed the other for having lost track of the camper van, which was patently absurd since the problem had arisen purely from a lack of the appropriate technology and other cops on the road being less observant than they might have been.

Pericles had ordered Dimitris to park up soon after they'd hit the coast, reasoning that there wasn't much point carrying on and wasting a load of fuel until they heard that the van had been located again. That was nearly twenty minutes ago, and since then, the text messages from her granddad had become rather more frequent but, mercifully, a lot more intelligible. She guessed this was because Frank had been doing the texting earlier while Eric was driving, but her granddad had taken over now that they'd come to a standstill.

The argument between Pericles and his constable had reached almost deafening proportions when, all of a sudden, Dimitris flung open his door and got out of the car.

'*Se gráfo sta archídia mou,*' he shouted, then slammed

the door and stomped off down the road, stopping a few metres away and lighting a cigarette.

Kate leaned forward in her seat. Pericles was breathing heavily, his hands resting on his knees and both were clenched tight into white-knuckled fists.

'I don't think I've heard that one before,' she said.

'What?' he snapped.

'I write it on my balls? Something like that anyway.'

There was a pause while Pericles gradually brought his breathing back to a more normal level, and his fists slowly unfurled.

'I'm sorry, Kate,' he said, turning to face her with the expression of a puppy who'd just been caught peeing on the carpet. 'That was... not professional.'

'So what does it mean? What Dimitris said.'

'Oh that,' said Pericles with a dismissive wave of the hand. 'A stupid expression. It means... I am not listening to you no more. That kind of thing.'

'I'll make a note of it,' said Kate. 'Might come in handy one day.'

'No, no. These are not the words for a lady to say.'

'Why not? Because "ladies" don't have balls?'

Teasing Pericles was like shooting fish in a barrel. He was less than half her granddad's age but twice the traditionalist, and she took a childish pleasure in chipping away at the pedestal he was trying to put her on.

'No, Kate,' he said. 'It is because men will think you are... *poutána* — a harlot.'

'A harlot?' she said, scarcely able to speak through her laughter. 'I don't think I've heard it called that since Sunday School.'

She pulled out a handkerchief and dabbed at her tears but immediately felt a pang of remorse when she noticed the pissing puppy had now been beaten with a very large stick.

She reached out and placed her hand on his forearm. 'Pericles, I'm sorry. I really didn't mean to upset you.'

'*Then peirázei*,' he said, faking a smile. 'It doesn't matter.'

His shoulders hunched into a shrug, and he turned away from her to stare directly ahead through the windscreen.

Uh-oh, thought Kate. Now he's got the sulks. Have to get him back on board again if only for Granddad's sake.

She was about to apologise again and launch into some serious ego massaging when her mobile bleeped. She opened the message and realised straight away that Frank must have taken over texting duties again: "Wot tge fvcks harPENING?".

44

Trevor's eyes stung from the sweat, and he used the tail of his T-shirt to wipe his forehead.

'How far down is this thing anyway?' he said.

'Can't remember exactly,' said Ingleby. 'It's been quite a while since I buried it.'

Trevor and Sandra had been taking turns with the pickaxe and shovel, hacking at the solid ground for nearly a quarter of an hour, but the hole was still less than a foot deep. Even Milly, who had reappeared after having apparently completed her inspection of the island, had given up after her initially enthusiastic scrabbling in the dirt with her paws. Ingleby, meanwhile, had sat on his tree stump — conveniently positioned in the shade — smoking and occasionally offering words of encouragement such as "Get on with it. We 'aven't got all day" and "Put your backs into it for God's sake". All he lacked was a shotgun across his lap and the chain-gang scene from one of those Deep South prison movies would have been complete.

Herbert was taking his time getting back too. Probably dragging it out so he wouldn't have to do his share of the hard labour. Getting lost wouldn't be an excuse either. He was supposed to phone for directions when he got back to the van, but what was the betting he'd claim there was no signal or his battery was dead or—

The opening bars of *Mamma Mia* interrupted Trevor's train of thought and announced that Sandra had an incoming call on her mobile.

'It's Herbert,' she said, and Trevor's twinge of guilt for doubting him was almost immediately overtaken by his relief that there'd soon be another pair of hands to help with the digging.

But it soon became clear from Sandra's end of the conversation that Herbert had his knickers in a twist about something and was in urgent need of their presence back at the van. Trevor was beginning to suspect that this was some other subterfuge for avoiding any part in the excavation work when Donna Vincent's name was mentioned.

'Sorry, Mr Ingleby,' said Sandra as she ended the call. 'Herbert's got a problem back at the van. — Come on, Trev. I'll explain on the way.'

And before Ingleby could utter more than a couple of expletive-ridden protestations, they were halfway across the clearing and heading for the woods with Milly racing along at their heels.

When they emerged on the far side, they spotted Herbert over by the van and peering in through the window.

'I haven't got a key or I'd have got rid of it,' said Herbert as soon as they were within earshot.

'Where's Donna?' said Trevor, fishing in his pocket for the van keys.

Herbert pointed up to the top of the castle tower. 'They drove off in their car, but I'm fairly sure they're up there.'

'Bird's eye view, eh?' said Sandra, shielding her eyes against the sun and squinting up at the turret.

Trevor went to the driver's door of the van and pushed the key into the lock, but before he even had time to turn it, a police car cruised around the corner of the building.

'Oh, bloody Nora,' he said, realising it was too late to do anything now, and took a step back, leaving the key in the lock.

Two uniformed officers got out of the police car and sauntered towards them, one male and one female, the male with the heel of his hand resting on the holstered gun at his hip.

'Good morning,' said the female officer with an unconvincing smile and more than a hint of Australian in her accent.

'Ah, great, you speak English,' said Sandra.

'Of course,' said the woman as if affronted by the notion that anyone could believe otherwise. 'So is this your van?'

Trevor, Sandra and Herbert all nodded in unison but said nothing.

'We've had a report that there is a certain object inside which is in contravention of quite a number of our laws here in Greece — and very probably most other countries of the civilised world. — Mind if we take a look? Good.'

She nodded at her partner, who had been checking the van out while she'd been speaking and was now hovering by the driver's door. He unlocked it and climbed in, then eased himself between the two front seats into the back and opened the tall fitted cupboard next to the cooker unit.

'Donna must have been very specific,' Sandra whispered to Trevor as the officer took out the rather grubby-looking coolbag and instantly dropped it on the floor, his head thrown backwards in evident repulsion.

He picked it up again by the carrying strap and, holding it at arm's length, slid open the side door of the van and stepped out, his features contorted into a grimace of disgust. Placing it carefully on the ground, he said something to his colleague in Greek, which she helpfully translated. 'He says it fucking stinks.'

With that, she crouched down and, keeping her face as far away from the bag as possible, slowly unzipped it and flipped open the lid. Millimetre by millimetre, she leaned forward as if daring herself to peer over the edge of a dramatically high precipice.

'Well, it certainly looks like a head,' she said, wafting away the cloud of flies that had already descended. 'And I suppose you have a perfectly satisfactory explanation as to what it happens to be doing in your van?'

She stood up and looked at the three of them in turn.

'It's rather a long story, I'm afraid,' said Sandra.

* * *

It had been touch and go whether the police would turn up before Trevor and the others could get rid of the coolbag, but in the end, their timing had been spot-on. Unable to contain her glee that she was at long last about to get her revenge on them for Harry's death, Donna had been dancing around the top of the tower like a whirling Dervish on speed, and if it hadn't been for Eddie's reflex reaction in grabbing her by the arm, she would very probably have gone flying headlong over the battlements.

'Take it easy, Mrs V,' he said. 'Plenty of time to celebrate later, eh?'

Donna nodded and took several deep breaths. Once she'd composed herself, she peered over the battlements with almost exaggerated caution at the scene that was being played out below.

'What are they messing about at?' she said. 'Why haven't they just carted them off?'

Eddie picked up the binoculars and focused in on the small group clustered around the camper van. 'My guess is they're tryin' to talk themselves out of it.'

'You kidding me?' said Donna, snorting a derisive laugh. 'They've been caught red-handed with a severed head in their van. What more evidence do they want?'

'Looks like the young lad's showing 'em his phone for some reason.'

'What?'

Donna snatched the binoculars from Eddie, and sure enough, the whole group had gone into a huddle while Herbert held his mobile up in front of them.

'No idea what's going on there,' she said and then swung the binoculars to the right at the sound of another vehicle approaching.

A second police car appeared round the end of the building and parked up close to the first. Two cops got out and strolled casually over to the group by the van. She was almost certain she recognised one of them as the sergeant who'd been waiting for them at the house when they'd got back from dumping Manolis's body — Pericles Something-or-other.

'Would you bloody credit it?' she said. 'Like flaming buses. Nothing for ages and then two show up at the same time.'

* * *

For the second time that day, Trevor was beginning to feel guilty about how he might have misjudged Herbert. The fact that the guy hadn't even realised he'd pressed Record on his phone's video was beside the point. No, the crucial thing here was that he *had* pressed it, and he'd filmed the whole episode of Donna and her pal putting the coolbag in the van. A little piece of footage which could very well be about to save them from a serious miscarriage of justice, although even after Herbert had shown them the video clip, the local cops seemed to be champing at the bit to arrest them — probably because they didn't usually have too many severed head murders to investigate round this way. But when Sergeant Pericles realised that this particular head had once been attached to his missing cousin and he recognised Donna Vincent in the clip, he'd convinced them that this was his case and that they should butt out and let him get on with it. At least, that was pretty much the gist of what Trevor could glean from their discussion.

'So you know where they are now?' said Pericles.

Herbert pointed to the top of the castle tower. 'Up there, I think.'

They all stared up at the battlements where two figures were momentarily silhouetted against the clear blue sky before they stepped back out of sight. Pericles said something to the other officers, and each of them drew their pistol from its holster.

'You three stay here,' he said, emphasising who he meant by eyeballing Trevor, Sandra and Herbert, one after the other. 'I still have many questions for you, but first I must speak to *kyría* Vincent and her friend.'

Crouching low, the four officers ran to the nearest part of the building and kept close to the wall before disappearing from view round the far corner.

Sandra gave Herbert a clap on the back. 'I think you may have just saved our bacon there, Herbert.'

Herbert's Cheshire Cat grin faded almost as soon as it had appeared.

'Hello,' he said. 'Who's the woman?'

Trevor and Sandra followed the direction he was looking in as a young woman with long black hair got out of the back of the second police car and slammed the door shut. At the same moment, a silver Toyota rounded the end of the building and came to a halt next to her. Two men got out. Eric and Frank.

'What the bloody hell are *they* doing here?' said Herbert.

'Come to join the party?' said Sandra.

Eric, Frank and the young woman had a brief

conversation and then came over to them.

'I don't believe you've met my granddaughter Kate,' said Eric with his trademark beaming smile.

The woman exchanged perfunctory nods with Trevor, Sandra and Herbert.

'You wouldn't happen to know the whereabouts of our friend Marcus by any chance?' Eric went on.

'He's busy,' said Trevor.

Frank took a step forward, his hand inside the bumbag strapped beneath his belly. 'We didn't ask you what he was doing. We asked you where he was.'

'*Il est occupé*,' said Herbert.

Frank fixed him with a malevolent, narrow-eyed glare as he pulled a gun out of his bumbag and aimed it at Herbert's chest. 'Go on,' he said. 'Piss me about some more, why don't yer?'

'Oh dear,' said Eric. 'You seem to have upset him now. It's really not something I'd recommend in the circumstances.'

Milly, who had been fast asleep in the shade ever since they'd arrived back at the van, peeled open one eye and then the other. She sniffed the air and surveyed her surroundings for anything that might be of interest, then did a canine version of a doubletake when she caught Frank's unmistakable scent and, more particularly, spotted his walking stick. Bounding over to him, she grabbed the stick between her teeth and yanked it from his grasp before he was even aware of what was happening.

'Oi! Bring that back 'ere!' he yelled as Milly ran round and round in an ever-increasing circle, her head held high and flaunting the stick with an occasional flourish.

Frank tracked her with his gun, and Trevor's body tensed rigid. He hadn't the slightest doubt that the idiot would shoot to kill, so he lunged forward and chased after Milly, as far as possible keeping himself between the dog and Frank's gun. This was no easy task, however, since Milly clearly delighted in this newly introduced element to the game and immediately abandoned her circular route for a far more unpredictable zigzagging motion. On his third attempt, Trevor managed to get hold of one end of the stick and after a brief tug-of-war and a lot of shouting, handed it back to its apoplectic owner.

'Next time, I'll pop her one,' said Frank, eyeing the saliva dripping from his walking stick with evident distaste.

'And now perhaps we can return to the matter in hand,' said Eric. 'You were about to tell us — or better still, *take* us — to Mr Ingleby.'

'We'd love to help you of course,' said Sandra, forcing a smile that oozed insincerity, 'but we're under police orders not to go anywhere till they get back.'

Frank waved his gun at her. 'Aye well, you're under *our* orders now, flower, so I suggest you get a bloody move on and take us to Ingleby.'

Trevor was doubtful that he'd actually start shooting with the police so close by, but it was difficult to be certain with a nutter like Frank. A quick glance at Sandra confirmed that she was thinking much the same thing, so he led the procession back into the pinewood with Frank bringing up the rear.

45

If the dark stains of sweat on Ingleby's shirt were anything to go by, his impatience had got the better of him and he'd carried on digging the hole himself. But if the absence of any discernible increase in the depth of the hole was anything to go by, his efforts had been short-lived.

'Where the fuck 'ave you been?' he said when the procession began to emerge from the pine trees, but his anger gave way to wry amusement as soon as Eric and Frank came into view. 'You two took yer time 'n' all.'

'You make it sound like you were expecting us,' said Eric.

'I've been expecting you ever since you got out of chokey.'

'So you're going to give us our share after all?'

'Why wouldn't I? Honour amongst thieves and all that crap. The three of us did the job together, and it was only luck that I got away and you two got nicked. Well, luck and the fact that Frank's a total fucking idiot.'

'You wanna say that again?' said Frank, swinging his gun round to aim it at Ingleby.

Ingleby got up from his tree stump and squared up to him. 'You're. A. Total. Fucking. Idiot.'

Before Frank had time to respond — either by pulling the trigger or with some insult of his own — Eric reached out and pushed down firmly on his gun arm.

'I think we can dispense with the firearms now, Frank,' he said and then turned back to Ingleby. 'So if you'd always intended to hand over our share, why all the prevarication? Why not just give us what we wanted in the first place?'

For a man in his seventies, Ingleby's impish grin was almost childlike. 'Thought I'd wind you up for a bit,' he said. 'I don't get a lot of fun outta life these days.'

'Oh great,' said Herbert. 'These two were going to start cutting bits off me just because you—'

A sharp jab in the ribs from Sandra's elbow brought the sentence to an abrupt end.

'A rather hazardous method for seeking amusement, as I believe this young man was about to point out,' said Eric. 'But all's well that ends well, I suppose.'

'This it then?' said Frank, who had wandered over to the half dug hole in the ground and was poking at it with his walking stick.

'No flies on you, eh, Frank?' said Ingleby, but either Frank didn't hear him or he decided not to rise to the bait this time.

'But why bury it so far away?' said Eric. 'Surely you could have hidden it somewhere closer to home?'

'After the job went tits up, I 'ad to get out of the country sharpish in case the plods came after me too. Crete was about the first flight out, so that's where I went. But then I decided I could probably be more anonymous somewhere on the mainland. Somewhere less touristy. So I 'opped on a ferry, and this is where it got me.' He pointed towards the wall of the port about half a kilometre to the north. 'I didn't wanna get caught with the gear on me, so I bought meself a shovel, and this seemed as good a place as any. Thought I'd come back and dig it up again soon as I got settled some place.'

'Why didn't you?' said Eric.

'I did. — Least, I came back for my share, but I left yours 'ere. Seemed safe enough, and I didn't know how long it'd be before you came lookin' for it.' He grabbed the shovel and thrust it at Frank. ''Ere you go, Frankie-boy. All yours.'

'With *my* leg? Piss off.'

'Perhaps our young friends here might oblige us,' said Eric, taking the shovel from Ingleby and handing it to Trevor, who immediately passed it to Herbert.

'Your turn, I think,' said Trevor.

Herbert scowled and drove the blade down into the hole with such force that the recoil sent it flying out of his hands.

'Bloody hell,' he said. 'This ground's like iron.'

'Isn't it just,' said Trevor.

* * *

The Heckler and Koch had been a present from Harry on his twenty-first birthday, and Eddie cherished it above all of his possessions. But this would be the first time he'd used it on real flesh and blood. He'd had plenty of practice on paper targets, bottles and tin cans over the years, but never once had he so much as pointed it at another human being. Donna didn't think that a shootout with four cops was the best time to start, and she told him to tuck it back in his belt.

'But how else are we gonna get away?' said Eddie. 'The filth'll be on their way up 'ere before we're even half way down.'

'And you think we can shoot our way out, do you? Four guns against one? You think Harry would have taken those odds?'

Eddie's chin dropped an inch towards his chest while he gave it some thought. When he spoke again, it was little more than a mumble. 'He'd have done anything to protect *you*, Mrs V. You know that.'

'Yes, I know. Which is why he wouldn't have done

anything that was more than likely going to get us both killed.'

His head sank even lower, and Donna laid a hand on his shoulder. 'Listen, Eddie, I don't want to spend the rest of my life in a Greek jail any more than you do, but at least if we're still alive, there's a good chance we can talk our way out of it. The police don't exactly have much in the way of evidence against us, and I can afford to get us the best lawyer in—'

Eddie's eyes sprang up to meet hers. 'Maybe I can hold 'em off long enough for you to…'

The look of inspiration faded from his face at the same time as his voice gave up on the rest of the sentence.

Donna peered over the battlements to the ground, forty-odd feet below. Even at the back of the tower, it was a good twenty foot drop to the sloping roof of the building it joined onto.

'Not sure how I'm going to manage that without a rope, Eddie love. Pity there aren't some bedsheets up here we could have tied together.'

She turned back towards him and saw that his chin was now almost in contact with his chest. The image flashed into her mind of the shy and futureless shambles of a lad who Harry had taken under his wing all those years ago.

'I'm sorry, Eddie,' she said, taking him by the hand and giving it a squeeze. 'It's not that I don't appreciate the offer. Of course I do. And you know what? Harry would have been so proud of you for that. Really he would.'

She let go of his hand and lifted his chin so that he was looking straight at her. He forced a smile to match her own, but it instantly collapsed into a frown.

'You crying, Mrs V?' he said.

Donna sniffed back a tear that she was unaware had even begun to appear. 'No, I'm fine. Just put the damn gun away, will you? Better still, chuck it over the edge so they don't catch you with it.'

Eddie stared down at the semi-automatic as if he'd forgotten its very existence, then went over to the battlements and held it out at arm's length. But before he could let go, someone shouted from the doorway that led out onto the top of the tower, and he spun round, the gun still in his hand. A gunshot exploded in Donna's ears, and Eddie's upper body jerked backwards, a bright red stain rapidly adding to the already garish blues and yellows of his Hawaiian shirt. He dropped the weapon and clutched at the nearest battlement, but his hand glanced off the weather-smoothed stone, and he toppled sideways from the top of the tower without a sound.

46

The dull "clank" of metal against metal was as melodious to Trevor's ear as a Mozart concerto, signalling as it did that the backbreaking hunt for Ingleby's treasure was almost at an end. Herbert had announced that he was too exhausted to continue after less than five minutes' digging, so Sandra had taken over and then Trevor. Every part of him ached as he pushed down on the shovel to lever himself upright.

'Some kind of metal box, is it?' he said.

'Far as I remember,' said Ingleby from his throne of a tree stump. 'Red, I think.'

Herbert stepped forward and snatched the shovel from Trevor, who almost overbalanced and fell to the ground after the sudden removal of his prop.

'My turn,' said Herbert and set about the last few shovelfuls of dirt with a previously absent enthusiasm.

Inch by inch, the lid and sides of a large, dark green, metal cash box were exposed to the air. Ingleby got up from his tree stump and advanced towards it while the others gathered round, forming a circle and gazing down at the box as if they were paying their last respects at a burial service.

'You gonna open it or what?' said Frank.

'It's your share. Yours and Eric's,' said Ingleby. 'One of you should open it, I reckon.'

Eric reached into his pocket and pulled out a coin. 'Perhaps we should toss for it. — Heads or tails?'

He held out the coin to Frank, but he brushed it away

with the back of his hand. 'What if he's booby-trapped it?'

'But how could he booby-trap a coin that's been in my pock—'

'Not the coin. The bloody box. One of us lifts the lid and — boom! Or maybe he's put a snake in there or summat.'

'Frank, if I'd put a snake in there, it would've croaked fuckin' years ago, wouldn't it?' said Ingleby.

'I suppose you still have the key, Marcus?' said Eric.

'Key? What key?'

'Er, to unlock the box?' said Frank.

'Don't think I bothered to lock it,' said Ingleby. 'If somebody'd found where it was and taken the bother to dig it up, I wouldn't 'ave thought they'd just walk away and leave it when they saw it was locked.'

'Well, get the damn thing open then.'

Ingleby said it would be a struggle for him to get down low enough to lift the box out of the hole, so he told Herbert to pick it up and take it over to the tree stump. The rest of the group followed, and Trevor noticed that Frank had positioned himself behind Eric — presumably bracing himself for an explosion — when Ingleby flipped open the lid.

'I knew he were bullshittin' us,' said Frank, moving alongside Eric and pointing at the box with his walking stick.

Inside, and filling the box almost to the brim, was a rolled-up denim shirt.

''Old yer 'orses, Frank,' said Ingleby, lifting the bundle out and knocking the box to the ground with his elbow.

He placed the shirt in the middle of the tree stump, and as he began to unwrap it, something glinted in the bright sunlight. With the bundle fully open, the glare was intense, and Trevor had to squint to make out the individual items within the small heap of jewellery. Rings, bracelets, necklaces, brooches, earrings — all heavily studded with diamonds and other precious stones. Very carefully, Ingleby eased the shirt out from under the pile and took a step back.

'There you are then, gents,' he said. 'Feast yer eyes on that lot.'

Eric leaned forward to examine the haul more closely, and Frank picked out a diamond necklace. He held it level with his face and gazed at it as it twisted this way and that in the breeze, dappling his ruddy features with the sun's shifting reflections.

'So 'ow do we know you didn't take more than yer fair share?' he said.

'You don't,' said Ingleby.

'Let's not quibble, shall we, Frank?' said Eric, holding a particularly large diamond ring up to the light. 'I think Marcus here has done us proud.'

Frank grunted and tossed the necklace back onto the pile.

'I need a piss,' he said and limped off towards a nearby pine tree.

'Me too,' said Ingleby and stooped to open the tap on his catheter bag.

Eric looped an arm round Kate's waist. 'Well, sweetheart, what do you think? Worth the effort?'

'Oh definitely,' she said, rising up on her toes and kissing him lightly on the cheek.

'Now, let me see,' said Eric and scanned the collection of jewellery briefly before selecting a ruby pendant earring and holding it close to her ear. 'Yes, I think this would suit you perfectly.'

She mirrored his beaming smile. 'Well, you can't say I haven't earned it, Granddad.' Then she nodded her head in Ingleby's direction and whispered, 'Does he have to do that in public?'

'Apparently so,' Eric whispered back.

Ingleby closed the tap on his catheter and pulled himself upright, wiping his palms on his shorts. 'Right then. I reckon this calls for a bit of a celebration, wouldn't you say, Eric?'

'Now let's not get too hasty, boys,' said Frank before Eric had time to reply.

They all turned as one to see Frank standing a little way off and holding his gun stretched out in front of him.

* * *

It was impossible to hear much of what was being said from behind the tree at the edge of the clearing, but Reynolds had no doubt now that he had reached the end of his sixteen year quest. Even from this distance, he had a clear view of the shimmering glare coming from the top of the tree stump, and it was almost unthinkable that what they'd dug up was anything other than the stolen jewellery. It was equally unlikely that Ingleby wasn't the third member of the gang — the one that got away.

But even though he'd dreamed of this moment for so many years, Reynolds was undecided how best to proceed now that the moment had finally arrived. Of all the many circumstances he'd imagined, the buried-treasure-on-a-wooded-island scenario certainly hadn't been one of them and nor was the presence of quite so many people. Most important of all was that he knew Frank Phelan had a gun, and if there had ever been one constant amongst all the variables, winding up dead was never going to be part of the equation.

He turned his lucky coin over and over in his pocket and pondered his course of action as he watched Phelan pick up what looked like a diamond necklace and dangle it in front of his face. Perhaps the best solution would be to prolong the waiting game a little longer. See what happened next and make his move whenever an opportunity arose that didn't involve putting himself in danger. After all, a few more hours — maybe even days — wouldn't make much difference, given the years he'd already spent on the case. Emerson and Phelan would probably be sloping off with their share of the loot before long, so all he had to do was keep tracking them till the time was right to strike.

Satisfied with his decision, and his rumbling stomach reminding him that it was almost lunchtime, the idea of adjourning to the restaurant at the head of the island was becoming increasingly appealing. Nothing much else was likely to happen here, and besides, the restaurant was perfectly positioned to spot anyone heading back to the mainland whenever the little band of treasure hunters decided to call it a day. Another decision made, he'd half turned to leave when his peripheral vision caught sight of Phelan hobbling off and disappearing behind a nearby tree.

Probably just having a slash, thought Reynolds. Still, I may as well hang on a couple of minutes to make sure.

But even before the allotted time was up, Phelan came back into the clearing and advanced towards the rest of the group as rapidly as his gammy leg would carry him and with a gun stretched out in front of him. Trevor, Sandra and Herbert immediately threw their hands up in the air while the others simply stared at him. Then Ingleby started mouthing off, and it was obvious that a full-scale row was developing. What was odd about it, though, was that Eric Emerson seemed to be taking Ingleby's side, and Phelan was mainly aiming his gun at Eric.

Dear oh dear, thought Reynolds. A lovers' tiff or something more serious?

His answer came a few seconds later when Herbert

gathered up the jewellery from the top of the tree stump and put it back into the metal box. After some more gun waving and chat from Phelan, Herbert walked over to the girl with the long black hair and handed her the box. Emerson was doing most of the shouting and pointing now, and when Phelan came up behind the girl and put his gun to her head, he took a step forward. But he stopped immediately when Phelan shouted something back at him and flung his arm around her throat, holding her in a tight headlock. As soon as Emerson backed off, Phelan released his grip on the girl, and she began to make her way across the clearing towards the pine trees. Phelan followed, walking partly backwards and partly sideways, his gun constantly aimed at Ingleby and the others.

Reynolds realised that once they reached the wood, they'd have to pass within a few yards of where he was standing, so he edged around the tree until he was fairly sure he was invisible to both Phelan and the Ingleby crew. The notion flashed into his mind that maybe he could use the element of surprise to jump Phelan and grab the gun off him, but the odds of getting to him before he heard him coming were far too great for his sense of self preservation. On the other hand, he needed to keep tabs on the jewellery, so he waited until Phelan and the girl were far enough ahead and set off after them.

* * *

The moment Frank and Kate left the clearing and entered the wood, Eric made to follow them, but Ingleby grabbed him by the arm.

'Wait,' he said. 'You wanna get yourself killed?'

'He's got my granddaughter,' said Eric. 'As far as I know, the gun isn't loaded anyway.'

'Oh yeah? You think he'd try a stunt like this if it

wasn't? Not even Frank's *that* stupid, and he's nutter enough to kill her too if you get too close.'

Eric thought about it for no more than a couple of seconds, then wrenched his arm free and hurried off towards the pine trees.

'For Christ's sake,' said Ingleby. 'You try to 'elp somebody and...'

He finished the sentence with a grunt and sat back down on his tree stump.

Trevor turned to Sandra. 'You think we should go after them?'

'I'm not sure,' she said. 'My guess is that Frank'll let her go as soon as he gets back to the car.'

'Yes, but what if—?'

He broke off when Milly flashed past him and hurtled off across the clearing, hot on Eric's heels. Either she'd been watching too many *Lassie* films and had got it into her head that there was a damsel in distress who was in urgent need of rescuing or she was still obsessing about Frank's walking stick. Trevor suspected that the latter was by far the most likely, but whatever the reason, Milly was certain to get herself into some serious trouble if he didn't catch up with her first. As he ran, he yelled at her to stop, but this was not to be one of those very rare occasions when she actually did as she was told.

Eric had already slowed down and was breathing heavily when Trevor overtook him, but Milly was nowhere to be seen. Then he heard the familiar sound of frenzied barking, and he quickened his pace. But when the barking abruptly stopped, he broke into a sprint. Twenty metres further on, he skidded to a halt. Milly had the end of Frank's walking stick clamped between her jaws and was twisting it this way and that to try and wrest it from his grasp. Frank staggered to keep his balance, his gun jerking from side to side as he fought to steady his aim at the dog's head. Trevor rushed at him, but before he could make contact, there was a loud "crack" and a flash from the muzzle of the pistol. A cloud of dust burst from the earth, inches from Milly's front paws, and she instantly let go of the stick. With his counterbalance so suddenly dislodged, Frank tottered backwards and was already on his way down when Trevor slammed into him. A second shot rang out, and the gun flew out of Frank's hand.

It landed a few feet from where Kate was standing, and she snatched it up and aimed it at the two bodies on the ground. More specifically, Trevor realised, it was mainly aimed at him since he'd fallen on top of Frank and was now providing him with his own personal human shield. Seeking a rapid exit from the firing line, he pushed down on the earth with both hands to launch himself upright, and a stab of searing hot pain flashed through his left arm. Then he felt the warm wetness on his skin, and he glanced down to see the blood streaming from inside the sleeve of his T-shirt.

'Bloody Nora, I've been shot,' he said to no-one in particular.

His vision blurred, and his knees went off-duty, sending him crashing back down towards the ground, but a hand under each armpit prevented a coccyx-shattering collision with the stone-hard earth.

'Oh my God, are you okay?' said Sandra, easing him down into a sitting position.

Trevor slowly twisted his head round to look up at her, but her face was swimming in and out of focus.

'I think I've been shot,' he said.

Sandra crouched down to inspect the damage and peeled back the sleeve of his T-shirt. 'Only skimmed you by the look of it.'

'Oh well, that's fine then if it only skimmed me,' Trevor said, making no attempt to conceal the sarcasm in his tone. 'So how come it hurts like—?'

'Stay where you are.'

It was Kate's voice. Frank had begun to get to his feet, and she'd taken a step closer to him, her arms straight out in front of her and holding the butt of the gun in both hands.

Frank's grin was dark and malicious as he continued to stand. 'You wouldn't shoot yer dear old Uncle Frank, would yer, flower?'

'Don't tempt me.'

Eric appeared at her side, sweating heavily and gasping to recover his breath.

'I'll take... over now, Kate,' he said and reached out for the gun.

'You sure you don't want to get your breath back first?'

'Yeah,' said Frank. 'Why don't you 'ave a nice little sit down, Granddad? Can't be too careful, man o' your age.'

'Shut up, Frank,' said Eric, taking the gun from Kate and aiming it at Frank's chest.

Frank snorted a laugh. 'Get real, Eric. You've never fired a gun in yer life.'

'Face down, on the ground. Now.'

The command was greeted with another snort of derision, and Frank took a couple of paces forward.

'That's far enough,' said Eric, but Frank kept coming, his hand held out for the gun.

'Hand it over. There's a good boy.'

Eric stepped back, struggling to control the tremor in his gun hand. 'I'm warning you, Frank.'

The words were scarcely out of his mouth when Frank lunged and made a grab for the gun. Eric threw up his arm so it was out of the shorter man's reach, but Frank drew back his fist and punched him hard in the stomach. Eric doubled over, and the pistol fell to the ground.

'Now then,' said Frank, stooping to pick it up. 'P'raps

we can carry on where we left off, eh? — Fetch the box, sweetpea.'

He nodded at the cash box on the ground and pointed the gun at Kate, who was gently massaging Eric's back while he bent forward at the waist, supporting himself with his hands on his knees and taking deep breaths.

'Fetch it yourself,' she said.

Frank stormed over to her and thrust the muzzle of the pistol into the side of her head. 'I ain't askin' you again.'

Kate straightened, and Frank backed off, keeping the gun on her as she walked over to the cash box. She was no more than six feet away from it when another gunshot reverberated around the pinewoods. Frank wheeled round and dropped to the earth, rolling from side to side, howling in agony and clutching at his shoulder as the blood oozed through his fingers.

A uniformed police officer appeared through the trees. Sergeant Pericles. 'Are you all right, Kate?'

She nodded, and Pericles picked up Frank's gun.

'Never mind her,' said Frank. 'I'm the one what's been shot.'

'You are very lucky I am an excellent shooter,' said Pericles. 'It could have been your head.'

'Yeah, I dunno 'ow I can ever thank you enough.'

Pericles cast his eye around the rest of the group. 'You are shot too?' he said to Trevor.

'Just a scratch — apparently,' said Trevor, pressing a bloodstained handkerchief against the wound.

'It would have been better if you had stayed where I told you.'

Trevor shrugged. 'We didn't have much choice, I'm afraid.'

'And now I have *more* questions I must ask you,' said Pericles but then explained that he had no time to interview them straight away as he had another shooting to attend to back at the castle. Instead, they would all have to come to the police station the next morning for questioning, and he issued a stern warning of the consequences if they failed to appear.

'Never mind all that,' said Frank. 'You gonna get me to a doctor or what?'

Pericles looked down at him with obvious contempt, then took hold of Frank's good arm and hauled him to his feet. He handcuffed his hands behind his back, and Frank's features twisted into a mask of pain. 'Watch what you're doin', yer stupid bubble.'

'Bubble?' said Pericles.

'I'll explain later,' said Kate.

'You will be returning by this evening?'

'I expect so, yes.'

'Then perhaps we could meet.'

'Tomorrow might be better,' said Kate. 'I'm going to be fit to drop by the time we get back to the flat.'

While she and Pericles were talking, Eric had sidled over to Frank and whispered something in his ear. Frank laughed in his face and said something which Trevor also didn't catch, then let out an agonised roar when Eric reached out and gave his blood-soaked shoulder a hefty squeeze.

'*Arketá!*' Pericles shouted and dragged Frank off through the trees with a parting 'See you soon' to Kate.

'Ow!' said Trevor, more in the anticipation of pain than the real thing when Milly paraded Frank's walking stick past him and came within an inch of swiping the wound on his arm.

'I guess Frank's not the only one in need of medical attention,' said Sandra.

47

By the time they'd made it back to the van, the blood had almost stopped flowing from Trevor's wound, but it was beginning to burn like crazy. He wasn't at all happy about the prospect of stitches or the tetanus jab that Sandra expected he'd need, but he was still keen to get to a doctor for something to relieve the pain.

'Where the hell are they?' he said.

It was the third time he'd asked the question since Sandra had called Herbert and told him to bring Ingleby and meet them at the van, and she responded with the same "any minute now" as before. Also waiting for Ingleby to arrive, Eric and Kate had passed the time by sifting through the jewellery on the bonnet of their car, and Milly, exhausted from her recent encounter with a near-death experience, was fast asleep in the shade, cradling Frank's walking stick between her paws.

Trevor was about to suggest that Sandra should try phoning again when he heard a cheery "*Bonjour, mes amis*", and Herbert and Ingleby stepped out of the wood.

'Is everyone okay?' said Herbert. 'We heard gunshots.'

'Well, thanks for rushing to the rescue,' said Trevor.

'Oh my God,' said Herbert, wide-eyed as he noticed the blood-soaked handkerchief which Trevor held clamped against his arm. 'Have you been shot? Does it hurt?'

'Yes and yes.'

'So what happened?'

Sandra launched into an explanation while Trevor tapped his foot impatiently and produced a series of heavily theatrical sighs.

'In your own time,' he said. 'I'll just sit here and quietly bleed to death, shall I?'

Sandra had just reached the part of the story where Frank had got the gun back from Eric when another figure emerged from the woods and strode across the parking area.

'Morning, all,' said Reynolds. 'Mind if I join the party?'

'Well I never,' said Ingleby. 'Detective Chief Inspector Reynolds, as I live and breathe. — Come to service the air-conditioning in the castle, 'ave you?'

'So you did recognise me then.'

'Not at first. Came to me later when summink came on the telly about pig farming.'

Reynolds grinned. 'I've been looking for you for a very long time, Ingleby. A very long time indeed.'

'Oh yeah? And why would that be exactly?'

'The third man?'

'Good film, that. Been a while since I seen it though.'

Ingleby lit a cigarette and exhaled directly into Reynolds's face, but instead of turning away to escape the smoke, he breathed it in with an expression of blissful ecstasy.

'You needn't worry,' he said, recovering himself. 'I'm off the job now anyway, and I really can't be arsed to deal with all the crap it would take to get you back home to stand trial, so I'm not about to arrest you or anything. I just don't like loose ends, that's all. Now I know who you are, I can close the case. Get some decent kip for a change.'

'Phew, what a relief,' said Ingleby, making a big show of wiping his brow with the back of his hand.

'There is one thing I *am* interested in though,' said

Reynolds and wandered over to where Eric and Kate had been busily stuffing jewellery back into the cash box. 'And I see you've packed it for me already.'

He held out his hand for the box, but when Eric failed to respond, he seemed to interpret this as an indication that further clarification was necessary. 'Consider it as my reward for finally tracking down the third member of your little gang after all these years. And the long lost loot itself of course. Compensation, if you like, for the time I've spent, the sleepless nights, the damage to my health — both physical and mental — not to mention a wrecked marriage and—'

'So you're just as bent as the rest of your kind,' Ingleby interrupted.

Reynolds spun round to face him. 'Never once in all my career did I take so much as a single brass farthing that I hadn't earned. This stuff's mine by rights like I told you. And in any case, I don't see why I should have to justify myself to a gobshite little villain like you.'

'One thing rather puzzles me though, Chief Inspector,' said Eric, clutching the cash box to his chest.

Reynolds raised an eyebrow at him.

'Simply this,' Eric went on. 'Why precisely do you think I'm going to hand this box over to you and let you just toddle off into the sunset without so much as a backward glance?'

'Precisely? — Well, precisely this, Mr Emerson. You see, if you *don't* let me toddle off into the sunset with it, as you so quaintly put it, I might just feel duty bound to have a word with the relevant authorities about a certain kidnapping incident which took place not a million miles from here and in which you yourself were very much involved. What with *your* record, I dread to think what sort of sentence you'd get for that.'

'Your word against mine,' said Eric.

Reynolds laughed. 'And who d'you think they'll

believe? A retired senior police officer with an exemplary record or an ex-con like you? Besides, it's not only my word against yours as I have three excellent witnesses who I'm sure will be more than happy to testify.'

He swept a hand in the general direction of Trevor, Sandra and Herbert and added, 'Unless of course they want to face their own charges for assaulting a police officer, kidnapping and false imprisonment.'

For the briefest of moments, Trevor forgot all about the pain in his arm as the image flashed into his mind of Ingleby's basement and Reynolds lying face down with a bag of frozen peas by his head. Almost immediately, the image was replaced by one of the inside of a Greek prison cell, which held more than a passing resemblance to some medieval dungeon that had been lavishly equipped by the Spanish Inquisition's most sadistic torturer.

'So what's it to be, Eric?' said Reynolds. 'I've heard some very unpleasant stories about what goes on in some of these Greek prisons.'

'Oh, just give him the bloody box, Eric,' said Ingleby. 'Then perhaps he'll piss off and leave us in peace.'

'It's all very well for you,' said Eric. 'You've already had—'

Ingleby held up his hand to silence him and asked Reynolds if he and Eric could have a couple of minutes in private. Reynolds said he couldn't imagine what else there was left to discuss but conceded that a couple more minutes wouldn't make much difference after all these years, so Ingleby took Eric by the arm and led him far enough away to be out of earshot of everyone else. With the sides of their heads almost touching, they went into a two man huddle, and when they eventually stood upright again, both of them were clearly attempting to stifle their smiles.

Eric walked straight over to Reynolds with the cash box held out in front of him as if it were some kind of sacrificial offering. 'Bang to rights is the expression, I believe.'

Reynolds took the box from him, his features apparently unable to decide between surprise and suspicion.

'Well, good,' he said. 'No hard feelings then, eh?'

No-one bothered to answer him, and with an awkward grin, he tucked the cash box under his arm and set off towards the far end of the building.

No sooner had he disappeared around the corner than Ingleby and Eric burst into an explosion of laughter that bordered on the maniacal. And amid the mutual backslapping and the clutching of aching ribs, Kate placed a concerned hand on one of Eric's rapidly convulsing shoulders.

'Granddad?'

'I'll tell you later, sweetheart,' Eric spluttered. 'I'll tell you later.'

'Do you think it might be okay if we went and found a doctor now?' said Trevor. 'If it's not too much trouble, that is.'

'Can we at least pick up some food on the way then?' said Herbert. 'It's nearly lunchtime, and I *still* haven't had breakfast.'

Trevor scowled at him. 'Huh, that's nothing. I once had to go almost three days with nothing more than a handful of biscuits because the van had broken down and I had to—'

'Bit of a long story, that one,' said Sandra, climbing in behind the steering wheel. 'Maybe you should save it for another time.'

48

During the long drive back to the villa, Ingleby was unusually relaxed and verging on cheerful. For once, he was even prepared to answer some of their questions, the most burning of which was why he and Eric had found it so hysterically funny when Reynolds had gone off with all the jewellery.

'Because they were fakes,' said Ingleby. 'The whole bloody lot of 'em.'

'What?' said Trevor.

'Fakes?' said Sandra.

'*Quoi*?' said Herbert.

Still chuckling, Ingleby went on to explain that he'd only discovered they were fake when he'd eventually found somebody in Greece who he could trust to value the stuff, and they'd told him that jewellers' shops sometimes put fakes on display as a condition of their insurance — especially if the shop had been robbed before and the insurers got twitchy about renewing their policy. They were copies of the real thing, and if a customer took a fancy to a particular piece, the manager would fetch the genuine article from the vault.

'So Eric and Frank went to prison for nothing?' said Sandra.

Ingleby grinned. 'Not quite. — See, not all of it was fake. Some of the stuff we got away with was the real McCoy and still worth a fair old sum as it happens. More than enough for me to buy the villa and live the life of Riley for the rest of me days. And that was just my share. Two thirds of it I kept back for the others, but now that Frankie-boy's outta the way, Eric'll get a nice little bonus, and there'll be a bit extra for me 'n' all. — Frank always was a greedy bastard, so I reckoned it was well on the cards he'd try something on whenever him and Eric came to collect. That's why I 'ung on to the fakes.'

Apart from Milly's snoring from the floor of the van, several seconds of silence followed Ingleby's revelation until Herbert broke it with: 'So where's all the real jewellery then?'

Ingleby tapped the side of his nose. 'Ah, now that would be tellin', wouldn't it? — But put it this way. If anyone ever tells yer they'd give yer the shirt off their back, take 'em up on it 'cos yer never quite know what else you'll be gettin'.'

Before he'd finished speaking, he unravelled the denim shirt he'd been hanging onto since he'd taken it out of the cash box and laid it flat on his lap, an obvious bulge in each of the two large pockets.

'What?' said Herbert, pointing. 'Is that all?'

'More money than sense what some people will pay for a shiny little trinket,' said Ingleby and rolled the shirt back into a tight bundle.

Another lengthy silence followed, and this time it was Sandra who broke it. 'So what about Reynolds?'

'What about 'im?'

'Well, he's not going to be very happy when he finds out that the jewellery he's got is worthless, is he?'

A snort of laughter. This part of the story seemed to please Ingleby even more than the extra cash that was coming to him.

'Yeah. Real shame that,' he said. 'I dunno what he plans to do with it, but my guess is he'll try and get it back to Blighty. He's bound to know a fence or two who owes 'im a favour.'

'But won't he just come after you again when he finds

out he's been had?' said Trevor. 'For the robbery, I mean.'

'Somehow I think he might've lost his appetite for it by then,' said Ingleby. 'Anyway, he still ain't got any proof I was involved.'

'Eric then. Won't Reynolds tell the Greek police about the kidnapping now?'

'So what if he does?'

'So what?' Trevor echoed. 'So he'll want us to testify, and if we don't, he'll drop us in it for knocking him unconscious with a bag of frozen peas and tying him up in your basement. That's what.'

'Not gonna happen.'

'You seem very confident,' said Sandra.

'Put it this way,' said Ingleby. 'First off, he's gotta get the fuzz to believe that Eric and Frank kidnapped him and the rest of you, and if you lot say you don't know what the fuck he's on about, then maybe he'll try and shaft you for what you done to 'im in my basement. But he was never even *at* my house, never mind tied up in the sodding basement, was he now?'

Ingleby gave each of them a long hard look, one after the other.

'And what makes you think they're going to believe our word against his?' said Trevor. 'Like he said, he's a retired chief inspector, and we're just—'

'Fine upstanding citizens without so much as an unpaid parking ticket to yer names?'

Ingleby posed it more as a question than a statement, and the other three nodded their agreement.

'And as for Reynolds being an ex-cop, I reckon he might lose quite a big chunk of credibility once he gets caught tryin' to leave the country with a whole bunch of knocked off jewellery.'

'Which happens to be fake,' Trevor reminded him.

Ingleby brushed the remark aside with a dismissive

wave of his hand. 'And 'ow long do you think it'll take 'em to find that out, eh? And even when they do, you think they're gonna take much of what he says as gospel after all that?'

'But who's to say he'll get caught with the jewellery anyway?' said Sandra.

'Oh, didn't I tell you?' said Ingleby with an exaggerated wink. 'I told Eric to 'ave a word with their police sergeant pal and get him to alert all the airports to take a special interest in a certain retired DCI of our acquaintance.'

49

The police station's reception area was mercifully cool, but after nearly three hours in the place, Trevor was more than ready to brave the heat outside again. He'd also left his painkillers back at Ingleby's, and the burning throb in his upper arm was reminding him he was well overdue for his next fix. At least Sandra had been wrong about the stitches. After a nurse had cleaned the wound — a procedure which itself involved a not inconsiderable amount of pain — the doctor had made some comment about having seen bigger paper cuts and patched him up with some little sticky strips and a big wad of gauze. Even the tetanus shot was in his arm rather than his bum, so Sandra had been wrong about that too.

As for the sling, the doctor had told him it was totally unnecessary, but Trevor had insisted. Okay, so maybe there wasn't a *medical* justification for wearing one, but its main function was to act as a warning — a kind of signal to others that they should keep well clear of his injured arm and avoid all agony-inducing contact, either deliberately or accidentally administered. So far, the strategy had proved almost entirely successful apart from the moment when Herbert had come out of his grilling with Sergeant Pericles and given him a cheery slap on the arm — a direct hit on the gunshot wound — and told him everything was fine and they had nothing to worry about before disappearing off in search of a cheese pie.

This was why Trevor's eyes had been streaming when

he was next to be summoned into the office at the end of the reception area, and Sergeant Pericles had taken one look at him and told him he had nothing to fear so he shouldn't get so upset. Trevor had started to explain that he wasn't at all upset and why it might have appeared that he was, but Pericles had cut him short and launched straight into his questions. During the whole of the interview, a plain-clothes guy — presumably Pericles's boss and some kind of detective — had sat near the back of the office with his arms folded and, for most of the time, with his eyes closed. This was either intended to aid his concentration or he was asleep. Judging by the slow, deep breathing, Trevor suspected the latter was the more likely.

The majority of Pericles's questions were, not surprisingly, about Donna Vincent and the severed head, and he'd been especially interested to know why she would have wanted to frame him and Sandra for the murder. Trevor had given him the trimmed down version of how they'd become involved with her husband, Harry, and why she might have thought they were somehow responsible for his death.

Pericles had seemed reasonably satisfied with this explanation and had then gone on to quiz him about the precise order of events which had led up to Herbert's filming of Donna and her accomplice planting the head in Trevor's camper van. This too had appeared to fulfil the sergeant's need to cross some T's and dot some I's, and he'd even confided in Trevor that there was more than enough additional evidence to put Donna and Eddie away for a very long time — if Eddie ever made it out of intensive care of course. Particularly damning was that most of the victim's body parts had been discovered on a rubbish tip up in the hills, and a few of these were found inside a suitcase bearing a luggage label with Donna Vincent's name and address on it.

'A stupid mistake,' Sergeant Pericles had said, 'especially when they had done the trouble to cut off his finger ends. They think I don't know tattoo of *Achilléas* on the arm of my own cousin? They think Greek police such barbarians we don't make DNA test?'

Then he'd sat back in his chair with a spectacularly smug grin and added, 'What is it you say in English? It's a fair cop glove.'

Trevor had agreed that this was exactly the right expression, but for some bizarre reason Pericles had responded by suddenly smashing his fist down onto the desk and going off on a mini rant about how he would be demanding the longest possible sentence for the bastards who'd murdered his cousin.

'Manolis was an *ilíthios* — an idiot,' he'd said, 'and I never like him from the first time I see him, but he was family, yes? And family in Greece is the most important of all.'

Once he'd got this out of his system, the sergeant had moved on to the matter of Frank Phelan and the shooting, which could have proved a good deal trickier if Ingleby hadn't spent half the previous evening schooling him, Sandra and Herbert on what they should and shouldn't tell the police. There was to be no mention whatsoever of stolen jewellery, and the reason Ingleby had wanted to visit the island was to mark what would have been the fiftieth anniversary of his marriage to his long-deceased wife. The island had been the place where he'd proposed to her, and Eric and Frank had agreed to come over for the occasion since they were old friends and had been guests of honour at the wedding. Unfortunately, an argument had broken out between the two of them soon after they'd arrived on the island, and it was this that had led to the shooting.

'And what was this argument about?' Pericles had asked.

'I'm not entirely sure,' Trevor had said, 'but I think Eric owed Frank quite a lot of money, and Frank was planning to take Eric's granddaughter hostage till he paid up.'

And that had been about it, apart from Pericles telling him he'd be needed as a witness at the trials of both Frank and Donna. Not a great prospect, but at least he and the others wouldn't be facing a murder charge themselves.

Next, it had been Sandra's turn for the interrogation, which, if it followed much the same pattern as Trevor's, should be over any time now. He certainly hoped so. The pain in his arm was getting worse by the minute, and his arse had gone numb from sitting too long on one of the two plastic chairs provided for visitors. Realising that it was within his means to alleviate this particular source of discomfort, if not the mounting agony from the gunshot wound, he stood up and strolled back and forth along the length of the reception area, taking only a vague interest in his surroundings — a long counter, behind which were a dozen desks, most of them unoccupied, and a uniformed officer at the counter itself, flicking through the pages of a magazine. The third time he passed in front of her, she eyed him suspiciously, so he moved on to the far end of the reception area where there was a small, glass-fronted office and another uniform — male this time — who was sitting at a desk, playing Patience on his computer.

Can't be a lot of crime round here, Trevor thought. Well, except for the occasional severed head of course.

Then he noticed that there was an open door at the back of the office, and beyond this, a cell. It was unlit, and it was difficult to see clearly, but the front consisted of floor-to-ceiling iron bars, not unlike those of the sheriff's office in almost every Western he'd ever seen. As far as he could make out, there were two or three people inside, and one had his — or maybe her — face pressed up against the bars and seemed to be staring straight at him. Not wanting to appear ghoulish, Trevor had turned and begun to walk away when a woman's voice shouted from behind him. Unmistakably, it was Donna Vincent's.

'Don't think you've heard the last of me, you bastard. I'll get you for what you did to my Harry. I'm not gonna be banged up for ever, and next time I won't mess about. You hear me, you—?'

The rest of what she said was drowned out by the duty officer yelling something at her in Greek and then slamming the door which led to the cell.

'Was that who I think it was?' said Sandra as she crossed the reception area towards him.

Trevor nodded. 'Watermelon Donna. The very same.'

'Not our biggest fan still, I gather.'

Trevor didn't answer. He'd gone into a mild form of shock and was sifting through Donna's words in his mind, trying to convince himself the threat was an empty one.

'Come on,' said Sandra, taking him by the hand. 'Let's go and get a drink.'

'Painkillers first,' said Trevor, mentally shaking himself back into the moment. 'Drink after.'

'You sure that's wise?'

'Probably not, but who cares?'

Sandra opened the glass exit door just as a marked police car pulled up outside and two officers jumped out. One of them went to the back and hauled out a ruddy-faced man whose hands were cuffed behind his back.

'Oh, bloody Nora,' said Trevor. 'Not him as well.'

Frank's eyes glowed with a venomous malevolence as soon as he spotted them. 'You two, is it? Well, you mark my words. First thing I'm gonna do when I get out is come lookin' for yer, and when I find yer, I'm gonna—'

'Oh, do shut up, Frank, you bloated old windbag. I've heard it all before, so you may as well save your ouzo-stinking breath for somebody who might be stupid enough to want to listen.'

The words were out of Trevor's mouth before he'd fully registered that he was speaking them, but he felt a faint twinge of pride when he'd finished. It wasn't often that he stood up to a bully like Frank, and he suddenly realised that the experience hadn't been at all unpleasant. Frank, on the other hand, didn't seem to have enjoyed it at all and, speechless for once, stared back at Trevor with his eyes wide and his mouth hung open.

A split second later, he howled in pain as each of the officers took an arm apiece and marched him off into the police station. 'Oi! Mind me fookin' shoulder, will yer?'

Trevor watched them go and then turned to Sandra. She was smiling at him with an odd kind of expression which he hesitated to interpret as... admiration?

'Right then,' she said. 'Let's get you those painkillers.'

A simple enough sentence, but one which could easily have taken the edge off the moment if Trevor had let it.

'Nah,' he said. 'Drink first. *Then* painkillers.'

50

'As I keep telling you, I'm a British police officer, and the only reason I have them is because they were stolen many years ago, and I'm taking them back to England to return them to their rightful owner.'

The customs official picked out a diamond bracelet from the pile of jewellery on her desk and held it up to the light for closer inspection.

'And as I keep telling *you*, *kírie* Reynolds—'

'Detective Chief Inspector Reynolds.'

'—we will have to make further enquiries.'

'Look, I've already shown you my warrant card. What more enquiries do you need to make?'

When he'd packed for the flight home, Reynolds had made no attempt to hide the jewellery because he knew it would be almost impossible to get past airport security without it being detected. Instead, he'd relied on his warrant card and the story about recovering stolen property to blag his way through. By rights, he should have handed in the card when he'd retired, but he'd decided it might come in handy one day — like now — and he'd lied about having lost it. What he hadn't bargained for was a jobsworth bloody customs officer with a conscientious streak as big as the Greek budget deficit. So much for Greeks being laid back and easy-going.

The customs officer gathered up the jewellery and got to her feet. 'You stay here.'

'Now what?'

'As I told you. Enquiries,' she said, opening the door to the tiny office.

Reynolds grunted. 'Christ, we're only talking about a few baubles here. It was a damn sight easier getting the Elgin bloody Marbles out than this little lot.'

The customs officer paused, her hand on the doorknob, and she turned back to him with a sly grin. 'You know, *kírıe* Reynolds, something tells me you might come to regret that remark.'

After she'd gone, Reynolds stood up and began pacing the room, rolling his lucky coin back and forth across his knuckles. On his third pass of the desk, he spotted the cigarettes and lighter that the customs officer had left behind, and he stopped dead in his tracks, staring at the packet like it was the crock of gold at the end of the rainbow.

'Special circumstances,' he said to himself, taking a cigarette from the pack and lighting it quickly before his brain had a chance to talk him out of it.

With his eyes closed, he inhaled deeply and held the smoke in his lungs for several seconds before releasing it with a sigh of intense satisfaction. He was about to take a second drag when a tinkling sound close to his feet distracted him. He looked down and saw his lucky coin spinning its final throes on the tiled floor and then rattle to a silent stop. Bending down to pick it up, he noticed that the coin had come to rest with the head side uppermost, and he snorted at the irony.

'Fat lot of good *you* did me,' he said, dropping the coin into the wastebin beside the desk.

51

Trevor was stuffed. He couldn't remember the last time he'd eaten quite so much food, and nor was he used to the quantity of booze that he'd poured down his throat since they'd arrived at the taverna a couple of hours earlier. It was a pleasant little spot on the quayside with a wood-floored terrace suspended above the water where the scent of the sea mingled with the jumble of aromas from the variety of dishes on their table.

When the waiter had brought their first round of drinks, Ingleby had stretched his arms wide and beamed an uncharacteristically bright smile. 'So what do you think?' he'd said as if he owned the place.

'Very pleasant indeed,' Eric had said, and Trevor, Sandra and Herbert had all muttered their agreement.

'Glad you like it, 'cos I own the bloody place.'

Ingleby had gone on to explain that he'd bought the taverna out of the proceeds from selling his share of the jewellery, partly on a whim and partly because he'd seen it as a sound investment. For the first few years, he'd been proved right, and the taverna had turned a decent enough profit, but since the Greek economy had "gone to bollocks", it had been struggling to make ends meet.

'Place over there's not doin' much better either,' he'd said, pointing to the much larger restaurant further along the quayside where Kate and Sergeant Pericles had gone to eat. 'But at least I know what goes into the moussaka 'ere, don't I?'

Since then, Ingleby had played "mine host" almost to

perfection and to such an extent that he was virtually unrecognisable from the grumpy old sod Trevor and the others had become accustomed to. He'd even gone inside to the Gents when he'd needed to empty his catheter bag and, to Trevor's knowledge, had only belched twice during the entire meal.

Now that it was coming to an end, one of the two waiters cleared away the plates while the other placed an enormous dish of sliced watermelon in the centre of the table. Trevor and Sandra leaned forward in their seats and fixed their eyes on it as if to confirm that it really was what it appeared to be.

'Is that…' Trevor began.

'…watermelon?' Sandra finished.

'Course it's bloody watermelon,' said Ingleby. 'Can't stand the stuff meself, but you lot get stuck in if you want.'

Trevor and Sandra sat back in unison and glanced at each other.

'Think I'll give it a miss this time,' said Trevor.

'Couldn't eat another thing,' said Sandra.

Herbert, on the other hand, plunged his fork into one of the largest slices on the plate and tore off a generous chunk with his teeth. Disappointment obviously hadn't affected his appetite — or his almost perpetual cheerfulness. His mother had phoned when they'd got back to Ingleby's villa after their grilling at the police station and told him the bad news about his A-level results. B in History and a C in English but only a D in French, which meant that he couldn't follow his dream of studying French at university. He'd taken himself off for an hour or so to "think things through", and when he'd come back, he'd been as bright and breezy as ever, announcing that "it wasn't the end of the world" and that he'd take a year out while he decided what to do with the rest of his life. Perhaps not surprisingly, he'd immediately ditched the beret, the red necktie and the hooped T-shirt and hadn't spoken a single word in French from that moment on.

'Delicious,' he said, spitting out watermelon pips into his cupped hand.

To Trevor's mind, the very sight of Herbert chomping away on the watermelon was little far removed from witnessing an act of cannibalism, and it combined with his recent over-indulgence to produce a distinct feeling of nausea. It was time for a stroll.

'Think I'll go for a bit of a stroll if that's okay with everybody,' he said, scraping back his chair and getting to his feet. 'Try and walk some of this food off.'

'Me too,' said Sandra and patted her stomach. 'Overdone it, I'm afraid.'

Milly, who had been asleep under the table after having gorged herself on the vast amount of titbits Ingleby had been feeding her, scampered after them, and they were halfway down the short flight of steps leading down from the terrace to the quayside when a voice called out from behind them.

'Mind if I join you?' said Ingleby. 'I mean, I don't wanna play gooseberry or nothin', but there's summink I need to talk to you about.'

'Er, that's okay, Mr Ingleby,' said Trevor, trying to suppress the wobble in his voice. 'We're not actually, er, you know... er...'

Ingleby frowned and looked from Trevor to Sandra and back again. 'Really? Well, bugger me. I could've sworn you two were— Still, none o' my business of course. — And by the way, you can forget the Mr Ingleby crap. It's Marcus to you from now on, okay?'

So saying, he gave Trevor a hearty slap on the upper arm, scoring a direct hit on the bullet wound. As a warning to others, the sling left a lot to be desired.

52

Kate had been dreading this moment from almost the very first time she'd agreed to go on a date with Pericles, and now here they were at the very same restaurant on the very same quayside, and she knew she couldn't put it off any longer. Her holiday fling days were well and truly a thing of the past, and she wasn't on the lookout for anything more serious any time soon. It wasn't personal. She'd probably have turned Brad Pitt down in her current state of self-imposed celibacy — well, maybe not Brad Pitt, but he would have been one of very few exceptions. She already felt guilty enough about having strung Pericles along to get information for her granddad, so she was even more determined to find a way of letting him down as gently as possible.

'Of course,' Pericles was saying through a mouthful of calamari, 'there has been much more crime in Greece since the beginning of the *kréesi* — the economic crisis. But this is not a surprise because the peop—'

'Pericles, my-grandfather-and-I-are-flying-back-to-England-the-day-after-tomorrow.' The words blurted out of her like a burst of machine gun fire.

Pericles's mouth froze in the middle of a word, a piece of fried squid clearly visible on the back of his tongue. He swallowed.

'But so soon?' he said.

'My granddad's finished his business here, and we have to get back.'

'I see.' His head dropped, and he stared down at the

remaining two rings of calamari on his plate.

Oh God, thought Kate, this is going to be even harder than I imagined.

His eyes crept back up to meet her own. The lost puppy look she'd seen more than once before.

'But what about... us?' he said.

Kate reached across the table and took hold of his hand — the one still holding the fork. 'Pericles, I've enjoyed our time together. Really I have.'

It occurred to her that people often overuse the other person's name when they're lying to them — a bit like somebody prefacing a racist remark with "I'm not racist but" — so she made a mental note to try not to say "Pericles" for the rest of the conversation.

He withdrew his hand from her grasp and put down his knife and fork. 'But now you are... What is the expression?... Letting me go?'

'Well, that's more when somebody gets fired really, but I guess the principle's much the same, yes.'

'But you said yourself that you have enjoyed our time together,' he said. 'So why can we not continue?'

She smiled weakly. 'I suppose it's because— You know, we have a saying in English about all good things must come to an end, and I—' Jesus, Kate, enough with the clichés, okay? Still, at least you didn't go for the one about quitting while you're ahead. 'I'd like to remember us exactly as we are now.' — Noooo. That's even more fingers-down-the-throat than the other stuff.

Pericles dabbed at his mouth with a napkin. 'I begin to ask myself if you like me at all, Kate.'

Uh-oh. Time for the bullshit *de grace*. Fix hurt expression on face. Go.

'How can you say that? I think you're a wonderful person, and someday I'm sure you'll—' Stop right there. That wasn't in the script. Grab his hand again and look deep into his eyes. And for God's sake, try to put some sincerity into it. 'If you want me to be perfectly honest…'

'Please do.'

'There are certain things — certain differences between us — which make me doubt that we could have any future together.'

Pericles raised an eyebrow and then made a show of pushing his plate of calamari away from him. 'I will give up eating meat.' He glanced down at the plate. 'And fish.'

Kate failed to stifle a laugh. 'No, it's not because you eat meat,' she said, wondering if there was a look of relief that flashed across Pericles's face. 'It's mainly about your job really. What you do for a living.'

'You don't like policemen?'

'No, that's not it at all. I think the police do a great job. It's just that — in this country anyway — you use guns.'

Another raising of the eyebrow.

'The thing is, you see,' she went on, 'as well as being a vegetarian, I'm also a pacifist.'

'Oh?'

'So I'd find it incredibly difficult to be in a relationship with someone who shoots people for a living.'

Oh, so now he's a professional bloody hitman, is he? Come on, Kate, Get a grip.

'I mean, not that you go round shooting people all the time,' she added before Pericles could respond. 'But you do have to do it sometimes, don't you? Yesterday on the island, for instance, when you—'

Pericles sat back in his chair. 'But, Kate, I was trying to save your life.'

'Yes, yes, I know that, and it's not that I'm not grateful. Not at all. But you have to understand how hard it would be for me to be in a relationship with a man who… Then again, it might be you who got shot. One day, I'd be sitting at home, and there'd be a knock on the door and… and…'

Cue a few well-placed tears. Rummage in bag for handkerchief. Click Send on mobile phone while you're in there.

'I'm sorry, Pericles. Truly I am.'

She blew her nose with rather more force than she'd intended and put the handkerchief back in her bag. This time, it was Pericles who reached for *her* hand.

'I could leave the police,' he said. 'Find another job. When I was a boy, I always wanted to be a butcher. — No, I mean a vegetable seller.'

Kate shook her head. 'But being a policeman is your life. It's what you live and breathe for. I know that, and I could never forgive myself if you gave it all up for my sake.'

Pericles gave her hand a particularly firm squeeze. 'I promise you, Kate, I would do anything if—'

Her mobile phone rang. Excellent. Granddad got the text then.

'I'm sorry,' she said, checking the display. 'I have to take this. It's my granddad… Hello? Granddad?… Oh, I see… Yes, of course… Straight away… Two minutes, yes.'

She hung up.

'Problem?' said Pericles.

'He forgot to take his pills with him. For his heart. He put them in my bag for safe keeping when we left the apartment, so I need to get them to him right away.'

She stood up and hung her bag over her shoulder.

'But he is only over there at the taverna,' said Pericles. 'You will come back here afterwards?'

'I think we might have to go straight back to the apartment. He doesn't sound at all well, I'm afraid.'

Pericles got to his feet. 'I see. — But perhaps we can

meet again before you go back to England. For a coffee or something.'

She looked down at the ground and then back up at him again. 'I think that would be much too painful for both of us. Better if we say our goodbyes now, I think. For both our sakes.'

He opened his mouth to speak, but she silenced him with a kiss. No tongues of course, but a kiss nevertheless.

'Goodbye, Pericles,' she said. 'I hope one day you'll be able to find it in your heart to forgive me.'

Right, that's it, Barbara Cartland. Get your arse out of here — now!

She turned on her heel and walked briskly away.

'But of course you will have to return for the trial of the fat Englishman?' Pericles called after her, but she pretended not to hear. As if that was going to happen unless they could be bothered to extradite her, which she very much doubted.

She quickened her pace as she made her way along the quayside, trying to convince herself that she hadn't been a complete bitch to the poor bloke. Okay, so maybe the whole pacifist thing wasn't that convincing as a brush-off line, but at least his ego hadn't been too badly damaged. Or she hoped not anyway. The male ego was a fragile creature at the best of times.

53

'So what d'you think?' said Sandra after Ingleby had left them to continue their walk along the quay.

Trevor wasn't at all sure *what* he thought. It had all come as a bit of a shock really. From grumpy old sod to "Call me Marcus" and "How'd you fancy running my taverna for me?" in less time than it takes to empty a catheter bag was too much to take in all at once. Sandra had pointed out that neither she nor Trevor were particularly knowledgeable about the culinary arts, but Ingleby had told them he already had a perfectly good cook and what he needed was somebody to manage the place. Someone to do the day-to-day stuff like ordering stock, keeping the books up to date, a bit of marketing now and again, that kind of thing.

'But why us?' Sandra had asked.

'For one, I need somebody I can trust,' Ingleby had said. 'I 'aven't known you for more than a few days, but from what I've seen, I reckon you're not the type that's gonna stitch me up. Second — and this is probably more important than all the admin-type stuff — I need somebody front of house who can do all the meet-and-greet kind of malarkey. Keepin' the customers satisfied kind o' thing. There's a lot of Brits come 'ere during the season, and most of 'em wanna eat out somewhere where they don't 'ave to get all hot and bothered pissing about with the Greek lingo when all they want is a relaxin' night out and a decent bit o' grub. Think you can 'andle that?'

Trevor and Sandra had thought they could probably 'andle that pretty well, and although the pay he was offering wasn't that great, Ingleby had talked about the possibility of some kind of profit share and a rent-free apartment above the taverna.

'Well?' said Sandra. 'You going to keep me in suspense all night?'

Trevor shook his head to bring his mind back to the here and now. 'Sorry?'

'The taverna?'

'It's a bit of a risk, isn't it?'

'What's risky about it? It's not as if he's asking us to invest in it or anything. We'll just be his employees, that's all. — Like we are right now in fact, except with the added incentive that we won't be having to sort out his catheter every five minutes.'

They'd reached the point on the quayside where the promenade turned sharply to the right towards the mouth of the harbour, but Trevor carried straight on, down onto a sandy beach, and headed for the gently lapping waves at the water's edge.

'What about the detective agency?' he said.

'What about it?' said Sandra. 'It's hardly been making any money in the last few months anyway, and business wasn't showing any signs of picking up any time soon either. That's why we took this job in the first place if you remember.'

'Oh yes, I remember all right,' said Trevor, ostentatiously raising his wounded arm. 'I also remember how you said what a doddle it would be.'

Sandra laughed. 'Well, yes, that *was* a bit unfortunate.'

'Unfortunate?'

'I'm sure you're not going to get shot at every time.'

'Every time what?' said Trevor, picking up a flat pebble and skimming it out to sea. It bounced twice and then sank beneath the surface.

'The way I look at it, there's nothing to stop us setting something up here,' said Sandra. 'A bit of a sideline to earn some extra cash. There's plenty of expats around, and I'll bet there's more than a few in need of a private investigator every once in a while.'

Trevor checked her expression to see if she was being serious. Apparently, she was.

'Look, Trev, I know decision-making isn't high on your list of personal skills, but I really do think this whole taverna thing is too good an opportunity to miss. We've got nothing to lose by it, and there's nothing to stop us jacking it in after a few weeks or so if it's not working out. — And here's another way of looking at it. We've got to be here for Donna and Frank's trials, and Sergeant Whatshisface says that could be months away. So why not just stay here and earn a bit of money while we're waiting?'

She picked up a stone and skimmed it. — A five.

They continued their walk along the water's edge while Trevor made a mental list of the various pros and cons involved and eventually had to admit to himself that Sandra was right on almost every point. A couple of Brits running a detective agency in Greece was probably little more than a fantasy of course, although that was hardly a deal-breaker. But then there was the issue of the rent-free flat above the taverna.

'This flat Ingleby's offering us,' he said.

'What about it?'

'He said it only had the one bedroom.'

There was a pause before Sandra replied. 'I'm sure we'll manage somehow.'

Trevor wasn't sure quite how the "somehow" would work, especially if it was a double bed rather than two singles, and his mind drifted back to the hotel room in the Cotswolds.

'You remember that hotel in the Cotswolds?' said Sandra with a slight chuckle and possibly a hint of embarrassment.

'You must have read my mind,' said Trevor, feeling the heat rise in his cheeks and grateful for the cover of darkness as a cloud slid in front of the moon.

Milly raced past them with an enormous clump of seaweed in her mouth, and they walked on in silence until Sandra suddenly stopped and turned to face him.

'Trev, I've got a confession to make. Something I've been wanting to get off my chest for quite a while.'

Trevor swallowed. Oh my God. What the hell is *this* going to be?

'It's been bugging me that I didn't own up to you at the time, but I didn't want it to spoil our, um, relationship... *professional* relationship, that is... our friendship, I mean.'

Bloody Nora, this *must* be serious. It wasn't often that Sandra got an attack of the blathers.

She took a deep breath and locked her eyes onto his. 'The mixup over the booking at the hotel? It wasn't a mixup at all. I booked a room with a double bed on purpose.'

What was the phrase they used in all the TV cop shows when somebody had been bludgeoned to death? Blunt force trauma. That was it. And that's exactly what Trevor felt he'd just experienced. A blunt force trauma that left him partly dazed but simultaneously filled his head with more conflicting responses than his brain could cope with. Eventually, he settled for the simplicity of 'Why?'

The moon reappeared from behind the cloud and bathed Sandra's face in light. She was staring at him with a curious expression that Trevor had never seen before. A weird kind of smiling anger he'd never have believed it possible to achieve.

307

'Why?' she repeated. 'Jesus, Trevor, why do you think?'

Trevor thought about it for a moment. 'Er, because it was cheaper than a room with two singles?'

The smiling part of her expression vanished from her face, and she whacked him hard on his injured arm with the palm of her hand.

'Owwwww!' Trevor cried out as a molten hot skewer of agony shot up into his shoulder and spread instantly through the rest of his body.

'Because I wanted us to make love, you bloody idiot!' she yelled. 'I wanted us to have sex!'

It was as if every pain receptor in his system had suddenly shut down, and the only sensation he was aware of was a strange chill in his veins which rapidly warmed to an intense glow.

Well, that couldn't have been much clearer, he thought, his eyes following in Sandra's wake as she stomped off along the beach. But why hadn't she said anything at the time?

Deciding that this probably wasn't the best moment to ask her, he set off after her and placed a firm hand on her shoulder. Spinning her round, his mouth made a dive for hers, but in his haste, it landed on the tip of her nose instead. He adjusted his aim, and their tongues met for what seemed like — well, about two seconds really because at precisely that moment, Milly came bounding up and planted her front paws in the middle of Trevor's back. Off balance, he staggered forward and brought Sandra down with him onto the wet sand, landing awkwardly and sending another bolt of pain through his arm. This time, he tried to repress the instinctive shriek of agony but was only partially successful, and he eased himself over onto his back while Milly enthusiastically licked his face in what was presumably the canine version of an abject apology.

'You know what would do that war wound of yours a power of good?' said Sandra, kissing him lightly on the cheek that Milly wasn't already dealing with.

'Stronger painkillers and a better behaved dog?'

'A good soaking in some salt water,' she said with what looked like a wink but was probably just a speck of sand in her eye.

Trevor followed her nod to the ebb and flow of the tiny waves a few feet from where they lay. It was certainly tempting. But then he remembered he was dressed for an evening out and hadn't brought his swimming shorts with him, and he was fairly sure Sandra hadn't brought her bikini either. Rolling his head to the side, he was about to inform her of the flaw in her plan when he felt her hand on his waist and the top button of his jeans being undone.

'Oh,' he said. 'I see what you mean.'

THE END

'LIFTING THE LID'
BOOK 1 IN THE SERIES

Heads You Lose is the second novel in the 'Lifting the Lid' series and the sequel to *Lifting the Lid*. It isn't essential to read the novels in order, and if you haven't read *Lifting the Lid*, you can find it in ebook and paperback formats at Amazon, Barnes & Noble and elsewhere.

There are some things people see in toilets that they wish they hadn't. What Trevor Hawkins sees might even cost him his life...

When Trevor hits the open road in his beat-up old camper van with his incorrigible dog, Milly, his quest for adventure soon spirals dangerously out of control. The simple act of flushing a hotel toilet transforms his life from redundant sales assistant to fugitive from a gang of psychopathic villains, the police and MI5.

Then there's private detective Sandra Gray, who could cheerfully throttle him for turning a well paid, piece-of-cake job into a total nightmare. Or could she?

With more twists and turns than an Escher-designed bobsleigh run, *Lifting the Lid* is a comic thriller about how a single, split-second decision can change someone's life forever.

'A superb adventure-comedy... *Lifting the Lid* will grab you and pull you along for a fun and wild ride.'
Jennifer Reinoehl for *Readers' Favorite*

'The story is just so much FUN! It is entertaining, well-written, cleverly planned and expertly timed.'
Joanne Armstrong for *Ingrid Hall Reviews*

ABOUT THE AUTHOR

Some readers have asked me if my comedy thrillers *Lifting the Lid* and *Heads You Lose* are partly autobiographical. Am I anything like the main character, Trevor Hawkins? The answer, quite simply, is: 'No, I'm not.' Okay, so I do own an elderly VW camper van (currently off the road), I do have a dog (five rescue dogs actually), I do have a low pain threshold, and I can occasionally be accused of 'anally retentive faffing'. But there the similarity ends.

Unlike Trevor, I live in Greece with my wife, Penny, two cats and the aforementioned rescue dogs. As far as I'm aware, Trevor has never written anything longer than a shopping list in his life, whereas I'm working on my third novel and two screenplays.

I hope you enjoyed reading *Heads You Lose*, and if you'd like any more information, please…

- visit my website at
  http://www.rob-johnson.org.uk (where you can also listen to my series of short, hopefully humorous podcasts)

- follow **@RobJohnson999** on Twitter

- check out (and please like!) my Facebook author page at
  https://www.facebook.com/RobJohnsonAuthor

REVIEWS

Authors always appreciate reviews – especially if they're good ones of course – so I'd be eternally grateful if you could spare the time to write a few words about *Heads You Lose* on Amazon or anywhere else you can think of. It really can make a difference. Reviews also help other readers decide whether to buy a book or not, so you'll be doing them a service as well.

AND FINALLY...

I'm always interested to hear from my readers, so please do take a couple of minutes to contact me via my website at:

http://rob-johnson.org.uk/contact/

or email me at:

robjohnson@care4free.net

I look forward to hearing from you.